97 or SEX and SENSIBILITY

LAURENCE BAILLIE BROWN

This is a first edition. Published 21st September 2023

ISBNs:
Paperback: 978-1-80541-381-3
eBook: 978-1-80541-380-6

For Jane, and for Stephen – for believing.

Other books by Laurence Baillie Brown

'Addictions' First edition 2000 Gay Men's Press

'At the Court of Broken Dreams: Love and War in the Middle Ages' 2022

'Addictions: Bears and Bitches' Second edition 2023

Contributor to:

'The Bear Book II' edited by Les Wright PhD Harrington Park Press 2001

'London Scene; the Gay Men's Guide' Gay Men's Press 1987

Acknowledgments

First, let me thank the Conde Nast organization who, as trustees of the Cecil Beaton bequest, allowed me (in return for a handsome fee) to use his wonderful 1968 photo of the great David Hockney, his then partner Peter Schlesinger and the ultra-elegant Maudie James as the basis for the front cover. I chose it principally because the image of Miss James personifies how I imagine Celia, my first heroine.

Secondly, I must thank my friend Mrs Judy Morgenstern for allowing me to use her photo of me (looking rather suave?) suited and booted, as the author image on the back cover.

Thirdly, as usual, I thank Publishing Push for their help throughout the publication process.

And, finally, I thank all my newly-discovered family and my friends for their toleration and support, as ever.

This is now. This is three years, less than three years, before the millennium. (Two thousand years since the birth of whom? And why?) No more historical novels, no more fey retrospectives. At this moment, eighteen endless years of Torydom are about to reach their long dreamt-of end and a new era to begin. April. A spring full of hope. The grey Major at the end of his rope. Jeremy is rich and famous and bitterer than ever, dear old Francis has been dead for six short years, Jonathan and Ben (or Jonathan at least) has got the seven-year itch, Celia has at long last left Pip in search of something or somebody, and George is beginning to see voices. Wait a moment and I'll explain. And soon New Labour will sweep all before it and joy shall (for a little while) reign broadly in the land, with degrees of disillusion/dissolution to follow. But this is now, as the poet said, this is now, here and in England. Our cool, rich, beggar-ridden, hopeless, hope-filled, dreary, grey, gorgeous England, this strangely dream-stirring spring of a year replete with signs and wonders, a year when, as the prayer book says, some shall live and some shall die, some shall be exalted and others put down. This is 1997.

PART I

Spring: Allegro con brio

George Eliot was a very good novelist because he understood how society of Victorian England worked. He had been born poor (fairly) and had risen through the ranks of a hierarchical society to the position of a lion though because he lived with a man it was not acceptable. In her earliest novels she wrote about the scum of society (well, the poor) but not in Daniel Deronda *which is mainly concerning with the upper classes. Not that means their behaviour is morally better as she explains.*

"Quite," mutters George, underlining the misspellings, non sequiturs and other outrages in red pen. Why do students write such crap? Why do teachers read it? An even better question but one which at ten o'clock on a Friday evening he is far too tired to try to answer. *But maybe not for much longer,* he muses with a little sigh of pleasure at the happy thought that his application for very early retirement cum redundancy has gone in to the college authorities and might – just might – produce that consummation devoutly to be wished: the end of teaching.

The end of the seemingly endless cycle of terms and seasons and cohorts of students, whom once like a passionate lover he had adored but now just longs to be rid of.

Actually, this is very much the feeling of Friday evening – and Monday morning for that matter. But in the middle of the week, yes, in the middle of the week there was even now a still small space when he could feel an echo of that early romantic commitment, those youthful days twenty-odd years before when college lecturing was a new and exciting profession for a bright young man and with its relaxed and easy ambience would serve as a pleasant almost pastoral backdrop for the poetry, novels and academic studies he was soon to write. In fact, once his PhD was completed, he would certainly be eligible for the university lectureship which his lower second in English Lit had made rather harder to obtain than he had expected. In fact he never had quite completed that PhD – yet, which ironically was to be on the subject whom his current students were in the process of tearing to shreds: Mary Ann or Marian Evans, Mrs (quasi-Mrs) George Henry Lewes, Mrs John Cross, the great, the inimitable woman/man, conservative and free thinker, master novelist and massive intellectual – George "Middlemarch" Eliot. But why, oh why, had they given his less than inspired or inspiring pupils neither the huge slightly stodgy *Middlemarch* – which at least they had heard of and could have watched not long ago on TV (or right now on video) – or indeed one of the earlier less complex (slightly, as a student might qualify at this point) novels like *Adam Bede* or *Felix Holt* – but instead the novel that he admired and worshipped above all others, the culmination as he saw it of her life's work, the deep and deliciously aristocratic yet also partly Judaic summit of her splendid oeuvre: *Daniel Deronda*.

Did the South Coast Universities and Polytechnics Examinations Syndicate – now known simply as South Coast like one of the new privatised rail companies – really have to ruin his (he hopes… no, prays) final year of teaching by allowing well-meaning but oh so woefully ill-educated young persons to tear her delicately ravelled skein into shards and shreds? This is the book – he tried to tell them – that Jane Austen would have written had she entered into a marriage of true minds (and lived a hundred years later, of course) or that one of Eliot's great admirers, Dickens or Trollope, might have produced had either been a woman – blessed with Mary Ann's intellect, her capacity to suffer, her ability to… But it was no use. He couldn't get it across to them and now it was certainly too late to try.

For Eng Lit lecturers – like almost everyone in the Department of Humane and Social Studies – were being dealt with in a manner most unsocial and utterly inhumane. They were all, in fact, redundant, or would be if they didn't re-train (again like one of the new privatised rail companies). For his younger colleagues redundancy could mean permanent unemployment, but for George, approaching fifty, it was just possible that he might be graciously awarded the longed-for prize known as "pre-premature retirement by way of enhanced redundancy". In other words, just about enough lolly to enable him to sail off into the sunset without drowning like Grandcourt (the villain of Mary Ann's masterpiece). But whether this boon would be granted depended entirely on the innermost workings of the great managerial mind – far too arcane a process to be fathomed by the likes of him. So now, in April towards the end of the summer term of this pivotal year, George waits to learn his future, continuing his enforced "reskilling" – in a choice between IT and ESOL, he chose computers over English for immigrants on the wise basis of going for the devil you don't know – and finds to his surprise that computers have a mind of their own which he is intrigued to infiltrate. Should freedom come, what precisely he will do with it he is unsure – maybe complete that magnum opus on his heroine or even write a play about her; he has (he always has had) lots of ideas (too many to bring to fruition; too many even to take seriously), but like the rest of Britain he waits, and despite the poet's injunction, he waits *with* hope for that brave, not quite socialist, not quite anything, new dawn.

II

The Coronet is lively on a Friday evening. It has that buzz of life, of liveliness that makes the English pub so English, so fucking English, thinks Jonathan. The smell of beer – it's not really hops nowadays, is it? More like chemicals – mingles with the scents of aftershave (*but not too much in this bears' pub,* thinks Jonathan thankfully), the pheromones of (mainly) fresh sweat, and the occasional whiff from the none-too-well-cleaned toilets to create a special odour of pubbiness, a home-from-home smell for most of the regulars like the familiar warmth of a child's long-cradled blanket.

Jonathan is used to seeing so many of these regulars – though he hates to admit he's becoming one himself. It's a rectangular bar, with another upstairs, on one of those remarkably, pleasantly, tranquil side streets off one of the busiest roads in the West End. Jonathan has taken to meeting Ben here after work whenever his other half's rehearsals or classes keep him late. It's awfully convenient, Jonathan muses, to have a lover (or partner as the in-phrase goes, or "significant other" to be really nauseating) who works – if work is the right word – in the heart of London, i.e. near to the liveliest, cruisiest gay pubs. In fact, it's awfully convenient. No, actually, it's bloody marvellous, in fact almost miraculous to find oneself having a lover at all – and a lover of seven years' duration at that. Jonathan had not really believed in his early thirties after more than a decade on the scene, with at least half a dozen failed (not so much failed, just disastrous) relationships behind him – plus countless (and I mean *countless*) one-night stands and quickies in numerous backrooms, bathhouses and cruising grounds – that *the right one*, Mr Right, destiny in 501s, would suddenly come along in the shape of a large, slightly naïve, opera-obsessed, basically sweet-natured, Californian baritone nearly ten years his junior – a man whom he had learnt/was learning to truly love as a partner, as a lover, as a special sort of best friend.

But love, like lust or grief, came in waves, in irregular patterns; it could not be measured or predicted or even (in oneself, at least) be relied on. At first, he had found loving, giving himself to the sensation of loving and being loved, extremely difficult. It had seemed unrealistic, over-demanding, too good to be true, too… sentimental. And when Ben had first said to him – when they had been sleeping and going out with each other for two or three weeks – in his warm, easy, gentle Californian way, "Hey, babe, I love you. I really love you," Jonathan had found it impossible to reply. He had just smiled sheepishly and felt tongue-tied. It was so unexpected and yet so very long longed-for, as to seem unreal, even untrue. He had come to believe in those ten and more years of singleness, of hard, proud gay singleness, that there wasn't really such a thing as "love" – other than the love of friends or family; that the other over-vaunted type of sensual love was in fact just a species of infatuated and inflated desire. But gradually it dawned on him that Ben's assertion wasn't untrue; that it actually represented an objective correlative, something real and perfectly *normal*, a predictable, human and unfathomably lovely experience that was actually happening – quite unaccountably – to both of them. After all, why should he be so different from everyone else, such an exile from the human race, as to be unable to form those perfectly everyday and essential things called relationships?

For years and years, it had seemed impossible, something that only other people could achieve, like whistling or swimming or speaking Italian. And yet now, without planning or any apparent transformation in himself, it was here and it had happened, and it seemed that everything had just spontaneously clicked into place. Otherwise why had he so easily and comfortably agreed that Ben should move in when he got his scholarship with the Conservatory, and why should he find it so pleasant, so easy and right that it should be Ben's broad, pale, rather handsome back he should wake up to every morning, and Ben's glorious baritone he should hear starting up between grunts and splutters each day from the bathroom, and Ben whom he should enjoy having sex with – no, making love to – two or three times a week. Well, it was three times a week for the first few months and then, like love itself, it began to come and go like the tide and presently, after seven years of ebbing and flowing, the tide seemed to be ebbing for most of the week – and for most weeks – in the sexual, but not, Jonathan was confident, the emotional aspect.

What Jonathan had always been afraid of in relationships was that moment – usually two or three weeks into coupledom but in a really good case it could be two or three months and, in a particularly bad one, two or three days – when the habitual need to scratch the itch of sexual variety produced an overwhelming sensation of stifling claustrophobia and all you wanted to do was scream and take back your accustomed sexual freedom and reassert the liberated gay man's natural right to shag every other gay man to glorious oblivion. Whether this was an irreducible aspect of the gay male persona or simply a matter of daily habit since the Stonewall Coming of 1969 was quite irrelevant; it was an irreversible fact and no amount of romantic sensibility or St. Valentine's Day gush could ever overcome it. And this knowledge of his own – and most other men's – prick-promiscuity had stood in the way of Jonathan being able or ready – as most Americans but not Ben would say – to *commit*.

With Ben, the act – or more accurately *inact* – of commitment had been extraordinarily easy, comfortable, almost like fitting into a perfectly knitted glove. But even so, two or three months into the relationship, the inevitable crisis had come. The point was that this time it did not seem to be such a critical crisis but, after a few initial squalls and tears, just another tricky but negotiable problem to be dealt with – and solved in light of their "love" (whatever that was, as Jonathan still thinks of it) and their ineluctable natures as sexually hungry gay men in a world of sensual delights.

There had been a few twists and turns to begin with. For example, at the very first party they went to together, put on by Celia and Pip – when those two were still, just about, together – at their lovely roomy old house in Hampstead, when Jonathan was just in the first flush of showing off his new boyfriend to all his friends and glorying in the novelty of relationship, they had a conversation with Pip and Jeremy about the whole notion of sexual fidelity. Pip – famous composer, and non-recovering alcoholic – smoking a cheroot dropping ash on his well-worn orange velvet jacket and gulping a large brandy, had said, "Relationships are very individual. Everyone's different. You can't make general rules."

And then Jeremy, looking terribly dapper in an embossed leather jacket in brown and tan which must have cost him a fortune, staring provocatively at Ben, said, "Absolutely. Though, of course, with a highly attractive young boyfriend one's bound to get a little paranoid. Just take it easy and don't get too wound up when one of you strays. Jealousy's such a *destructive* emotion."

"And I thought you were such a romantic, Jeremy," Jonathan smiled.

"We all are, dear. We old theatrical queens," Pip put in, in his languid drawl. "But we're also realists and as far as I'm concerned if I get cruised by some gorgeous lad anywhere at all I'm not going to say 'Sorry, love, I can't possibly suck you off 'cause my boyfriend – or wife – is waiting for me at the other side of London.' That's more than human flesh can bear. And it works both ways, of course."

Ben – who had been standing in his quiet, stolid way drinking a beer and smoking (one of those occasional habits Jonathan was hoping to cure him of) – spoke up. "I totally agree. That kinda freedom comes with the territory. Just go with it."

This was an immense relief to Jonathan. Not that at that point he wanted to rush off and cruise other men or look for a raunchy threesome. Not at all. He was in that first full flush of romantic feeling, like the bright early days of spring, when the first (naïve) thought of the morning is "this is another day for

Ben" and the second "when am I going to see Ben today?" and you feel united in a warm oneness with somebody deliciously attractive and other. They were heady days, of course, and at one point later in the evening when he and Ben were seated on the carpet with Ben's bulky, handsome legs around him and they were looking into each other's eyes he heard Jeremy saying to Celia – a touch of envy in his voice, "My God, look at those two boys. They're practically having it off."

To which Celia, in her husky laidback tones, had answered, "And why not? There are plenty of stains on that carpet already."

But as a realist Jonathan knew that a time would come – not so far off either – when one of them would be put into that ever-so-tempting situation and would, indubitably, fall. At least he knew now that Ben wouldn't be fazed by it. What a sensible, mature boyfriend he had got for himself.

About a month after this, things were continuing to go well, very well, between them and already the thought had occurred to both of them that maybe they should consider moving in together. That first flush of infatuation had already lasted longer than it usually did for Jonathan – and also it was different. It wasn't the kind of sickening lust he had experienced previously or a wild passion that was "simply too hot not to cool down". In every previous relationship Jonathan had known at the back of his mind that things were not exactly right, that this queasy infatuation was not love, that the hot desire was not a substitute for tender loving care. Always there had been disparities, distances between him and the other, because the other was *too* other, or, in a few cases, not other enough. But this time, at last, the miracle had happened. But do miracles last for seven years?

"'ello, you slag. Where's the husband?"

Jonathan smiles wryly at the fat bastard who's addressing him. "Singing his balls off I expect. Unless he's already on his way. Which he should have been twenty minutes ago."

"Probably got a cock in his mouth I shouldn't wonder. How are things, you old slapper?"

"Pretty good. And how about you, Grant?"

Grant is six-foot and weighs around eighteen stone. He's a big lad, in his early thirties, with snake tattoos peeping out onto his wrists beneath the cuffs of his check shirt and, as Jonathan knows, a magnificent multi-coloured tattooage of St. George and the dragon empanelling his broad lightly mottled back. He wears a suede-head cut and short brown beard. Jonathan also knows that Grant has tattoos of blue manacles around both his ankles suggesting that this indolent, green-eyed rugby forward actually requires the domination he projects.

Our boys had first seen him in this very pub a couple of months into their relationship. It was Saturday evening and they had spent the day shopping in town. As soon as they had come through the door, Jonathan's long-trained eye had spotted the new face, the broad shoulders and the flicker of the green eyes registering their entrance.

"Seen who's at the bar?"

"I ain't seein' nothin' till I get a drink, babe."

"Well, go and get the drinks and take a look at the big bugger with the light beard. Just picking up a pint."

"Okay. But why?"

"Christ. Well, apart from him being pretty sexy, he's the guy from the bears' video we were given by your Belgian friend."

"No way. That guy's Belgian. Kinda similar I guess."

"Kinda the same you mean."

"*Possiblamente.* I'll get the drinks."

Jonathan with lubricious excitement saw Ben at the bar apologising to the big boy for jostling him and exchanging a few more words with the fat – increasingly gorgeous – bastard before coming back with the drinks and a little smile.

"Well?"

"Well what?"

"Is it the same guy?"

"Oh sure."

"What d'you say to him?"

"I just said, 'Pardon me, sir, but do you have a really impressive tattoo of a dragon on your back?' And he said, 'How do you know that?' So, I said, 'My boyfriend and I think we may have seen you in a movie. Is that possible?' He kinda gurgled and said, 'It's possible.' I gotta admit he's cute in a real British kinda way."

"Meaning he's working class and eminently fuckable."

"*Baby*, you sure don't pull your punches. I repeat, my dear, he's kinda cute. And working class. But not stupid."

"Never said he was, my angel. Shall we go and speak to him before anyone else does?"

"Why?" said Ben, playing as straight a bat as any first-class cricketer.

"Well," said Jon gingerly feeling his way towards as yet uncharted ground, "I suppose we *could* consider inviting him for a threesome – if that's what you want, and he's agreeable?"

There was a three-second pause in which Ben stared straight at Jonathan as if in utter shock. *What a great acting career you have before you*, thought Jon.

"Let's do it."

And done it they had – and Grant too. The sex had been highly recreational, light-hearted, and contrapuntal like a three-way conversation. It gave opportunities for voyeurism/exhibitionism which were, frankly, more exciting, more satisfying than the direct interchanges themselves.

And so, they entered a new phase of their relationship. Now you may think this second phase – happening as it did no more than about six to eight weeks after Jonathan returned to London from Amsterdam and they began seriously going out together – was a little too early for comfort. True – you may be saying, dear reader, especially if you are a dear *gay* reader – it is inevitable for all or at least most gay couples to move on from the gooey romantic love of first infatuation, the love which is always merely an egotism *à deux,* an immature extended self-obsession – to a more mature, laidback objective and long-lasting kind of emotion in which both parties acknowledge their need for external stimulation and learn that they can have sex outside the relationship – usually within certain agreed rules or guidelines – *but* that such a development will usually occur about six months to a year (or even longer) after the start of the relationship.

You may be shocked, dear gay or non-gay reader, or even disgusted (though your disgust, I suspect, will be seasoned with just a little vicariously lubricious excitement). But do not be. For the proof of the pudding is surely in the eating, and this relationship having lasted nearly seven glorious years is clear proof that our boys moved on to stage two at the right point *for them*. Of course, my heterosexual readers (if I have any – and if such persons still exist – and if so I welcome you with kisses on both cheeks, my dears) may be astonished or amused or contemptuous that such a partnership is considered to be par for the gay (male) course. But – and here I address the ladies whose sensuous sensibilities are generally so much more refined and monogamic than our own – just consider the "natural" proclivities of men and how they would behave without the civilising influence of women; where straight men would fight to assert their male dominance over the bodies of their womenfolk, we, dear ladies, *fuck* (not necessarily literally, of course, but in some manner express our man-obsessed carnal desires). Perhaps our more feminine side (and remember that brilliant German – I forget his name – who proclaimed that the future is female) is expressed in our warm and loving relationships while the masculine urges – the ineluctable explosions of testosterone, those firecrackers of hard-faced tenderness – find fulfilment in the freedom of sex encounters without context or emotion.

At any rate, J and B's sex life took a definite up-turn after their first six-handed sex fest, while their emotional contentment simply grew more clear, more settled. And if, beloved reader, your thighs are aching for a little more explicit exposition of their three-way encounter – ah no, this is not the time, nor the place. But be patient. I suspect they'll meet Grant again.

|||

A woman at fifty. A woman of no importance. A woman of substance. *Yea, well, that one's true*, thinks Celia through a fog of cigarette smoke. "Your fifties can be beautiful" smirks the headline of the article she's browsing in her *EG* – the magazine for women in their prime. (What *did* it stand for? Egregiously Gorgeous, Easily Grateful… Extremely Gross?) Weren't these the people who were coming to interview her next week? And one mustn't disappoint one's public – or pubic, as Pip would say. *But why the fuck should I care what Pip would say? – that sodden washed-up faggot of a soon-to-be ex-husband of mine. If he thinks we can go on being married while he lives his single life of Scotch and buggery he's quite wrong*, she thinks as she lifts her twelve-year-old single malt to her rather parched lips.

For Celia, the menopause had come and gone without effecting the massive change she had been led to expect. HRT had helped, of course, and fashionable acupuncture and the fact that she had never expected or wanted to have children, but nothing had lifted her up, re-filled her sails and revivified her hormones more than her singing, the joy of performance on stage. Yes, she was still a woman of substance, a woman of style, a woman of character. Well, characters. Creating characters, *being* other people, possessing other personalities was what had always excited her; had she always been more of an actress than a singer? *I could have gone to Italia Conti,* she thinks, *when I was twelve. They practically begged me, but no, my parents insisted on my staying at the Hampstead High School for the Daughters of Distressed Gentlefolk and taking my A levels – I suppose it was good for my languages – and then off to the Conservatory. I never wanted to go to that bloody snob-pit; the Guildhall would have been far more my scene, but no that wasn't good enough for Daddy. "Not sufficiently academic" meaning not sufficiently posh. Of course, it did mean I got to meet Phillip, the brilliant young composer on his day trips up from Cambridge. Christ, did he seem glamorous. And without Pip I would never have played his* Lady Macbeth of Stepney *which was* the *most fabulous role since Ben Britten's heyday. Which actually I would play better now. But how many roles are there for fifty-year old sopranos? If only Pip would write me a Cleopatra or a… or a Potiphar's wife or anything big and bold and middle-aged and glamorous and* for me, *I'd be happy – overjoyed – to drop the divorce just for that. If Helen Mirren can do it, so can I. And just look at Cher – and I don't believe all that stuff about plastic surgery; they're just jealous. Wish they were jealous of me. But am I attractive enough, sexy enough? Thin enough? Christ, that Twiggy's got a lot to answer for. How the hell do I know after twenty-odd years with a bi – no, come off it – a homosexual, a raving flamboyant poof for a husband?*

Will you please stop thinking about him, woman? she tells herself, turning the page to the centrefold – a hunky young man wearing a mock sultan's outfit revealing a surprisingly unwaxed, hairy chest. *Interesting, very interesting,* she thinks, *but no sensible woman of my age is going to get involved with a boy in his twenties, even with such a furry chest. But a nice mature man, a handsome, intelligent heterosexual man – just for a change*

*– that would be something. And the world, my dear, is my…
ashtray.* She looks round for one as a long wobbly column of
ash falls onto the Afghan rug. *Yes, what I need's a real Anthony
to my Cleo. I've practically forgotten what it feels like to have a
multiple orgasm. Shit, I've forgotten what it feels like to have* one.

But the new role, which frankly she has been desperate
for for several months, is something – a real delight. She has
always wanted to play Elizabeth I, even if Donizetti's Elizabeth
wasn't quite the Virgin Queen of her English history O level.
Rosemary Angmering being a couple of years younger and
blond got to play Mary, Queen of Bloody Scots, whore and
murderess as Elizabeth accurately thinks of her. *Of course,
Rosie's a dramatic and I'm a mezzo and a mezzo is never the
heroine. But still, Eliza is one hell of a fabulous role and who
knows it may be my last – but three or four,* she thinks, refilling
her glass. *If he thinks I'm finished because I'm finished with him,
he's got another think coming, as my old dresser used to say.*

"A woman at fifty can be beautiful. But a woman at fifty
needs to watch the bottle – set the bottle aside," she says aloud
matching the deed to the word, "And do some bloody work."
She looks a little blearily round for her score, but is saved by
the chirping of the phone.

"Hello, my cherub, having an evening in?"

"Darling Harold, I have so much work to do, how could
I think of going out? Unless you're looking for a partner for
dinner with HRH again. I could always manage that."

"Sadly, not tonight, sweetie darling. HRH is touring
Botswana with those lovely Allspice ladies. Didn't you know
they're on a joint tour? I fixed it up, darling. You know me;
always a fixer."

"So, who are you fixing me up with, darling?"

"Nobody tonight I'm afraid, love, but I wonder if you're free tomorrow? I've got tickets for the Met – the new production of *Otello* with that gorgeous young black man in the role, Paul Robson. The trip's on me, sweetie. I've got the flight tickets, first class, of course, and everything. And they say young Mr Robson adores older ladies. And he's got the biggest dong this side of the Zambezi."

"Darling, he may have a dong as long as a barge pole, and it's all very kind of you and everything, but tomorrow I have to be at rehearsals. I do still have a career, you know, and Queen Elizabeth is a very big role. Anyway, who's let you down?"

"Nobody, sweetie, how could you? You were my first choice. Now I'll have to start trawling the old address book. But your loss etc. Still, why don't we go out for a drinkie later? It's only 6.30. I've got so much dirt to dish you wouldn't believe it."

"Oh yes I would, dear. But your dirt is always so pungent I just can't resist. And you must tell me the cause of this sudden New York trip, you lucky little poof."

"Aren't I just? But, of course, it is work for me, dear. And an opportunity to meet the scrumptious dusky Paul. I'll pick you up at eight thirty."

Two hours later – including a productive thirty minutes of vocal acrobatics and thirty of digesting Donizetti – and Celia feels like a new woman. *Or rather,* she thinks, *I feel like a new man. Pity that appellation wouldn't quite fit an old queen like Harold, bitter and twisted old fag that he undoubtedly is. So, why do I hang around with him? Because he's charming, or can be; because he gets tickets to every opening night on three continents; because he knows everybody, including cabinet ministers and royalty; and because I'm an outrageous and appalling old fag-hag. But,* she thinks looking in the mirror at the still (naturally) auburn hair, the crimson lipstick, the almond, grey, naughtily sparkling eyes and the lime green crepe de chine cocktail dress draping the still sensuous full-breasted figure, *a woman of substance. A woman at fifty can still be beautiful.*

IV

It's 5 a.m. Only three hours' sleep, if that, but that's never bothered Harold. Celia's just getting to sleep properly after their drinks together the night before; George is getting back into bed, grumbling, for another couple of hours after peeing to calm that weak bladder, but Harold, lithe and lissom, is up before the lark and quickly tidies his already immaculate bedroom before packing in ten minutes, showering, taking the lightest of breakfasts and changing the message on his answerphone. He glances at the fake ormolu clock on his mantelpiece: 6.05. He'll make it provided the traffic's not too heavy which is unlikely at this time. He's not at all sleepy. The thought of twenty-four hours in New York sends the adrenaline whizzing round his neat, impeccably attired, forty-five-year-old frame.

"This old kosher queen ain't dead yet," he mutters, shoving a couple of files into his smart leather briefcase and just in time remembering to chuck in his golden tickets for the Met.

Then he takes a file out again, glances at a letter in it with a red rose in the corner, smiles and puts it back. In the hall he adjusts his mauve silk tie with a swift look in the mirror. *Not pretty*, he thinks for the umpteenth time, *but attractive and very* alive. He walks the two flights down to the ground floor and, opening the heavy front door, emerges into Lisson Grove.

Harold gets into his new Audi with some pride. He always describes himself as a "deferential Tory", but with the Audi, the Paddington flat, his connections both political and artistic, the deference has actually worn rather thin. Eighteen years of Tory rule have, of course, done him no harm. Quite the reverse. Indeed, Thatcherism (and its watery successor) have shaped his whole career as they have the lives and careers of a whole generation. He was always a Conservative – because of parental example and his own complex character: conventional on the surface, rebellious and daringly reckless at a deeper level, but then profoundly devoted to stability and the social order at the deepest level of all (at least I think the deepest level of all) – but when the blessed Margaret hove into view he became a true blue Thatcherite, despite having progressive social views that would turn her blue rinse grey. She became his icon, the shrine at which he worshipped.

And Harold Rosen is justifiably proud of his rise as part of the Thatcherite revolution, as one of Thatcher's older children; though in fact his ascent from "humble" beginnings as the product of lower middle-class, respectable, ostensibly orthodox parents in Jewish north-west London had started when he was named after that Harold whom his father had so much admired, the future prime minister Harold Macmillan, and educated under the aegis of that other *Labour* Harold, that Mr Wilson who had done so much to shape the sixties. Our Harold – or *Henriette* or *Haroldina* as his operatic friends variously called him – feels a certain warmth towards them both. But for La Thatcher he preserves his adoration. Although a certain type of queen does not wish to sleep with women, he has a desperate need to worship one or two of them, and for so many his icon fulfils that role.

Thanks to the progressive policies of his namesakes, Harold had won a scholarship to a posh and highly academic school where his considerable talents allowed him to win a further scholarship to one of the quieter, more conservative Oxford colleges to read English, which he did with enthusiasm while joining the Conservative Club and the Union. Coming down from Oxford in the mid-seventies and determined not to teach (oh, how George would sympathise!), he had qualified, somewhat ruefully, as an accountant and, due to his impeccable self-presentation and intensely hard work, had got into one of the biggest and best firms of accountants and risen without a trace. But then as a well-paid, always busy but very junior, partner in the early eighties his career had seemed becalmed. Though his bosses admired his financial wizardry and self-discipline at work they had been discreetly informed that – outside work – he was the campest and wildest of queens. There were tales of SM, of private (and not so private) orgies, of whole nights squandered on Hampstead Heath, of designer drugs, of whips and chains and yellow water sports. His active membership of the Party was not enough to counterbalance these slightly disturbing rumours and his *professional* masters felt it was more prudent, at least for the time being, to keep him at a harmless, if comfortable, level within the firm. In '87 he tried for a winnable constituency for which his background should have ostensibly fitted him precisely. But he didn't even get onto the shortlist. Was he just too flamboyant, too camp, for Margaret Thatcher's Tories? A certain bitterness began to appear in his already brilliantly bitchy humour and his social life became even more *outré*, trying out a whole host of life-enhancing substances and techniques; he even tried heterosexuality – once. His partner in the experiment – a secretary at work who had long had a crush on him – found his technique surprisingly good (he'd had plenty of analogous practice), but Harold couldn't really see the point. For a time he couldn't see the point of anything apart from Celia Greyfield and Montserrat Caballe (another of his icons) whom he flew to see in performance all over the world. A visit to Toronto for the purpose – where he was unexpectedly offered a highly attractive job in management – even led him seriously to consider emigrating.

And then suddenly his luck changed. An old school friend had acquired a key post in the Number Ten policy unit and brought him in informally to give advice. Harold was in his element and happy to oblige with ideas, intelligent observations and discreet assistance at no charge whatever, whenever called upon. In straight company he was urbane and only subtly camp; in private consultation he worked ferociously at any task assigned. Now he was really in demand, with a busy social round in the salons of the great. Finally, his bosses, realising their error, offered him that elusive equity partnership he had so longingly coveted. With immense satisfaction he told them, politely, where they could stuff it. He was leaving to set up an independent political consultancy. He had discovered his vocation; not as an accountant or a politician in office but in oiling the wheels of business that keep government – and opposition – on track. He would be that most essential synapse in the brain of the body politic, the unattached lobbyist and fixer.

Now – seven years on – Harold is driving confidently to Heathrow, a little worried by the traffic and wishing they'd already opened the promised fifteen-minute link between Paddington and the airport. It would certainly get plenty of use from him. But he makes it with just forty-five minutes to spare. He quickly checks in and goes through to the business class lounge – first class seems a little over the top even to Harold despite his fib to Celia – though his sponsor for this trip would not have demurred.

An hour later he is sitting on Concorde with champagne in one hand and *Opera Today* magazine in the other, reading Jennifer Tench's article on the decline of British opera in the nineties, bemoaning the lack of another *Lady Macbeth of Stepney*, asking why Jeremy Groves' programmes at the BNO have become so predictable. Isn't it time for him to make way for new blood? Harold giggles like a naughty child; he must keep this for Celia who'll be highly amused, if not outraged. *Oh yes*, thinks Harold, *this is the life – unencumbered, single, ready to make that daring leap, and always, always with the right connections, the right links to form the perfect chain.* "Only connect" was too good a motto for that charming old queen Morgan Forster; it should be the logo of this, the new communications/information age. And on he flies, buoyed up by confidence and daring through the sound barrier, the time barrier, even the political barrier, over the sparkling Atlantic towards the New World.

V

The same bright breezy fresh spring morning in April. George is getting ready for work. George is not very happy. But then George is never very happy going to work; at least not these days. Time was when he was a young and eager lecturer, a teacher with a vocation, his hands filled with the wonders and jewels of English literature, ready to spread them out in all their richness and beauty, all their revealing and life-enhancing depth (life-enhancing, he remembers, pulling on his battered brown boots, was a favoured phrase, especially of his as of many English graduates, back in the seventies, the youthful permissive life-enhancing seventies) before the glistering eyes of the keen young men and women who attended his college then: St. Pancras Polytechnic. Which, despite being known to its students and staff as St. Pancreas ("Same thing anyhow," says George, always fascinated by the origin of words) had been – even more in retrospect but also at the time – an institution long-established and of some esteem and self-esteem. *And what*, thinks George, having a pee for the third time, anxious yet stubbornly unhurried knowing he has only fifteen minutes to do a forty-five-minute journey, *what had St. P.* (fourth time, stimulated by the letter) *become?* The University of Bloomsbury – as he had always dreamt – and even thought feasible when a plethora of polys were universitised in the late eighties – or even remained St. Pancras Poly, a not unworthy title, a title sanctified by nearly a century of usage and respect? No. It had first transmogrified into Euston and St. Pancras College (as if the addition of a second railway station would give greater upward mobility, or were the board of governors embarrassed by their canonisation?), and then – *oh, how low can you stoop*, thinks George touching the door handle five times for luck, or just for neurosis – in a last humiliation to be degraded into Euston Adult Education Centre, or "EAdEC".

"Eadec here," said the telephonists, as if a mellifluous and witty acronym had been coined instead of an empty and ugly euphemism – *or malphemism*, thinks George with a sardonic leer returning to the door one last time to check it's locked, taking for granted his ever-present and burgeoning *folie du doute*.

The bus journey takes even longer than usual. *The traffic just gets worse and worse every day*, he thinks. *How long am I going to have to go on doing this? In theory another fifteen years to serve. No, it cannot be possible. This* must *be inhuman and degrading treatment, surely the Court of Human Rights will have something to say?* But the first day of term is always the worst. And then it strikes him. Being the first day of term the students' presence is not today required.

"Is it ever?" mumbles George relaxing into his seat as he recalls that instead of a 9.30 class, he has today a 10 o'clock meeting. Not that he enjoys the monotonous and interminable staff meetings at which the pomposity of a lavishly paid management is displayed in all its garish splendour. Yet this is something he quite looks forward to – as being so crass it's almost appealing. Of course, looked at objectively from outside the college – sorry, educational centre – this new management (new from the early nineties) is efficient, business-like, smart, impressive. Even George and his fellow luddites concede that it's good at PR and creative accounting, maybe even grudgingly good at management. But to George, a scion of the old school, dusty relic of an age when education was meant to be freely available, liberal and emphatically *non*-business-like, they stink of money, ambition and empty words.

The meeting has, of course, begun as George makes his ironic, shambling way in, deliberately knocking over a couple of chairs. The second executive officer (management titles changed to business style only a year ago, to keep up with the times) Dr De'ath – the apostrophe, as George likes to say, is optional – is addressing the meeting and soars over the minor commotion.

"… which I felt it would be helpful to flag up at this time. Because, of course, we must always keep the core entitlements of our customers before our eyes…"

"Excuse me, Dr Deeth, did you say 'customers'? Have we opened a shop?" shouts George over the six or seven rows in front of him, suddenly having a problem with the good doctor's name.

"Yes, John, customers," says the SEO smiling, well-knowing George's name. "Our students today *are* our customers, our consumers *and* our end product. They're not just numbers as I don't need to tell you, though student numbers are, of course, terrifically important."

Polite laughter at this scintillation, as George mutters to his neighbour Frank, an ancient woodwork teacher forcibly converted like George and other colonised peoples to IT, "First one."

"But the principal aim of this morning's programme evaluation is to bring you all up to speed on the new action plan for assessment and monitoring of the acquisition of competencies, as flagged up in our terrific updated mission statement."

"Two," says George.

"Now, if you have in front of you your FTR6DA pro forma…"

"What?" says George.

"It's a form," whispers Frank, "It's yellow."

"What isn't around here?" mutters George, holding up a crumpled stained form, "I'd used mine as a coffee mat."

Frank guffaws as several younger lecturers look horrified.

"There's a whole pile of them here, John," says the good doctor condescendingly.

"Thanks, Doc, and it's George, George Darkside."

An acolyte of the SEO brings George a new form and the management wannabes tut-tut.

"I'm surprised they don't all try to sit on me like the Mad Hatter," mutters George.

"Jenny can sit on me any day," growls Frank, looking diagonally at a well-proportioned woman in her late forties a little behind them.

"They'll get you for sexual harassment, Frank, watch it."

"I am watching it."

"Sh, sh, please," says Jenny looking daggers at them.

"… most helpful for our records. As the chief EO – Phil, I should say – has so often emphasised…"

"Chief Teletubby," whispers George.

"We are totally committed to a non-action scenario in terms of the redundancy situation and terrifically determined…"

"Three – not many so far."

"… to guarantee a purely and wholly voluntary policy of self-determined selective severance…"

"Of limbs," says George.

"And protuberances," adds Frank.

"… with extremely generous benefits as compared with other similar institutions. I'm sure you see where we're coming from…"

"Yes," whispers George, "And I also see where you're going to."

"The fiery pit if there's any justice," spits Frank.

"Can we have silence please?" Jenny bursts out.

"… because it continues to be the policy of the board of direction…"

"We sure are."

"What?" says Frank.

"Bored, Frank, bored of direction. Keep up, love."

"… to ensure that all needs are addressed, with staff constantly upskilled wherever possible and downsized when unavoidable. I'd be terrifically grateful to have feedback on that."

"Only four," says George. "He's getting lax in his old age."

"I presume there are classes this afternoon?" Jenny asks aloud.

"Why do women teachers always want to work *more*?" asks George quietly.

"Why do male teachers always want to do *less*?" retorts Jenny more loudly, then, noticing a few men frowning, adds, "With notable exceptions, of course."

George's mind drifts off – as it so often does – to George Eliot, that extraordinary woman-in-drag, and her long romantic, illicit affair with that other George – Henry Lewes. And our George melds himself with the Georges of his imagination and wonders whether even now he might be able to fabricate, to create *ex nihilo* a magnificent all-embracing intellectual life of the great Madam George, remembering that it was she who said, "It is never too late to be what you might have been." And he hears a great organ swelling as the figure of Madam George rises before him… and Frank is tapping him quite heavily on the arm.

"It's finished, my old love, we *are* allowed to leave."

"What happened, Frank, apart from boiling hot air?"

"Faintly veiled threats of redundancy if you didn't notice, old pal. Voluntary at first, compulsory if it comes to it. However, if you condescend to peer at your yellow pro forma do-da you'll observe that it's a bloody good deal if you're fifty plus. And it won't be repeated," he says getting up from the table buttoning up his ageing corduroy jacket, the uniform of the older generation college lecturer.

"That's what they always say."

"True, but with a new government virtually certain, they probably mean it. This new lot'll make Maggie look maternal."

"Oh, go on, you old sixties leftie… Are you going to take it? You're older than me."

"I'm well aware of that, my old chum, but with two kids at uni I can't afford to. They'll be abolishing grants altogether soon. And Jill's been offered it at her school, so she's entitled to first go. But *you* can take it, you old bachelor boy. Get a bit of part-time work. Why not?"

There are no classes that afternoon, just a continuation of meetings – *always meetings,* thinks George, *interminable, ineluctable* meetings – in "subject groups". ("What's wrong with the word 'departments'?" he mutters.) As George had dropped hints to the English group that he would be attending IT and vice-versa, he feels free to stray in body as well as mind this afternoon. Of course, the total control mentality of new management (everything new, including "New Labour", George regards with extreme caution) will surely catch up with him, but he is thinking only in the short term. And he needs time to think. So, he sidles surreptitiously out of the spanking new glass and concrete management block where meetings are usually held into the older largely Edwardian college buildings next door with its old classrooms where he has taught Eng Lang and Lit for nearly twenty-five years. It is one of those classic, generously proportioned pre-World War l buildings with gabled roofs and a big wide staircase from the foyer up the three floors. And today, first day of term with meetings in progress, it is deliciously quiet and ruminative as George wanders around. He loves the faintly rancid smell of the old college – so different from the plastic and paint of the new block – composed of accumulated year upon year of students, some fragrant, some foul, chalk dust (though chalk was long replaced by whiteboard markers), thin old trodden-down carpets, the smells of old books and the atmosphere so many times inhaled and exhaled of teaching and learning, learning and teaching over almost a century. When the big old classrooms are empty like this – and George feels sure this building will soon be demolished – he can feel them peopled with the ghosts of former students, students whom, collectively and in the Platonic sense, he had loved. The old order had certainly passed, giving way to new, and without doubt this would be the last year when he would be teaching English Literature, as both A levels and GCSEs were being phased out. After all, the CEO had said at a recent meeting to "consult" on those long-taught examinations, "We have a completely open mind about whether to continue running these courses in the future." In other words, they were indubitably doomed.

Of course, he may be lucky enough to be timetabled to teach liberal studies – no, they were long-outmoded along with liberal values – "communicational competencies", to the great British unwashed on day release, but that was hardly a consummation devoutly or even faintly to be wished. Instead, he would be translated across to the vast new Teaching Resources Information Centre (the "TRIC") where he would be supervising students – that is, customers – teaching themselves the tricks of the new trade of superfast communication and instant access to knowledge – or at least facts. And much as he resents it, George has found the world wide web quite breath-taking in his beginner's course in the TRIC and for the first time he is tempted to jettison his old typewriter and splash out on a computer of his own. But fascinating as this world of the third millennium might be, would he feel interested or qualified to teach it to others? Was that why he had taken his BA at Durham, his MA at UCL? What had happened to those profoundly innovative novels he had planned to write or that great tome that would unlock the arcana of Victorian literature? Maybe if he volunteers for this advanced redistributional severance – or whatever the damn thing is called in this sense-obscuring post-Thatcherite jargon – he can write them now, in what a recent Radio 4 programme on ageing had called his "advanced middle youth".

In his mind's eye he sees the sweating middle-aged host of a glitzy TV show in a sparkly gold lamé jacket with masses of shiny black hair leaping down a huge staircase towards the camera saying with an enormous grin, "Can life begin for you, George Darkside, at fifty? You bet!" And then he is back in the empty classroom, looking out of the second-floor casement window across the variegated roofs of West London into a bland pale blue, early spring sky.

Getting into bed that night, George is still weighing up the pros and cons of his future. At forty-nine he feels neither old nor young and the thought of being middle-aged, middle-class and middle-brow sounds horrendously dull. Advanced middle youth; yes, that's a more attractive nomenclature. He likes it. He warms to it. But how to adapt to it, to feel truly at ease with it? At least, unlike Frank, he doesn't have teenage appendages to earn for. George enjoys his bachelor status; in fact he relishes it. That's not to say that he is without certain needs, needs of the body, desires of the flesh. George's sexuality is of an indeterminate and flexible nature. Since his early short-lived marriage to a domineering (but not adequately dominant) lady, George has remained largely celibate; in body, but absolutely not in mind. For over twenty years he has lived alone, but in a mental world rich in diverse and complex imaginings. The fantasies and images that have remained unwritten and unabsorbed into novels, plays or short stories have flowered in his fertile brain: historical, contemporary, surreal, neurotic and above all, pansexual. George's sex life is, in the bold world of make-believe, immensely exciting, highly promiscuous and filled with every possible variation, deviation and perversion. Twosomes, threesomes, orgies, exhibitionism, sadomasochism

– some mild, some disturbingly extreme – and lots of voyeurism in every possible context. But, dear reader, you are gagging to know if these lurid fantasies are of a homo, a hetero or even a bisexual nature, and your inquiry is quite apt. As a matter of record I should say they are largely homosexual, though the orgies and tableaux often contain an intriguing and piquant heterosexual or rather bisexual element, and his frequent, thrilling excursions into the realms of masochistic submission usually – no, always – saw him grovelingly abject before a magnificent madame, a dominatrix of middle age and grand proportions and even grander personality.

So, the hour he spends in bed before sleep each night – an hour he particularly anticipates all day – is sixty minutes in an erotic subaqueous world of gorgeous young men, some hunky, some lissom, and huge domineering ladies, like a canvas jointly painted by David Hockney and Beryl Cook. This evening, in a mood decidedly gay, having enjoyed a late night pop concert on TV he would never in a million years admit to having watched, he plays one of his favourite games: toying with the lubricious concept of matching up contrasting pop and rock stars in exciting combinations. And for a while, a long while, he plays with an intriguing mating of that luscious young Robbie from the boy band he had drooled over on the telly with a much bigger and maturer rock star. Meatloaf seemed to fill the part – in more ways than one. Then their long-drawn out wrestling match is interrupted and overwhelmed by a superb black dominatrix: Tina Turner cracking a ferocious whip. But the music scene fails to hold his attention for very long and drifting into images from the well-illustrated sports pages of his daily *Times* he begins to imagine a bout – several rounds of boxing leading then to wrestling and finally to a more total and satisfying submission between a huge black heavyweight, handsome as morning with brightly coifed dreadlocks, and a lithe and lovely well-oiled lightweight of Middle Eastern appearance and equal eagerness for the contest. And if, dear reader, I draw a veil at this point preferring not to name these imaginary – or imagined – figures and leave to your own vivid imagination what George is so avidly creating in *his* – well, would you blame me, discretion being, as Falstaff so wisely warns us, the better part of valour? Eventually, satiated and damp, our anti-hero slips off contentedly into the strong and welcoming arms of Morpheus – or should that be Orpheus? whatever – proving once again the astonishing fertility of the human brain in pursuing an activity totally harmless yet immensely fulfilling.

VI

After a three-hour rehearsal of *Mary Queen of Scots*, Celia is not at all in the mood for giving an interview to a woman from *EG* magazine or from any other mag for that matter. But as with all PR work she knows she has to grin and bear it. Not that she hates being a diva – quite the contrary. As she readily admits she relishes such fame as she has – being widely and well esteemed amongst opera lovers – and would love to have more. To be an opera singer is to aim for stardom – nothing less will do – and Celia has never forgotten those heady days fifteen years ago when she created the title role Pip had written for her – for *her* – in *Lady Macbeth of Stepney* and on the nerve-racking first night emerged from the stage door of the Whippo – sorry, the Western Hippodrome – to be greeted for the first time in her life by fifty or sixty fans and autograph-hunters, including Stefan the strange tall Pole with the intense gaze behind the little round glasses who had passionately kissed her hand after she had signed his programme and who had never ceased stalking her since. He was totally harmless and she rather enjoyed it. If anything, he was too harmless. Their relationship had never progressed, apart from her learning that Stefan, whose knowledge of opera dwarfed Celia's or even Pip's, had a wife also Polish and two children; the wife having gone off some years ago and more recently the now grown-up children too, leaving him, an electrician by trade, more than ever devoted to opera and his personal diva. But Celia had not seen him in over a year, not since her recital (with Jeremy accompanying her sonorously on the Bösendorfer, his favourite concert grand) at the Wigmore Hall. *God, those Richard Strauss songs had gone down superbly well; eat your heart out, Dame Janet.* Stefan had raved at the stage door, much to Jeremy's predictable chagrin. (As Pip said, "More shagging, less chagrin.") Since then, nothing. And just when a dash of masculine adoration was most requisite. Thinking which, as she prepares her late light lunch, she guiltily puts on her latest Take That CD; the quite unnecessary guilt just adding that extra frisson to the enveloping miasma of teenage testosterone.

Having devoured her meagre lunch and the luscious sounds of her favourite boy band she toys with the idea of snatching a nap – one of the few pleasures she has discovered in middle age – but the appointment was made for 2.30 and it is almost that. The journalist was called Mavis something and was well respected in the field. Suddenly Celia realises there might be a photographer. In fact, she hopes there is. A photograph adds so much to an interview, but she also hopes there isn't. Glancing in the mirror she sees the Queen Mum before her daily makeover. A woman at fifty can be… appalling? *Christ! But who cares,* she thinks, *about Mavis Whatshername. We can arrange a separate photo session. Or I could just palm her off with…*

The doorbell rings and Celia goes to answer.

"Miss Greyfield?"

It is not a woman. *It's certainly not a woman,* thinks Celia. It is a young man, early thirties, medium height and build, with an intelligent oval face, pale blue dreamy eyes, and fashionably short light brown hair. *His body seems*, she thinks, *remarkably well shaped beneath his cream blouson and distressed pale blue Levis and his accent very hard to place.*

"You're obviously not Mavis Do-da."

He smiles. "No, I'm Jeb Walters. Our editor sent me instead. I hope you don't mind."

"Mind? Not a bit. I prefer men." She makes a dramatic pause, thinking he sounds subtly and attractively Irish. "Do come in."

My God, I must look like shit, she thinks, *and, of course, they had to send an attractive young man. The voice. Remember your best asset: the voice.*

"Would you like a drink? Sherry? Whisky? Or a nice cold beer? I know what young men are into these days." *Christ, that sounded terrible*, she thinks.

"Beer would be great."

"Do come through to the kitchen. Forgive the mess. My home help hasn't been in for a few days."

"Miss Greyfield led me through to her dishevelled but charming kitchen where I asked her if her much talked-of separation from her composer husband, Philip Travers, had been traumatic." He gives a low chuckle and looks coolly at her from beneath ice-blue eyes. *My God, he's gorgeous*, she thinks.

"And I thought you were here to talk to me about my career and in particular my new role as Queen Elizabeth," she almost purrs. "Molson or Stella?"

"Molson, thank you."

Now she thinks he sounds American, maybe Canadian.

"D'you mind if I record? I just want to have your voice on tape."

She opens two beers.

"You flatterer. Keep going."

"You're as good an actress as singer. Would you take on pure acting roles?"

"I'd take on anything, darling. Or anybody. But opera singing *is* acting because opera is theatre. There's no distinction."

He takes out a little notebook.

"And how do you look after your voice?"

"Oh, lots of booze and fags – can't get away from fags – and very little exercise; you know, the usual things."

He gives her a very cool, level glance.

"It works, Miss Greyfield. Or do you prefer Mrs Travers?"

Very straight bat.

"I've never used my married name. Are you married?"

He gives a wry, dry smile.

"Nice beer. Tell me about your new role. Do you identify with Queen Elizabeth?"

"Very much. She was a remarkable woman, who somehow found the power to rule triumphantly over a whole society of men. Through the use of brains and sexuality. It's a powerful combination. Don't you agree?"

"And how do you get on with your opposite number playing Mary?"

He has a way of almost muttering his words that makes it impossible to place that accent. So intriguing. It's the way a lot of young people talk, she thinks.

"My... oh, Rosie? Rosemary Angmering and I are just like sisters. Always have been. We have a wonderful relationship."

"There were those rumours, of course, of her having an affair with Mr Travers…"

You cheeky, cute bastard.

"Don't make me laugh, please. It never happened. But, quite off the record, of course, she and Jeremy Groves, our brilliant conductor, are very close, like that." She crosses her first and second fingers tightly. "*Very* close. But that's just between us, sweetie." *That'll do wonders for Jeremy's reputation,* she thinks.

"Are you happy, Miss Greyfield?"

"Profoundly, my dear. Never been happier. I think I've found a kind of still centre now, approaching my middle years, which I've never known before. And very ready for new challenges."

His steady look gives her no indication if he believes this drivel. "Such as?"

"Who knows? Straight acting perhaps, as you suggested, or directing, that's always appealed to me." *And terrified me,* she thinks. "But I have a good five years of singing at the top level in front of me and – to put aside false modesty – I know I'm singing better than ever before. My voice certainly has new maturity, added nuances, as Jeremy was saying only yesterday."

"And what are your views on the election?"

"The election? I didn't think *EG* was a political magazine but… I'm not a terribly political animal myself, unlike my dear friend and colleague Jeremy who is very closely linked to New Labour. I think he even gave a donation to Tony's election fund. You know, for the leadership, but that you *really* mustn't mention. As for me… well, frankly I'd be very glad to see a change after eighteen years of a pretty philistine sort of government. Norma Major's very nice by the way – we have some friends in common – and very much *au fait* with my world but as for the Tory Party… no, we certainly need a change. Personally, I'd be in favour of giving the liberals a chance, but then my grandfather was a liberal MP, you know, back in the forties…"

"Thank you so much, Miss Greyfield. It's been a pleasure." He is standing up, packing notebook and cassette recorder back into his elegant tan leather backpack.

"For me too. Will there be photos with the article?"

A moment's silence. "I'd guess so. That's really not my department."

"Of course. I'll give you a couple of publicity stills but your editor can call me if she wants a shoot somewhere."

She brings back the photos – no more than a couple of years old.

"There we are. Jed, was it?"

"Jeb. An honour to meet you, Miss Greyfield. And thanks for the beer."

"Not at all. If you want tickets for a performance, just call me. Here's my card."

"Thank you."

And he is gone.

Don't suppose I'll see him again. Hm. She puts the kettle on, feeling the need for a strong, black coffee. A woman at fifty. A man of about thirty. *You bloody fool*, she thinks.

VII

Jonathan's career has not been a brilliant success in the last seven years. In fact, like one of Pharaoh's cows in the years of famine, it has grown progressively leaner. At the fall of Thatcher, he was one of the most successful and envied young conductors in Britain; to be acclaimed for your performance of *Lohengrin* at the BNO in your early thirties was to be almost a prodigy – especially without the advantage of foreign birth or name. All his life Jonathan had been something of a prodigy – at least, in certain phases. And that had been a truly glamorous, glittering phase, his artistic achievement culminating in his meeting with his long-time companion, his partner of preference, his beloved Ben.

But then things had begun to go – to use the in-phrase of '97 – pear-shaped. Jonathan had read the cache of letters which Ben had brought over amongst Francis' effects; the bitter, mocking ironic letters which had passed between (thought Jonathan) those two sad old queens. He had at once become utterly disillusioned with his mentor at the Western Hippodrome, the man to whom in fact he owed his glittering career but whose corrosive jealousy and spite had eaten into the very microchips of his PC, Jeremy Groves. In Jonathan's opinion the man was a louse, not the latter-day Marquise of

Les Liaisons Dangereuses, but a jealous, bitter, rancid old queen.

"No wonder the man lives alone," he had said to Ben, "His vital juices dried up long ago."

And so, in a fit of pique – and with a touch of anxious jealousy over Ben whom Jeremy clearly coveted – Jonathan had announced that he would spend six months of the '91 season with the BNO and then resign to spread his wings abroad. First, he needed those six months in London to trial his relationship with Ben and to give him time to look around for a long-term job; for he was confident that with his recent success, great offers would be in the offing. So, at the end of his stay in Amsterdam he rejected the twelve-month music fellowship he had been offered at the university there and returned to London. But he forgot – or hadn't learnt - two things: that the last six months of a contract are usually the worst and, in relation to Jeremy, that revenge is a dish best served cold.

Jeremy – unsure why his erstwhile protégé had taken this decision and (like most of us) both infinitely worse and infinitely better than Jonathan took him to be – was both complacent and appalled. As Jonathan thought, he had certainly been jealous of the younger man's budding success and had done his utmost to rein him in, but now he was quite genuinely horrified to see his brilliant protégé throwing away a sparkling career at the Whippo. He had pleaded with him to stay on, conduct any opera he desired in the '92/'93 season, even offered to recommend him to the board for the title of assistant MD of the BNO. But Jonathan had made up his mind that he could not possibly continue to work with this snake in the grass in the sure knowledge that his huge success here had guaranteed him plenty of offers in the wider world. He was too inexperienced to realise that most people who work together at the top of organisations – especially in the media – exist in a state of smiling mutual antipathy and distrust.

Jonathan had actually hoped and lobbied for a post, even a relatively humble one, at the Garden, but relations between the Whippo and the Garden had never been good and were going through a particularly bad patch then. (What garden would welcome the offspring of a hippo marauding through it?) Next, he had heard of a very promising opening at the Met, which would be excellent as Ben was also quite eager to live and work for a while in New York City. On and off negotiations had gone on in secret for several months and he was finally offered a junior but remarkably well-paid conducting post subject to the formal agreement of the new president of the board, a vastly wealthy businessman whose identity was being kept secret and who could not be contacted. In the meantime, Jonathan accepted a quite appealing job to start on 1 July '92 as director of the Flemish Masters Orchestra of Bruges, a well-established ensemble whose recordings of rococo and Romantic works had won several awards. That was an excellent fall-back position – though Ben, fully occupied with various odd singing jobs in London, would not want to join him there full time. But New York beckoned and he even received his tickets on Concorde in early June. He had done most of his packing when, on the twenty-first of that month – his letter of regret to the Flemish master already etched on his PC screen – when he received a letter from New York, baldly stating:

Dear Jonathan,

At the recent board meeting, which was the first of the new season, your proposed appointment was laid before the board as newly constituted.

Regretfully, the board was unable to confirm such an appointment at this time. They have asked me to pass on to you their best wishes for your future career. You are at liberty to dispose as you wish of the airline tickets already dispatched to you.

Yours most sincerely,

Elaine Rosenbloomberg-Smith

Secretary to the Board

Jonathan was physically unable to breathe for almost a minute after reading this letter, which he then read through time and time again with waves of nausea, gradually turning to anger, sweeping over him. A week before, he would have said that Bruges was almost as appealing as New York and that the post in Europe had many advantages, but now he had to admit – even to himself – that he had passionately desired and expected to be going to live in that big juicy sexy green apple and work in one of the greatest opera houses in the world. He felt profoundly shaken, shaken to his roots. And he suddenly saw that life is not, as he had hitherto imagined, an ever-advancing and rising path up the mountain from promising beginnings to ultimate glory but something far more devious and complex with sudden highs and swooping falls, less a draftsman's drawing than an Escher sketch.

At home that evening, as Jonathan tearfully adapted his letter to Bruges into one of apparently cheerful acceptance, Ben was immensely consoling and loving. He read him, from his favourite anthology of verse given him on high school graduation by his congressman father, the beautiful poem by Walt Whitman, the American apostle of manly love: "We two boys together clinging, one the other never leaving…"

The next morning, he read him something else. "Hey, Jon, do you see this in the *Herald Tribune*?"

"Hardly, dear, I never read it."

"'The Metropolitan Opera's new board held its first meeting last week under its new chairman, Mr Mostyn Sinclair. As one of New York's leading attorneys and patrons of the arts Mr Sinclair has long been considered the ideal holder of this most coveted position.' He's the guy who backed our production of Jeremy's *Streetcar*, isn't he?"

"You mean the one that was almost as good as *The Simpsons'* version?"

"Hey, don't be so bitter, babe. New York's loss is Bruges' gain. And you're incredibly well placed there to find jobs in Germany. In fact, why don't I look for a job in one of the German opera houses – that'd be fantastic experience and we can spend huge amounts of time together."

"And who contacted Mostyn Sinclair and warned him off me? Who do you think? That bastard Groves, of course, who else?"

"Well, possibly. Or maybe Mostyn already had some blue-eyed boy of his own lined up. That's how it usually works, believe me, babe. Just let it all wash over you. Rise above it. Take deep breaths and plan your future in Bruges. And you just insist on a humungous bed for your amply proportioned boyfriend to wallow in, every possible weekend I can get over there."

Bruges is, like Amsterdam, a city of waterways and bridges, but, unlike Amsterdam, its arteries debouch into no wide and generous harbour and its bridges are a closure not an opening up. Pretty and historic, taciturn in a land of three languages, it enfolds its visitors in a haze of unknowing, a moody forgetfulness beneath its folding star. Jonathan could not feel settled there. One weekend a month Ben would come to stay in his quaint but cosy studio apartment overlooking a secret garden in an internal courtyard and another weekend he would fly to London – which was painful and disturbing as London meant not only home but also freedom, expansiveness and cultural plenitude. When he visited Ben in London their nights were romantic, warm and comforting. But when Ben came to stay with him in that dark, inverted city, the sex between them was hot, yearning, penetrative, intense. It was like two sides of a coin, both enhanced by the fortnight it took to turn the penny over.

The members of the band, the eponymous old masters, were business-like, competent, naff, like most orchestral players. And being Belgian they had little or no time for their unknown English MD whom they regarded with glazed indifference. They responded adequately to his baton but without his ever feeling an emotional or spiritual interchange had taken place between him and them. Just once when he was playing a Mozart piano concerto with them – the ethereally beautiful "K.491 in C minor" – directing them from the keyboard (not easy in any circumstances), when they began the serene slow movement and the woodwind players came in to envelope the pianist's repetition of the divinely simple theme, he experienced a melding of sounds that felt almost a melding of souls. This delicious ecstasy – a correlative in exquisite sensation of a spiritual high – buzzed and sang right through to the end of the extraordinarily refined finale. At the end he looked round at the players, his face radiant with exultation, to hear, through the polite applause of the local audience, the German horn player say quietly to the Scottish clarinettist, "My piles are killing me. Do you have those pills with you?"

As a professional he should not have been fazed or surprised, but he could not help feeling that it summed up his experience of making music in Bruges.

Reader, in one life we follow so many roads, drink from so many cups, kiss so many mouths, touch so many hands – and never know till far too late the destination of the road, the value of the cup, the beauty of the mouth, the integrity of the hands. Gentle reader, prepare yourself, if you are young or untried, for the inconstancy of lovers, the egotism of colleagues, the unkindness of friends, the unbearable pain of loss. Disappointment, disillusion, frustrated ambition, grief like a knife (for during this period Jonathan suffered the death of his mother to whom he was so close that he had not even felt able to mention her, let alone dissect his feelings about her in his autobiographical *Sketches*) – all these and many other painful occasions Jonathan experienced and somehow survived.

But everything passes, even grief is absorbed, and hope like the seasons is miraculously renewed. Jonathan's contract was for two years and though it felt like twenty it eventually came to an end. He had nothing to return to in London – except home and Benjamin, which was a thousand times better than the Flemish masters. There was also a letter awaiting his arrival which read as follows:

My dear Jonathan,

You must be heartily sick of boring old Bruges. Welcome back to civilisation. I wish I could offer you your old post back at the Whippo – we've gone through several replacements since your (quite unnecessary) departure but I now have a super deputy called Adelina Majorca, who learnt her trade in Sydney and is certainly destined for big things. She's a woman who likes women, if you know what I mean, and you must come and see her – she's doing Dutchman *next month. I'll send you tickets. And it's so trendy having a woman deputy – I've had so many accolades for it. But you don't want to know that. What you do want to know is that I have quite a lot of freelance rapporteur work for you to do here with voice coaching etc. – all the sort of stuff you're really good at – and once you're here who knows what conducting opportunities might arise? And I don't want to hear any false pride or such nonsense; you need work and there's work here. That's all there is to it. Give my love to your gorgeous hunk of a boyfriend and remind him to come up and see me sometime – also about work. Oh, how I miss Francis – the only person in the world with my warped sense of humour. Call me within a week or the police will be round.*

Your friend,

JG

Jonathan hated having to go back to Jeremy, especially for the sort of work he had been doing for him nearly five years before, but the letter was accurate: any pride he felt would be false and stupid. So, he buckled down to it, took up the offer and got other part-time work teaching piano and conducting a ladies' choir in South London. But the carrot of conducting the BNO orchestra again stayed beyond his grasp; Adelina was just too damn good, and visiting conductors filled any gaps. His ambitions as a writer had largely withered, except for a lingering feeling that he would love one day to write opera. Despite Jeremy's hints, it seemed most unlikely he would ever conduct again. And in relation to any other post he applied for – and in the first couple of years there were several – he sensed there was always the unspoken question of "Why *did* you leave the BNO so suddenly, after such early success?" People knew something had gone wrong, and as Jeremy Groves remained a figure to be reckoned with, it was he himself who took the weight of suspicion. But elevating him above it was the experience he had been waiting for all his life – the experience of joining the human race by living with the person he loved, and that proved well worthwhile. He may not have been a genius or an incandescent star, but he was living a fulfilled if low-key life in their two-bedroom rented flat in West Hampstead while Ben developed his singing career, working as a singing waiter, giving private tuition and benefiting from subventions from the inconsistent but generous congressman, his dad.

And so passed another five years: of John Major and Madonna, and Charles and Di's divorce, and the death of John Smith, and Tony Blair becoming king-in-waiting, and the internet, and the Spice Girls until we arrive, as if by magic, at spring 1997 and *now*.

VIII

"... our five pledges... trust me on this one... bringing hope..."

Tony Blair on TV looking halfway between manic and messianic, Jonathan sprawls on the couch watching the final stages of this long election campaign. A large, well-built, naked man with a lurid snake tattoo emblazoned across his broad back wanders in from the bedroom.

"Shove up, you slob. Not him again."

"What's Ben doing?"

"Having a shit. Which is better than watching it."

"Oh, come on, Grant. Don't say you're gonna vote Tory."

"Tory? No way. They're all useless fuckers, politicians."

"What about gay rights? The homeless?"

"Jonathan, mate, your heart's dripping on the sofa. Politicians don't give a fuck about anyone but themselves. They're all the bloody same."

"So, you're not gonna vote?"

"No way."

"So, you want everything run by the military?"

"Couldn't make a worse job of it."

Jonathan thinks, *Do I really want a fascist in my home? Sitting sweating naked on my couch?*

"Come here, you silly sod."

He grabs Grant's arm and the bigger man begins laughing – a really dirty, dry, sexy laugh. They start to wrestle and briefly Jonathan, having seized the initiative, is on top.

"You're a stupid wanker. What are you?" He holds Grant down by both arms – or Grant lets himself be held down.

"Whatever you say, sir."

And with that, he's reversed the situation, and both are on the carpet rolling over, Grant still laughing inanely and Jonathan puffing as he strains every sinew to get back on top.

"They're all empty-headed cunts, that lot," shouts Grant as he pinions Jonathan to the floor and they stare at each other sweating heavily, Grant looking amused, tolerant, Jonathan staring goggle-eyed, almost hateful.

Grant holds both of the smaller guy's wrists under his one actually quite small, but strong left hand and with his right hand grabs Jonathan's balls and twists them – just enough to cause him to shout out.

"Ooh, you bastard."

"You love it, don't you? Ask Daddy for more, beg for more. Ha, ha, ha."

Jonathan says nothing but looks up into Grant's incredibly shiny green eyes with his mouth wide open. Grant quickly moves his hand up to get a hold on Jonathan's very hard prick.

"Don't you love it? Filthy little bastard."

He spits on his right palm and then, grabbing the prick again, jerks it quickly, still laughing, with Jonathan crying out like a muted foghorn.

"Just carry on, you guys, don't mind me," says Ben ambling into the room fat and comfortable in a pair of briefs as a jet of spunk shoots out from between Grant's tightly clasped fist and he falls back laughing uproariously and slapping Jonathan heartily across his wet belly.

"… a new tomorrow," perorates Tony on the box to massive applause.

IX

"You will come over to Jeremy's Thursday evening, darling, both of you?"

"I think we were planning to stay in and just pig out – as Ben would say," says Jonathan, winking at Ben who looks unamused and whispers, "Who is it?"

"Celia. Now if you'd invited us to *your* place that would be different."

"Yes, dear." She sounds a bit pissed off at that. "But *my* place used to be *our* place and till I've got that whole divorce thing sorted I really can't entertain here. But we do expect to see you, Jeremy and I."

After that faux pas, Jonathan sees he has no choice.

"Let me just consult with my husband… Darling, do you want to watch the election results at Jeremy's?" Receiver in hand, he grimaces and rapidly shakes his head.

"Love to, babes," replies Ben, not even looking up from his *Classic FM* magazine.

"Shit."

"Sorry?"

"Sure thing," says Jonathan, "We'd love to. I hope Pip will be there."

"Doubt it, sweetie darling. He was invited but I don't want to share the evening with his new boyfriend – apparently, he's virtually geriatric and Mitteleuropean – and he won't come without."

"Sorry about that."

"I'm not. By the way, did I tell you the weirdest thing about my interview with *EG* magazine? A rather attractive young man – very attractive actually – came round to interview me, did it charmingly with notebook and everything, then Mavis Do-da called the next day to apologise that she hadn't been round! So, I had to do it all over again. Can you believe that?"

"I can believe anything connected with you, dear."

"Do you think he's a stalker or a secret agent or something? He was gorgeous in a sleek, held-back sort of way."

"More likely a burglar, love, in a sleek, held-back sort of way. No, not really. Don't worry about it. Anyway, I read the piece. It was great."

"My taxi's here for the rehearsal. See you Thursday."

"Bye." Phone already dead. "Why the hell he has to use Celia to send his messages I don't know. And I really don't want to go there on Thursday as you would have known if you'd just looked up."

"What, babe? Sure, I knew you wanted to go. It'll be a real blast. Have you seen they've re-mastered these recordings by Karajan?"

X

"Exit polls very promising, boys," shouts Celia as Jonathan and Ben come through the door of what was once Francis' very elegant Knightsbridge apartment, before his premature demise in the Californian haze handed it over to Jeremy.

"The fucking thing's over, dear. We've won. It's just a matter of numbers," calls Jeremy, making coffee in the kitchen. "As Peter Mandelson was saying to me last week…"

Jonathan splutters. "I thought you'd gone over to the Liberals."

"Rubbish. I got fed up with the old left, but as for Tony and Peter…"

"Would you like something a bit stronger than coffee, boys?"

"More like the Democrats, I guess," says Ben. "The Third Way, Clinton calls it. My dad thinks its brilliant: an empty vessel each voter fills up with his own dreams and wishes. You know he's standing for the Senate next year?"

"I'll stick to coffee till the news is more definite, my dear. So, it's just the four of us?" asks Jonathan.

"Unless Pip calls in later, which wouldn't surprise."

"And Adelina may show her face at some point," says Jeremy coming in from the kitchen. "You always stare at that

Raoul Dufy whenever you come here, Jonathan. I could leave it to you in my will if you like."

"My favourite painter – when I was a teenager. But I grew out of it."

"So, I won't then."

David Dimbleby is asking Cecil Parkinson something about fertilisers to everybody's amusement.

"This could be like the '64 election," says Celia. "I remember it well. I was just about to start at the Conservatory; they were wonderfully exciting times…"

"Of course, darling," says Jeremy bustling in with the drinks. "And next you'll be telling us how you nearly broke your crinoline when Dizzy got back in. Think *now*, dear."

"Shit, they've taken Basildon. That's it. We've done it." Jonathan hugs Ben who smiles wanly.

"Let's open a book on the majority."

"Fifty, at least."

"A hundred and fifty, I'd guess."

"Ben, you gorgeous hunk, when we want an opinion on American politics – such as they are – we'll ask you," says Jeremy, patting Ben's bare left knee. "Of course, you're our expert on senators and things. I'll put a bottle of champers on eighty."

"Can we just see what they're saying on ITV?"

Jeremy intervenes. "Celia, love, a general election has to be watched under the cultivated eye of a Dimbleby. That's the law!"

The intercom buzzes.

"Would one of you boys get it? I can't be disturbed at this point."

Ben opens the door to two middle-aged men – one quite short with greying hair and a warm diffident smile, the other tall, lanky with round glasses and a very serious expression.

"Sorry to disturb you," says Pip, "But isn't it fabulous?"

"Absolutely," mutters Celia in a pissed off sort of voice, not bothering to look round.

"By the way, everybody, this is Stefan."

Celia turns her head so quickly she cricks her neck. *What the hell is my erstwhile Polish stalker doing going around with my husband? So, it* is *true: all men are gay.*

"I think you two have met, darling. Stef's one of your greatest fans."

"An enormous pleasure to meet you once again, madam," says the tall Pole, moving forwards to take Celia's hand tenderly in his, smile at her stigmatically, and kiss it.

A frisson passes up her arm. The man, though plain, has charm; she can almost hear the gallant Polish cavalry. Then he sits close to Pip who smiles at him possessively.

"My God, Finchley's gone to Labour. Finchley's gone to Labour." Jonathan is dancing round the room with Celia.

"Probably more than a hundred and fifty," says Ben, "With all due respect, maestro."

Jeremy ignores this. "I shall have to call Peter personally on his mobile. What a wonderful night for Socialists."

Pip kisses Celia. "It was worth waiting eighteen years for, darling. We are still friends, I hope?"

Stefan is staring at her with those small intense eyes.

"We're all friends here, my love. After all, it's the Socialist millennium."

Jeremy is trying to get through on his mobile phone.

"Tell him it's Jeremy, Jeremy Groves… He's just about to speak to the next PM…? Oh, of course, just put me on hold… Someone go and break open the Bolly for God's sake. It's on ice."

Another buzz on the intercom. Ben goes over. "Sure, come on up, Adelina, everyone's here."

A tall, handsome, very confident woman of about thirty-five comes in. She has dark Mediterranean eyes.

"Hi, guys. Is it party time yet?"

"Definitely, Adelina, now that you're here, come and sit down. We women should stick together."

Celia – who has often worked with Adelina in the last five or six years – has never realised until now how attractive, almost beautiful, the woman is, in a rather unusual style, somewhere on the spectrum between lipstick lesbian and butch dyke.

Pip and Stefan are both staring over at Celia as she takes Adelina's free hand (the other is holding her champagne glass as Jonathan fills it) and puts it tightly between her knees.

Adelina sips and watches the box.

"Isn't that that Portillo character we all love to despise? Though he's actually quite handsome," she says in a contralto voice halfway between Germaine Grier and Greta Garbo.

"He's lost it, he's lost it," shouts Pip.

"And to an out poufter," screams Jonathan. "It's a fucking miracle."

"What do you mean he's speaking to the palace? Oh my Lord, yes, just keep me on hold."

"Celia," says Pip, "Isn't that your camp Tory friend? What the hell is he doing at the RFH?"

Celia peers and, indeed, it can only be Harold, the egregious, ubiquitous Harold, somewhere in the crowd not far behind the Labour leadership and speaking to another younger man, attractive with a close-cropped head, whom she feels she knows.

The scene switches back to Basildon where Portillo is now conceding defeat.

"So, *he* won't be leader of the opposition. He's being quite gracious about it, don't you think?" says Adelina in her clipped Aussie tones.

"Shit, that was the bloke who interviewed me for *EG* or pretended to."

"Excuse me?"

"What the hell is going on?"

But Pip and Stefan have both lifted her up and are dancing a kind of Polonaise with her around the room, Ben is giving Jonathan a huge kiss while Jeremy is still shouting into the phone.

"Now, yes now, the White House will have to wait."

Adelina sits and sips her Bollinger quietly. She seems quite sanguine about the Socialist millennium. She's already planning for the real one.

PART II

Summer: Andante cantabile

"Nice room this. Roomy. Lots of room."

The vice-principal's secretary – a dour slightly frumpish woman – looks up from her work at a shiny state-of-the art PC and gives George a snarling smile.

"Quite a bit bigger than the cupboard I share with two smelly colleagues and an old filing cabinet that won't open properly."

"I'll have another look to ask if he's ready to see you yet."

George smiles wickedly to himself having clearly succeeded in driving the woman to distraction, and action.

"Dr De'ath can see you now."

"Do come in, Jeff."

The good doctor is not a bad man, though he is by most people's reckoning an ugly one. He is making a genuine effort in his cold and calculating way to balance the demands of his boss, the Department of Education, two hundred lecturers, his wife, three kids and a remarkably ugly female catering lecturer who lives behind Battersea power station in a property which has recently become a lot more valuable.

"Jeff."

"Let's go over to the table, George."

It's a massive office and apart from the VP's elegant desk contains a large boardroom table. They take chairs at one corner. Dr De'ath has a voluminous file in front of him which he glances at from time to time. He smiles and the skull-like face lights up with remarkable, if insincere, brilliance.

"George. We've never really spoken till now but I'm sure you realise that you're terrifically valued by all of us as one of our most experienced lecturers."

"I'm certainly one of the oldest."

The VP cackles.

"Well, you're looking good on it. I see you've indicated an interest in our advanced self-determined selective severance scheme."

"Redundancy."

"Now there is no obligation on either side, of course, as a result of these preliminary enquiries. It's simply—"

"What's the deal, Doc?"

"I have the figures here."

That's almost frighteningly good, thinks George. *They're clearly desperate to get rid of me, which gives me some bargaining power.*

"You know I taught for two years in a private language school before I started here, so you should take that into account."

"That's a little irregular but I think the chief could probably be persuaded to add one year..."

"No, *two* years."

The Veep smiles again.

"Anything for you, George. Perhaps you could stay on as part of the management negotiating team?"

"Don't patronise me, Doctor."

The doc's smile hardens.

"Is there anything else you want to discuss? No obligation on either side at this point as I said. I shall submit your application to the chief and then it comes back to you for signature before final submission to the board, though that's generally a formality, of course. Anything else?"

Anything else? *Just that I've given this fucking institution the best twenty-five years of my life, that it's all turned sour and rancid, that I came here as a bright young man and I'm leaving as a bitter old bastard, that I had a passion for teaching that has turned to dust and ashes, that I once loved my students now can't stand the sight of them, that the very sight sound or stench of you and your cohorts just makes me want to puke...*

"No," says George with a look that he hopes – like Dirk Bogarde as Aschenbach in *Death in Venice* – sums up his whole life and all his feelings at the moment when, at Visconti's gesture, he stands up in the gondola and Mahler's *adagio* rises with him to a breath-taking orgasm, and walks out of the cold doctor's office and back towards life.

II

"Holy Christ," says Ben.

"What?" Jonathan doesn't like talking over breakfast. He definitely prefers it if Ben either gets up and out before him or is still lazing in bed when he goes out to work. In fact, he doesn't really enjoy having any meals at home with Ben nowadays; they seem to have run out of conversation. So, he buries himself in *Platitude, The Post-Gay Lifestyle Magazine* (whatever that means) over his Rice Krispies, while Ben reads his ever-voluminous correspondence.

"My dad's getting married again. The old goat."

"Really?"

"Yea. Mom's going to be at the do – hey, it's gonna be in the Library of Congress… OK… he wants me there…"

"The Spice Girls are saying Maggie Thatcher was the original Spice Girl. Weird idea and yet…"

"There's an invitation to follow. Sounds like a real big affair… Shit, Bill and Hilary might even be there, Hilary almost certainly. I gotta go, babe."

"What was that?" says Jonathan suddenly tuning in. "Did I hear first person singular there? Isn't the famous congressman inviting his son's partner to his second wedding? Or do I mean third?"

"Second, baby, and you gotta remember the old man's a Republican but he's probably put you on the invitation. You must come over with me anyways. This big envelope's gotta be the invite and here's a letter for you. It got mixed up with my stuff."

"Yea, right. Well, I do get letters just occasionally."

The letterhead reads "Gay London Opera Works" and for some reason Jonathan can't help hearing the letter in his head in a rather nasal camp voice.

My dear Jonathan,

As chair of London's only gay and lesbian opera company I am a great admirer of your work both at the BNO and with the Hendon and Edgware Ladies Choral Partnership, of which my mother is actually the president. You may remember her; the lady with masses of mauve hair, and a Chihuahua (also mauve, sometimes)?

We – GLOW – have been in existence for nearly five years now. After a shaky start we have come into our own in the last three years since my election to the chair. The donation of a six-figure sum to our coffers by dear Mummy certainly did no harm either! Our productions have come on in leaps and bounds – you may have seen the "glowing" reports in the local and gay press of our recent Mikado – but we are keen to tackle more complex and modern works and clearly all we are now lacking is a musical director of high calibre.

Our present MD has truly done wonders but the world of haute couture is demanding more and more of his time. While we operate in general on an amateur basis, we are very willing to offer a substantial fee to a musician of your quality for a commitment of say twelve hours a week. A figure of £1,200 to £1,500 a month springs to mind but we are open to negotiation. Should you feel tempted by this little offer I should be delighted to hear from you by phone or e-mail.

I feel sure that GLOW will shine ever brighter in your capable hands!

Yours very truly,

Peter Hore-Commodore

Jonathan's response is immediate. He has sworn never to work with amateurs and these people sound pathetically limp-wristed. However low his funds are he isn't going to be tempted simply by a regular income. And whoever had heard of a gay opera company? Ridiculous!

"What is it?"

"Oh, just an invitation to be MD of a stupid-sounding amateur opera club called… GLOW."

"I've heard they're pretty good and rolling in dosh. Look, babe, the wedding's next week and I'm gonna have to book my flight. I could fly out in a couple of days. Why don't you come with me? We can have a great vacation in D.C., go down into Virginia…"

"Am I invited?"

"The old fool's forgotten to put your name on the invitation, but I can sort that out real fast. *I* want you to come."

Ben looks up into Jonathan's eyes. A couple of years ago – maybe even a couple of months – the magic would have worked. But this time the magic seems very faint, just like an echo.

"Look, Ben. I've got my teaching and I've got some work coming up at the Whippo. *And* I need to investigate this GLOW business. Could be the break I've been looking for. You go and enjoy it. Sometimes it's good to have a couple of weeks doing separate things."

Ben looks profoundly pissed off. He blinks a few times and takes a large draft of cold coffee.

"OK. Sure." He looks down at the invitation. "At least I like the woman Dad's marrying. She's an old family friend."

"Oh well," says Jonathan a bit sardonically, "Maybe this'll be your dad's happy ending."

"There *are* no happy endings," says Ben.

"Bollocks," says Jon.

|||

It's June; a lovely late spring day in London. Jon has still not replied to the letter from Mr Hore-Commodore; he's in one of his states of indecision and self-doubt. And now that Ben has flown off to his father's wedding in the States – in the Library of Congress no less – he regrets his hasty, haughty decision not to go with him. After all, Congressman Schlesinger has a lot on his mind and would probably have been perfectly happy to see him at the wedding once they had arrived. And it would have been a great opportunity to see his old friend Beauregard, Francis' old flame, and check how well he was responding to the new combination therapy. But at the same time, he still feels resentment at being ignored by Ben's father whom he has met and liked. And surely if Ben had been so keen to take him along, he could have called his very *important* father in the States and demanded he change the invitation to include his lover. But then Ben wasn't that sort of person. He was too laidback, too *Californian* to take such drastic or dramatic action. And maybe that was the root of the problem between them. Or maybe it wasn't.

But now it is Thursday evening and Jon has the flat to himself – and the whole of London. Why not take advantage of it? One thing he likes to do whenever freedom beckons is to visit one of London's burgeoning gay saunas, or bathhouses as

Ben annoyingly called them. (Why is it that those very features that Jon had found most attractive in Ben are now the ones he finds most irritating?) Ben never really liked the sauna, perhaps because as a big man he felt embarrassed to strip off in public especially before the super-critical eyes of other gay men, and Jon is uncomfortably aware he had never really made sufficient allowances for that, never shown enough empathy when he had tried, often unsuccessfully, to persuade him to come along to the baths. Anyway, now it is like the old days – temporarily. He is a free agent, "as wide as store" in the words of his favourite metaphysical poet, and, boy, is he determined to soar – and score. Strange, isn't it, that those very features of the gay scene he'd so desperately wanted to escape – the sleaze, the sexual easiness, the lack of commitment – suddenly seemed intensely attractive? So, which "bathhouse" would it be tonight?

There was a new, luxurious and spacious, sauna in the Farringdon area that Jon had heard about, with a proper swimming pool, several Jacuzzis and very good bar food. So, he doesn't want to go there; *that* isn't what he is looking for. Instead, he heads for a small place he's visited several times already called "Friendly Faces – your local sauna for local people" neatly tucked away in the back streets near King's Cross. On the tube he has that slightly queasy ambivalent feeling he hasn't felt for a long time; the sense of adventure, of freedom, of naughtiness. This is the queer life!

It is just an ordinary shop front and as you go in there is a window with a guichet on the left.

"Welcome to Friendly Faces or Frisky Arses as we prefer to call it," says the lanky young man behind the window – a

Charles Hawtrey-lookalike – in a pissed off sort of voice. "Have you been here before? You look familiar."

"Not as familiar as you, dear! Yes, course I have. Always enjoy it."

"You can enjoy paying ten pounds in that case."

"With pleasure."

"Pleasure's extra," replies the young queen predictably, opening the door.

It is a small sleazy place on two floors, the dry social area on the ground floor and the wet more sensual area below. Jonathan goes through the lounge with its serving counter, TV high on the wall and its big battered sofas and easy chairs, and into the lockers section where he strips off with a sense of liberation and ease – *is this what nudists feel like?* He wonders – ready for whatever action may result. The faintly stale, boiled air stokes his sense of anticipation.

Slipping back into the lounge for a moment, glancing casually around with a practised eye, he notices no one of particular interest. It is the usual crowd here, ordinary-looking, chatty, some on the scene, others married, a few pretty young things but mostly fleshier and older. And Jon is surprised to realise he is fast becoming one of these older (and just a bit fleshier) types. True, he is not yet one of the "dirty old men" – the admirably persistent old lags in their sixties and over who evidently have more time and pension money than anyone else to cruise the bathhouses of London town, and profit surprisingly often from their persistence with young men; for as the ancient Greeks knew, which young man does not need and enjoy being treated occasionally as a desirable girl? And while none of us relish the thought of joining that band of the elderly and undesirable (who nonetheless provide that essential audience of lubricious admirers for self-regarding young men), do we, pray, prefer the alternative? And tell me, gentle and probably gentile reader, how many of us when presented with that ineluctable choice of oblivion or old age do not plump for the latter, despite all the opprobrium and contempt we have heaped upon it when younger and prettier ourselves? And in the gay world, let me ask you, how much respect, how much affection is there for age – unless, of course, it be accompanied by wealth, prestige and power?

So, while our friend clearly has not yet reached that age at which anything is excusable – the "old man Steptoe" era of near-senility – he is well aware that he is no longer the slim svelte young thing of the mid-eighties, when desirability could be taken for granted simply as the tribute owed to youth. He is at that age when even the most Peter Pan-ish of boys becomes a man: nearing forty. And perhaps it is this knowledge – allied with a niggling, insinuating sense of claustrophobia and irritation with his once lovably naïve and American boyfriend – which has inspired Jon's intoxicating need for escape. He feels that now he is becoming that very thing he has always wanted, changing into the object of his own desire: the chunky, hairy mature man they call a *bear*. An eerie sensation: to morph into the object of your own lust, and perhaps a resolution of that age-old question of gay and possibly all desire: to have or to be? Not that our man has put on much weight, but just a little alters the distribution of the body and combined with the full beard and maturity imports a weightier aura. Anyway, thus configured, wrapped in a tawdry towel, he descends the staircase into the warm and hellish depths.

Peering through the glass panel of the sauna cabin, he sees a motley crowd, too many for comfort, and walks past to the neighbouring steam room where the light is pleasantly dim. The hot sticky air is immediately relaxing and through the mist he makes out a few bodies draped round and along the benches which line the walls. Spotting a comfortable enough gap, he sits down, easing himself into the atmosphere which is at once and in a peculiar way both easeful and tense, both totally laidback and watchfully alert, soporific and exciting. I think I have made my point. Half closing his eyes he notices near him a man who attracts his interest, though he'd be hard put to say why. Far from being the bear of Jonathan's imagination – or the chubby baritone of his marital bed – the guy is moderate in build but quite muscular, suggesting a regular attendance at the gym. The body is comfortably fleshed out but not fat. And the face, topped by a fashionably short-cropped – or is it balding? – head, is languidly handsome in repose, or rather not handsome but pleasingly fresh, clean-shaven and cheeky. It's an oval face, not his type at all, but Jon – through half-closed eyelids and in the semi-dark – is already alert and turned on. After a few minutes he senses some, not unusual, activity: another man, taller, bearded (a rival) has drawn closer to Mr Languid, their knees touching and then – with the astonishing speed and ease with which these intimacies happen – they are feeling each other's bodies and in a few seconds stroking each other's cocks. There is no great sense of drama or even excitement about it, and certainly no obscenity; it is simply a perfectly natural way for two men to enjoy themselves and each other in this humid, torrid ambience. And, intriguing feature, Mr Languid has next to him a little pot of something into which he dips his fingers before pulling on his neighbour's dick.

Jonathan keenly wants a piece of this action. And, as if in a dream – a highly erotic dream – he moves closer to the man with the smooth shapely body and languid look and begins to tweak his nearer nipple. (There is no point in being shy or retiring about this; in such a situation, daring and decision are all.) The nipple is brown and well-rounded and evidently sensitive. Mr Languid turns his gaze slightly, smiles a little (*I'm in*, thinks our man), then dips his free hand into the pot and creams up Jonathan's alert and burgeoning dick. His hand has a lovely easy movement, languid again and very effective. Jon now has his full attention as the hairy rival is being slurpingly fellated by a fat OAP with a circlet of scrubby hair, and is lying back with an ecstatic face. And then Jon does something he knows he is not supposed to do, reserved as it usually is for that special relationship that prevails between him and his lover. He leans slowly forward towards his interlocutor's increasingly beautiful and expressive face and begins kissing him. The lips are very sensuous, velvety and soft. He sees Mr Languid's eyelids close but keeps his open as he dips his own hand into the honeypot and lavishly creams his partner's long slim shapely uncircumcised cock. (Just the opposite of Ben's fat and circumcised member.) He registers – or feels – how the whole room is now alive with activity and a lanky, unattractive older man is now feeling up Mr Languid from the other side. But Mr Languid, in a pause from the long sensual kiss, seems quite unconcerned, gives the old man a grin and gently pats him on the back. And while Jon resents the interruption – in sexual pursuit he has always commanded the ruthlessness he lacks at work – he somehow admires Mr Languid's gentle and unrejecting response to the guy. With renewed intensity he hugs then kisses him and then suddenly the crisis is approaching for them both and – almost uniquely and unplanned – both cocks are gently spurting a thicker gooier cream into the one around them. Relaxing, the two strangers smile at each other, a little shyly with a touch of humour and embarrassment, but feeling for that moment suddenly and warmly close.

"I'd better get cleaned up," says Mr L. His accent is maybe Irish, maybe American, his characterful voice a light and pleasing tenor. "Thanks, that was lovely."

As he gets up to leave, Jon is in two minds: leave it there, a delicious memory floating in the void or follow it up, find out the guy's name and more. He knows which course is wise. So, he does the other and gets up to follow the languid and beautiful man out of the steam. In the tacky row of three tepid showers divided by soggy plastic curtains, they exchange a few more pleasantries. Mr L is blinking as if in need of his glasses.

"I'm Jonathan, and you?"

"Jeb. The water could be hotter, don't you think?"

"Definitely. Still, we don't come here for luxury, do we?"

"I hope not. You'd be sadly disappointed."

He certainly sounds Irish.

"Do you live in London?"

"For the time being."

"Going off somewhere?"

"I was living with my ex in Canada for a couple of years and I might go back there soon."

"And what do you do here?"

I'm asking too many questions, and anyway, I have a boyfriend – a lover.

"Do a bit of recording from time to time, and a bit of writing."

Now he really sounds American, or Canadian.

"Have we seen you in the Coronet? I go there a lot with my other half. He's away at the moment."

My conscience is assuaged; I've mentioned him.

"The bar off Oxford Street? I think I've been there once, maybe twice. I tend to drink near here, at Traffic."

Mental note: sleazy pub two streets from here. Must give it a try.

While Jonathan is deciding whether to risk suggesting going there for a drink right now, Jeb turns off the tap, puts a hand seductively on Jon's arm and says, "I really must get off now. Got lots to do tonight. Been great. Thank you." He kisses him on the mouth, and is off.

And Jonathan spends the rest of the evening guiltily thinking over the brief and beautiful experience and wondering, *Shall I see him again?* Should *I see him again? Of course not. Forget it.*

IV

Adelina is a tough Australian cookie, born in the suburbs, drawn into Sydney, and educated there. Adelina is a lipstick lesbian, a bright tall beautiful gender-bending tomboy of a girl who respects Dr Germaine Greer but feels she doesn't need her; a nineties woman, a post-feminist dyke, butch on the streets, femme in the sheets – or sometimes vice-versa. Adelina is a second-generation Aussie of Catalan ancestry, whose grandparents fled Barcelona in the *any zero* of 1939 when the generalissimo's Moorish troops goose-stepped down the Gràcia, with further back in her family line a mélange of Catholic and Jew with splashes of Saracen. (The only race her family had never married into was the unloved Castilians.) They had bought and sold in Catalan marketplaces, sailed to Naples and traded in the Maghreb, and made lovely antiphonal noises in the gothic churches of the Barri Gòtic. One day Adelina intends to write a brilliant panoramic novel of her ancestors' bustling lives in medieval Barcelona – in the style of George Eliot's *Romola*, a novel she read for her final school exams loving its vivid pictures of Renaissance Florence – but at present, and she lives intensely in the present, she is far too busy.

Adelina is also the mother of Lesbia Brandon Majorca (pronounced, of course, *Mayorca*) – named after an unfinished novel by Algernon Swinburne. In fact, had she been a boy, she would probably have been named Algernon, which, for all her post-feminism, Adelina was secretly pleased she was not. Lesbia is a two-year-old of egregious precocity who, her mother knows, will in the new century be president of Australia if not the world. Adelina herself is named after (or *for* as the Americans more appositely say) Adelina Patti, one of the great opera divas, whom her mother Carmen – a singer-actress manqué – had always wanted to be (or to have). But though musically gifted (she was a fine pianist) Carmen – or Carme, in the authentic Catalan form – born in the romantic little resort of Sitges but brought up in New South Wales, had a weak voice and not much luck, and her biggest roles were bit-parts in Australian soaps. Adelina's dad on the other hand was a tough businessman who lived up to their Catalan forebears by creating the wherewithal through a network of employment agencies to send her to academic private schools and the Sydney Conservatoire. Adelina and her adoring daddy have always identified strongly with each other; her little brother Manel, though her mum's favourite, never got a look in. Adelina knew from the beginning she was a special, independent, *unusual* girl but it was only when, drawn as if by an electric charge, she picked up a weathered copy of *The Well of Loneliness* in a second-hand bookshop at age thirteen that she saw herself as in a mirror. And what she saw she liked. The well of loneliness was for her the well of loveliness, of pride, of womanly love, and she longed to bathe herself luxuriously therein. She saw herself in the noble, misunderstood Stephen Gordon, striding across the green pastures of her father's estate in England – a country she had never visited and had never even heard mentioned by her parents who spoke only of Spain and France, but was immediately determined she would live and work in. And what Adelina was determined to do she did. Its temperate climate, its kings and queens, its association with Radclyffe Hall, Oscar Wilde and so many great figures of lesbian and gay history increasingly appealed to her. Her identification with the man/womanly Stephen Gordon also had the odd result that when, some years later in the mid-nineties, she met Jonathan Gordon at the British National Opera in London she at once thought of him as Stephen's long-lost brother and therefore hers too. (It took Jon rather longer to warm to this super confident Aussie who had taken his place at the Whippo, but by the time we meet her, he had… just about.)

Adelina is, like her dad, a strong and very gifted personality – a dramatic soprano, brilliant pianist, musicologist, feminist, opera fanatic, and above all, operatic conductor. Having taken Sydney by storm, she has swept into the Western Hippodrome like a whirlwind, perfectly sure that she will be the first woman intendant of a European opera house. And much as she admires the Garden, it is the cabbage patch as she likes to call it that she has set her sights upon – at least in the first instance. *Mirabile dictu* Jeremy appears quite unfazed by her glowing ambition and fascinated by her vivid appeal. After all, he is over fifty now and is thinking about moving on to take over one of the great London orchestras he is so often now asked to guest with. And he has more than enough money and fame not to feel threatened by anyone – *apart*, thinks Adelina, *from his own paranoia*. (All that eludes him now is an honour or a title. Ah, if only…) Meanwhile, Addy as he calls her has been his *numero duo* at the Whippo – a post Jon was never anointed for – for nearly three years, and their odd coupledom continues.

Adelina lives in a small but trendy house she has bought in fashionable Clerkenwell with baby Brandie (yes, even Adelina balks at addressing her daughter as "Lesbia") and girlfriend Tallulah. Tallulah's mother – to whom she is close – is a Trinidadian actress and her father is a white rock singer whom she has never met. She does nothing to discourage unlikely rumours that he was Mick the Lips, though as she sardonically points out, "My lips are full and sensuous enough without those particular genes." She was very bright at school in South London and read law at St. John's College, Cambridge. She practises at the common law bar (specialising in employment law and has recently been junior counsel in a test case with Cherie Booth – this girl knows all the right people) and plans to be the first black high court judge – and eventually Law Lord (Lady?). But having lived with Adelina for two years – very exciting and enjoyable years it must be said – she has decided to buy her own place, her own space – partly for investment reasons and partly because she is fed up with baby-sitting, but mostly because she is not convinced that this relationship is going to be permanent.

Late one Tuesday morning in early June the doorbell buzzes at Adelina's small, very chic Clerkenwell home. A middle-aged white woman stands outside admiring it while a younger black woman comes to the door; she is about thirty, with short straight black hair, a cappuccino complexion and a strong Roman nose. Having been doing her aerobics she is wearing a shell suit and Is not in the mood for receiving visitors.

"Hello," says Celia, "Is Miss Majorca in? She's expecting me, I think." She smiles politely. The other woman does not.

"Really? Wait a moment."

She's awfully well-spoken for a cleaner, thinks Celia, *if a bit off hand.*

"Addie," she shouts upstairs. "Someone for you?"

She comes back to the door and turns on a massively brilliant and patronising smile.

"I'm Tallulah Quartermain, Adelina's partner. I don't think I've had the pleasure. Do come in."

Celia hides her discomfort almost totally as they shake hands.

"I'm Celia Greyfield. Adelina suggested I come over to go over a new score."

"Of course. I should have recognised you from *Maria Stuarda*. Very… unusual production. Do go into the living room. I have to change. I'm in court at two."

Celia looks round the colourfully busy room, like a set designed by Kaffe Fassett – so fashionable it hurts. A superb volume of lesbian icons is lying on the low coffee table – she can see the Editions Aubrey Walter logo on the spine. Hand embroidered cushions are scattered with Afghan throws over the two comfy sofas. In the corner is a Bechstein upright with a couple of scores on the music stand. She is just thinking, *Thank God I didn't tell Adelina how neatly her home-help keeps everything*, when her hostess comes in very fast saying in her clipped bright New South Wales tones, "Show me your CV and we'll have a very quick interview but you realise you're at least an hour late, sweetie."

Then she sits down and looks at Celia who glowers back at her, aghast.

"Oh my God, Miss Greyfield, I completely forgot. What a dickhead – me, that is. I assumed you were a potential nanny for my daughter, Brandie." She bursts out laughing with huge boyish gusto, and after a moment so does Celia, a bit more gently but much taken by Adelina's openness and warmth. Of course, she has occasionally worked with her before but never been here or got to know her intimately.

"Well, you mistook me for a nanny and *I* nearly... but never mind that. Your friend's awfully nice. Very attractive."

"Tallulah? Thanks. She's a bit stressed at the minute."

"Hardly surprising if she's in court today. Nothing serious I hope?"

This time Adelina erupts into vast guffaws, *rather like an Australian rugby player*, thinks Celia. *What have I said now?*

"She's in court because she's a barrister, you dildo!" says Adelina between splutters. Then adds, "Don't be offended, Celia. I love dildos."

Now it's Celia's turn to laugh, a tad nervously.

"I've never been compared with a dildo before. Anyway, I thought you ladies didn't use such things in these liberated days."

"We use anything we damn well like, Celia, and if you hang around long enough, girl, I might even show you. Grolsch or Earl Grey?"

"You don't have any whisky, do you? That would *really* suit me."

"Excellent. Course we do. Chivas or Glenfiddich?"

"The pure malt please. I've got Scottish blood somewhere. And you?"

"Catalan through and through, and one hundred percent Australian. Would you be any good as a nanny by the way? Got your own kids?"

"Not even one. I envy men being able to say, 'Not as far as I *know*.' Mind you, most of the men I know are gay anyway so…" Then she has a thought: there have been some rumours about Adelina and Jeremy when she first arrived, which he had assiduously promoted by an astute mixture of nonchalance and denial. "Does Brandie's father take an interest in her? There's so much fuss about absent fathers these days, isn't there?"

Adelina presents a long, lovely dark and very serious face. "You mean Mr Bank? That's her father. His first name's sperm." Then she smiles.

"Touché, my dear. Serves me right for prying. Now was it *Ariodante* you wanted to read through?"

"Sure, Celia. Just to help us get a handle on it. Geddit?"

V

7 June 1997

Dear Chief Executive Officer,

Once the opportunity for re-evaluating my third-age career choices had become evident in light of your flagging-up of incoming staff re-adjustment consequent upon down-sizing, it seemed to me that my personal and professional goals (or should I say professional fouls) would be better enhanced by a re-accreditation of my own vocational development. Having been brought up to speed on this by the vice-principal for human entrails (Bill to all of us), it became evident that my own learning outcomes and indeed my acquisition of skills (sorry, competencies) would be best served by a programme overview leading to re-evaluation of my personal mission statement and to owning my share in the new deal. My future action plan has now been extensively resourced by the relevant funding council thus releasing essential energies for integrated estates development.

In other words, the college having descended into anarchy and filth, I'm leaving you stupid tossers as soon as you hand over the gelt.

Thank you profoundly for a quarter century of vast initial enthusiasm drowned out by anger, frustration, self-hatred, exploitation, oppression, contempt, semi-penury, boredom, envy, unhappiness, wasted years, longing for holidays, disappointment, depression – oh, and acres and acres of guilt.

To you, Pete, and your lickspittle cohorts I can only say: good riddance and fuck off.

Thank you so much.

Yours in profound disgust,

George Henry Darkside

George types up this letter on his new home computer with immense satisfaction, then drafts a second version, which is rude only by reason of its acute brevity. He puts them both in envelopes addressed to the CEO, closes his eyes, then plays "eenie, meenie, miney mo". When he opens them, his finger is resting on the less egregious version; at least he thinks it is. Without more ado he picks up the letter, pops in the aptly named "release form" which he has signed, throws it into his bag for the college post and chucks the other one away.

George is back at work. The die is now cast. Whichever letter has gone will make no difference; his career is over. After all what was a career but a downward trajectory, careering onward towards a preordained end? And here at last is the long-awaited *Götterdämmerung*, the final melodramatic showdown of his clattering, sputtering professional life. Now he must be careful not to allow gloom to overtake his last few weeks in the college or to overshadow that glimmering light at the end of the tunnel entitled *release*. It draws him with a great power of attraction and he knows that when soon the magic day dawns he will greet it with the utmost pleasure to be followed by a long period of profound relief. The release date: what every prisoner longs for. And for him it will come with a large handout (about one and a half year's salary) and a small pension, so that in combination with the substantial savings his parsimony has amassed over the last twenty-five years, in theory he need never work again. Oh ecstasy, oh bliss!

It is that same class, again intent on destroying the acute beauty of his favourite novel *Daniel Deronda*. Though he concedes that his own teaching methods have become dreary and dried up over the years: "Have you considered the use of the overhead projector, George?" as an officious, dowdy female inspector had suggested to him a year ago.

"Have you considered the use of make-up?" was the reply he had made – *sotto voce*, of course.

It is the typical class he would expect these days, even for the A level course which he knows is bound to be abolished soon. Eighteen on the register, eight in the room; a motley group, his jaundiced eye surveys, of people of assorted ages with hopes and interests but no *grounding,* no *hinterland* on which to base an understanding of such a work. If he spoke of the nineteenth century, what would that import to them? Did they have any knowledge of Queen Victoria, of British Empire and imperialism, of the background of classical and European learning that lay at the fingertips of that remarkable, masterful woman, that dominatrix of the English novel whom George worships? And now at last he will have the freedom to research her life in depth and write that definitive study he has always dreamt of…

The class is drawing near to a close; they had been going through the text with George dictating notes, and very little feedback or commentary from anyone else. He had been using these same notes for at least ten years, but after all, the classic text didn't change, so why should his interpretation? And rarely these days did a student have anything fresh to add that might stimulate further thought from him.

"So, the question of Gwendolen's guilt in relation to Grandcourt's drowning remains an open one, and what can one say of Daniel's gloss upon it…?"

"What's a gloss?" asks a hunky young Caribbean man at the front of the group.

"Well, in this case it means an interpretation or commentary. It's related to the word 'glossary'."

"What does that mean?" says a small mousy woman sitting a bit too far away for George's comfort.

He sighs. *What do they teach them at school these days? Nothing.* "A glossary is a list of terms you would find at the start or the end of a book explaining technical expressions, or legal phrases that are used in the book."

"There's one of those at the end of my home insurance policy but the way everything's explained makes it just as difficult," complains the woman.

"Bit like this class," mutters the Caribbean guy.

"Now let's concentrate please," says George rather sternly. "We've only another ten minutes to…" He was going to say "get through". "… To go before lunchtime." Then, remembering he's just put in his release form and has nothing more to fear from the authorities says, "Actually, that's a good place to end. Bye."

He'll probably be released – oh, that blessed word – before they take their exam. Most of them will be taking it in December and even a few months ago that would really have pricked his conscience but now he's way beyond all that.

A young man, about nineteen with a beard and a yarmulke, in a dark maroon V-necked sweater and pinstriped trousers, has approached him. George is already salivating at the thought of his homemade mature cheddar and tomato sandwiches and had assumed the class was over. But there is something serious in the boy's eyes that holds him.

"Sorry to hold you up, Mr Darkside, I know it's your lunchtime."

"That's all right, erm…"

"Daniel."

"Yes, of course. That's a coincidence, isn't it?"

The boy clearly doesn't see it that way.

"Was it something about the book? As you say, it *is* lunchtime…"

"Well, yes…" Daniel appears rather diffident. *An unusual characteristic,* thinks George, *amongst the self-obsessed students of the nineties.* "You've heard of the Talmud, Mr Darkside?"

"Indeed."

"It just occurred to me… Some rabbis have argued – I can give you chapter and verse – that a recalcitrant husband is a 'wrong-doer' and therefore he may not be rescued, according to the law, if he falls into a river. It just struck me that possibly Daniel Deronda may have been aware of this when he gave his advice – his rather comforting advice – to Gwendolen about her responsibility for her husband's death. Do you think that George Eliot might have known that, being a very great scholar as you were telling us?"

George is gob-smacked, transfixed. *Is this young man taking the mickey, or is he genuinely and astonishingly engrossed in the literature which they are supposed to be studying? And if so, what is he doing in this college?*

"That's very… interesting, Daniel. I don't remember reading an essay of yours about the book."

"No. Unfortunately, I wasn't well for a couple of months, so I missed a lot. I did tell you about it and that I was copying up the notes and things."

"Good, excellent. That's certainly a thought-provoking idea of yours. Are you enjoying the rest of the book?"

"Well, yes…" He looks very serious. "But I do feel a bit disappointed at the end – very disappointed, actually – that Daniel doesn't marry Gwendolen. It just seems the right thing to happen. But, being orthodox myself, I feel rather guilty about that. I should be pleased that he marries a nice Jewish girl instead. But I'm not." He suddenly laughs then looks serious again. "How do you feel about that?"

"Well… Gwendolen's very selfish, you know, and very materialistic and George Eliot is a very moralistic writer, in the best sense, and she feels that Gwendolen simply isn't ready for marriage to someone like Daniel, whose character is possibly a bit too good to be true. But I do understand what you mean. Perhaps that tiny moment of regret on our part is intended by Eliot. She's a very complex writer after all. Let me see your essay about the book anyway."

"I've got it here for you, sir. And sorry for holding you up before lunch." He flashes a smile, looks serious again, and is gone.

If that had happened yesterday, thinks George, *if I had known – like that moment in the Bible, in the story of Sodom – that there was even one serious student left in this damn college, would I have signed that letter and ended my career?*

Of course I would. Forget it.

VI

"Curiouser and curiouser," says Harold, sipping a huge mochaccino in a giant and very handsome cup. "So, you *really* think that your darling mad genius of a husband – and don't say ex because you're still married and you still love him deep down in that squelchy old cunt of yours – is actually fucking an old skinny Pole who you thought for *yonks* was stalking *you?*"

"It certainly looks like it, doesn't it, sweetie? There they were at Jeremy's on election night bold as bloody brass, with the Pole, Stefan, still staring at me as if my face held the secret of the universe…"

"So, was he stalking *you* to get to *him* or – the reverse?"

"Christ knows, darling, and probably cares but I don't. I've given up on men at this point. I prefer giraffes – or even women."

Celia and Harold are sitting at an oblong table in The Sphere, an elegant café looking onto Soho Square, neither gay nor straight but decidedly *queer* in the jargon of the mid-nineties. The décor is in a selection of pastel shades with a silhouette projection of "The Sphere" in a lemon lozenge moving hypnotically across the pink ceiling. The waiters are tall and slim and queeny in white tailored T-shirts and the place is packed with young people talking very loudly against a barely audible background melange of Britpop and hi-energy house music.

"Is that why you've been seen *more* than once in the glittering dykey company of Adelina Majorca, with or without the black barrister girlfriend?" Harold smirks, his face – like a Jewish version of Kenneth Williams – all pursed up beneath large shining half-impish, half-malevolent eyes.

"Isn't it lovely being able to sit out on the terrace like this in the warm sunshine, almost like being in Paris? I think we're going to have a very hot summer, you know."

"You can't evade the issue, duckie. Are you dabbling in dykedom – about to plunge irretrievably into the great muff of loneliness never to be seen or heard of again? Will you be featured on the cover of *Diva* just like your girlfriend the adorable Adelina has been?"

"Oh, don't be ridiculous, Harold. Though if I did, it would serve the male species right – I hate the lot of them. I don't count you, of course, dear. You're not one really, are you?"

"Look at these photos before you make your mind up on *that* point, dearie."

Harold opens up his slim, elegant Toshiba laptop and begins a slideshow.

"They were taken at a little do I went to last weekend. A gaggle of MPs were there, but they all covered their faces I think – very wisely. We were all coked up to the nines, of course."

A waiter is momentarily transfixed as he passes by, looking over Celia's shoulder at a picture of a man bent over with large weals on his bottom while another rather chubby man in a mask and little else holds a bullwhip over him.

"That's me bending over, of course," says Harold loudly, as the waiter pretends indifference and moves on. "Oh, the youth of today," he continues, "Have no idea how to enjoy themselves. Not unless you pay them to do it, of course."

Celia cursorily looks through the rest of the photos – all par for the course with Harold. "I thought you'd grown out of this sort of thing, dear. It's all very old hat now, you know. We're back to hearts and flowers, in a bisexual sort of way. That's the fashion."

"I know, dear, but I can't resist going to those kinds of parties. And you *do* hear the most intriguing gossip." He leans over conspiratorially. "They say that Diana could be on the verge of a *big* romance; one the royals will not like one bit. Mark my words, dear, in a few weeks the papers'll be full of it. I heard it from someone with contacts at *the highest* levels."

"Another coffee, darling, or whatever it is? What astonishes me, sweetie, is how you've managed to keep in with these highest levels despite a change of government and your contacts for the last twenty years – always in fact – being with the Tory side."

"My dear," replies Harold, attracting the attention of the same waiter, who pretends not to notice then sends over a colleague, "In my line you have to be flexible, have to be a sort of chameleon. I always kept channels open to the other side – and the gay world helps a lot with that, you know. Not *this* gay world but the more secretive one that celebrities feel free to move about in. George Michael, cabinet ministers, royals who like a dabble, that sort of thing. Another giant mocha please and a medium cappuccino for my guest."

"My God, Harold, I suspect that even if the bloody National Front got in you'd be in there advising them."

Harold's pale face looks genuinely shocked.

"My dear, I may dabble in SM and the occasional designer drug, but I do have certain standards. I'm a deferential Tory at heart and after all what is New Labour? As for the highly distasteful NF, they'd have my queer Jewish balls for earrings in no time – and rather lovely danglers they'd make I'm quite sure."

Celia smiles. *So, does even Harold have standards after all?*

The coffees arrive, remarkably fast.

"And what were you doing in New York just before the election, darling? I know it wasn't merely an opera trip. You must have had a political motive."

"Well, light of my anus, all I can tell you is *this* – and it really must go *no further* [*which means he's already told everyone,* thinks Celia] – certain people almost embarrassingly close to La Blair need to have informal channels of access and information to certain other people very intimately linked with Le Clinton; plausible deniability assured, of course. Thus the great men and their official channels are totally out of the loop. I, moi, my dear, *am*, in this context, the loop. *Compris?*"

"Not a word, sweetie. Anyway, I think you've made it all up. But then that's probably what you want me to think. Well, anyway, I'm glad you're supporting Labour now. Just think, we're on the same side at last."

"New Labour, darling, in fact not really Labour at all, more… Blairism. Sounds better in French actually – *Le Blairisme*. The French'll love him. For a while anyway."

"Well, at least it's compassionate," says Celia, "As compared with your previous heroine."

Harold's slightly singsong voice suddenly sounds fierce and focused. "Do you know what Blairism is, Celia? Thatcherism with balls. Let's say you lose your job. Blairism simply removes the cushion, the semi-comfortable cushion of benefits that even Margaret left in place. So, what do you fall back on? Pins and needles, Celia darling. A great big, bloody bed of nails. And you either bounce back, or bleed to death. *That's* Blairism."

Celia stares back at him open-mouthed.

"Thanks for the tirade. I can never tell if you're serious or not."

Harold's very serious expression lights up in an impish grin.

"It matters not whether *I'm* serious, darling, just whether *they* are. Nothing to worry that magnificent larynx of yours about."

"And by the way," she adds, remembering something almost subliminal, "You don't know a rather nice tall hunky young man called Jeb, do you? The one who called on me for that interview? Because I'm sure I saw him on the box at that election night binge for Labour. I bet you know him."

Harold blinks a couple of times.

"Still hankering after the lost young man, eh? No idea *who* he is, darling. Some insignificant journalist. You're a diva. You deserve someone who's been on the cover of *Diva*. Stick with the divine Ms Majorca. Though I must say I prefer Ibiza myself."

VII

Jonathan is missing Ben who has been away for about eight days now. His calls have not been immensely forthcoming. Yesterday (another humid and uncomfortable day in London) the phone rang by the bed at about 7 a.m.

"Hello."

"Hi, gorgeous. Did I wake ya?"

"Uh yea, but I should be getting up to go to the Whippo. How are you?"

"Fine, babe, fine. Great wedding. You shoulda been here."

"I wasn't invited, remember?"

"That's crap. Anyway, Dad asked after you. The new wife's great. She's a writer, a novelist, a big lady, very stylish, loves opera. Dorothea. Great name for a fag's step-mom, eh? You'd get on real well."

"Good. How long are you staying?"

"About another week, maybe ten days. I wanna spend a bit more time with Dorothea, and I need a few days in NYC for that audition, you know? It was great meeting the Clintons – for a few seconds. Beau sends his love by the way."

"How is he?"

"He's good. Hates taking all those fuckin' pills but he's almost gone undetectable now. Funny how Dad's got real close to him."

"Have you seen your mother?"

"Had dinner with her last night. She might be getting married soon as well."

"Great. Maybe *we* should."

"Maybe. Anyway, I'm missing—"

The line goes dead.

Presumably, thinks Jon getting up, *it's me he's missing but then again... Am I missing him? Yes and no. I'm certainly missing cock.* He looks in the bathroom mirror. *Christ! That's what nearly-forty does to you.* The shock first thing in the morning. A forty-year-old face with huge bags beneath the dull brown eyes glares glumly back at him. *Is that me or my late wrinkled Auntie Rose?* He smiles and immediately thinks of a tall smooth shapely man with a warm smile and an intriguing Irish Canadian accent he met in the sauna – and possibly last night in his dreams. Why not look for Jeb just once in the week he's got left before the boyfriend returns. Why should it bother Ben? He's in the States in the ample bosom of his prosperous well-connected family. Clearly having a fabulous time. *I'm entitled to a little fun of my own*, thinks Jon. *A little romance even.*

He goes into the kitchen, fills the kettle and puts out two mugs. He smiles. *No, only one needed.* He thinks maybe he *is* missing Ben, just a little. But at least he can make himself a proper pot of tea, without having to bother about the coffee that every American has to drink at breakfast. And then again he's aware of a smile and an accent that isn't Ben's but has somehow penetrated into his consciousness. *And what the hell does "Jeb" stand for anyway? Is it short for Jeremy? Heaven forbid,* he thinks. *Not another one. Or is it some unusual Irish saint's name?* Jeb, almost like jab, and he would certainly like to jab that lithe manly body with the erection that's hardly softened since he got out of bed. And the face, the smile; such Irish charm, and the slightly vague myopia of his lusciously bright blue eyes like sapphires – *or might be*, thinks Jon coming out of orbit, *if I'd ever knowingly seen sapphires.*

Having finished breakfast and bathing, he has a few minutes spare and, without further thought, sits down at the computer.

Dear Mr Hore-Commodore… he types, and then deletes.

Dear Peter,

Apologies for the delay in replying to your very kind invitation to become musical director of GLOW – I've only just returned from a very pleasant fortnight working in the Netherlands [he lies]. *It sounds a very interesting proposition, although my having to give up the opportunity to take on various other projects I have recently been offered may necessitate a re-negotiation of the proposed salary. But I'm sure all this can be most amicably resolved when we meet in the next few days. Would you be kind enough to call me on the number above or at the Western Hippodrome where I am working as repetiteur most days? I haven't yet joined the mobile fraternity though taking on yet another job may make it inevitable!*

Sincerely,

JG

*P.S. I do indeed recollect your charming mother —
known affectionately to the ladies choir as the Babs
Cartland of Hendon, I believe!*

King's Cross. 10 p.m. Jonathan is emerging from the
tube. Busy and noisy and crass; like London, like life. No
pretences. A line of taxis waits to carry passengers arriving
from the north, as Jon so often has when his parents were
alive. *Mais ou sont les neiges d'antan?* he thinks. But this feeling
too takes him back, as he stands for a moment, orientating
himself, savouring the taste of freedom, thinking, feeling his
way back to the years when he was single. A singleton as they
say now. *And what's a gay singleton?* he wonders. *A gingelton?*
He turns right into Lancaster Way, wide, industrial, empty.
On the corner a working girl sweltering in a fur coat – and
little else presumably – gives him a gap-toothed grin. He half-
grins back then hurries on. The street name reminds him of his
Cambridge college. *Does Jeb have a degree? Did he go to school
or college here or in Canada or in Ireland? What does he do for a
living? And why do I care?* He hears his own footsteps; solitary,
solid, safe? He looks round, but there's no one. Across the
road is a huge hangar-like building with a strange Germanic
name across the old fascia in massive letters. He wonders if
that was where they filmed that Cold War movie of Michael
Cain's, back in the sixties, where he's been brainwashed and
has to choose between two controllers. And he feels a little
guilty because he's chasing cock – no, worse, one particular
cock – *because* Ben is away. It's not a comfortable feeling. But
he wants to see this man; is beginning to ache to see him. And
that's bad.

He turns right and there's Traffic. He hasn't been here for years. It does have bears' evenings, but this isn't one of them. Though looking round the ground floor bar, he sees quite a few beary types. He certainly fancies them: their roundness, fleshy blokeyness, their lack of pretension, which was part of the reason why he originally fancied Ben. That and his exotic Americanness, his chocolatey baritone, his slightly off-beam self-absorption. And the appeal of Jeb is his exact oppositeness to all that, his not-Benness, his not-bearness. But as Jon goes up to the bar and orders his Scotch on the rocks, he realises that the desired one, the pursued one, the not-bear, is also not here. A couple of bears further down the bar eye him up surreptitiously, giving nothing away.

"Is it open downstairs?" he asks the barman.

"Yea, but there won't be many down there yet."

Still, it's worth a try, thinks Jon, in his curiosity to see if his quarry might be there.

At the top of the stairs down to the cellar is a huge transvestite in an almost elegant red velvet gown and two inches of make-up with thick eyelashes.

"Hiya, sexy. Don't often see you here. Where's your man tonight then?"

"He's visiting Daddy and Mummy in the States for a while."

"So, while the cat's away... hmm?"

S(h)e gives Jonathan a lipstick kiss on the lips as he passes. Miss Fleurice is *the* diva of the fat men's scene in London – a scene on the verge of exploding into fashion, when bears will be the new clones – and had once some time ago on the Heath had a brief, sweaty session with Jon, but that was not Miss Fleurice, that was Mr Brian.

Jonathan feels his anticipation mounting; this would be the perfect opportunity to meet up with Jeb. It's a very raunchy, sensuous atmosphere below in the cellar and maybe something might happen here between them or he could take him back… *Whoa,* he thinks. *Hang on there. Don't go too fast.* He looks round the smoky backroom. A few guys in, but not many.

And then suddenly the tension gives way. He feels deflated and a bit silly. Why on earth is he standing here cruising the cellar of a sleazy bar in King's Cross on a Tuesday evening, when he has a boyfriend he loves in America and lots of work to do tomorrow morning? *What's the point? It's not the early eighties now,* he thinks, *and I'm not twenty-five. I'm not even* thirty-*five anymore. Still, you don't have to be young on this scene, as the Old Abe makes all too obvious. Not that I've been in there for a while either. Maybe tomorrow night…? Oh, come on, love. Drink up and go to your nice warm bed.* But he doesn't, not immediately. After all, the beautiful stranger, the not-bear, may yet turn up.

He looks at his watch: 11.15. *Is it worth getting another drink? Probably not.* He looks at the door. It opens and in comes a *big man*; big and handsome in a rough way, with a goatee beard and magnificently broad shoulders under his white T-shirt which has a roughly hand-painted bear – a real one – on it. Jonathan feels knocked sideways. He's the not-not-bear and he's beautiful.

"Hello, you old cunt, what you doin' 'ere?"

Shit, of course it's Grant, realises Jon slightly abashed but still impressed.

"Well, hello, Grant," he says feigning suavity, "And how's tattooed lover boy?"

Grant gives a huge guffaw, massively masculine, the sort that gay men aren't supposed to give.

"Mind your language, you tart. Where's the gorgeous American then?"

"You know, I don't think I'm a person in my own right anymore, Grant. Everybody always asks about Ben before they even ask about me. He's away in the States."

"So, you're out on the pull. I won't cramp your style then. Unless I can get you a drink?"

"I'll have a Scotch please. You won't be cramping anything, big boy. Unless you want to."

"There's nothing wrong between you two, is there?"

"Nothing that a couple of weeks apart won't solve."

"He's a real nice bloke. Don't throw seven years away for Christ's sake. *I* did that and look where it got me. Mind you, mine was a right cunt."

Grant turns to order and he is standing so close Jon can smell the testosterone, feel the massive warmth of his body.

"Don't bother to order," says Jonathan. "You can have a beer at my place. It's time we had a one to one."

Grant turns, smiling, and suddenly embraces the smaller man as if he could crush him. Their faces just brush and Jonathan smells hops and tobacco, feels stubble.

"So, what are you waiting for, you whoreson?"

Jonathan stares.

"Never read *Henry IV*? Get on with you."

Grant never ceases to amaze, thinks Jon as they swagger out of the pub, lots of eyes jealously following the big man and the small.

VIII

George, at last, has his own "desktop" computer. He had thought a laptop would be twee and fiddly and far too expensive and, maybe, just that bit too trendy. He prefers something solid and clunky and a little bit out of date. So, for a few hundred pounds – a mere snip out of his £40,000 pay-off, neatly added to his cosy investment package – he now sits facing his very own shiny artificial brain, his plastic and silicon monster, filled with complicated chips and brilliant semi-conductors (whatever *they* are), and all derived, as George often ponders, from the extraordinary mind of that mad, maligned, misunderstood queen, Alan Turing, prime begetter of the Enigma machine. *Oh England, my England. Only England,* thinks George, *would drive its most inventive genius in centuries to bite a poisoned apple because he preferred to sleep with boys. And we're shocked at what Athens did to Socrates; not that any students these days would have heard of* him.

This creature – is it a creature, or merely a creation? – this *machine* will soon – when the end of term, that blessed consummation, dawns in three weeks' time – become his chief interlocutor, his interactive partner in life. To George, who has never had a partner before, or even, outside work, many friends, this is quite a daunting, but also an exciting thought. He is determined to get to know his computer, to cherish it, even to love it.

And why? What is the goal of his delving into this new and hitherto alien world of megabytes and rams, of a world wide web of virtual reality, when all the reality he ever dreamt of has come from the well-thumbed pages of novels and his own steaming churning unconscious? It isn't so that he can surf the internet for pornographic websites or chat groups to discuss the works of his favourite writers, though he may do that too. Or so that his Victor Meldrew-type letters of bilious complaint to monstrous utility companies can impress with ever greater erudition. No, it is to help him come closer to the matriarchal ideal of his fantasies, the huge dominatrix-mother of his imagination, that man/woman who bestrides the great tradition of the English novel like a golden colossal: Marianne or MaryAnn or Mary Ann Evans, Aunt Polly (to her nieces), Madonna (to her "husband") or even, as she dared to call herself (illegitimately) Mrs George Henry Lewes, and eventually (and legitimately) in her final months and incarnation, Mrs John Cross, but always and forever simply: George Eliot. Her great brain, he hopes, will emerge from the confrontation between *his* brain and the artificial intelligence housed in the square, squat plastic box before him, from which he will produce, almost like Casaubon's *The Key to All Mythologies* in *Middlemarch*, a masterpiece to sum up all the manifold aspects of her character and achievements; almost like, but not exactly so, because, unlike that fusty old scholar's magnum opus, *his* tome would be finished, born like the phoenix from the smouldering ashes of his collapsed academic career.

They had asked George at Compunerds 2000, the highly recommended computer outlet near Staples Corner, whether as a tyro – actually they didn't use the word "tyro", it was "web self-starter" – they should install the internet for him, and he said, "Why not?" So now, on this bright sunny Sunday morning, he takes out their booklet of child-friendly instructions on how to use this "internet". *And what, after all*, thinks George, *is the internet? Is it a web of souls reaching to the stars filling the universe with energy and ideas, is it a linking of minds amazingly fast across continents buzzing with thoughts both pure and impure, both evil and good (which being the product of humanity is not a surprise), or is it just a lot of over-hyped crap for naff people (mostly men) without the imagination to enjoy a good book or conversation? Right, now we are going to find out.*

He finds the page on how to use search engines, which makes George think of a battering ram or a rather cruel interrogation technique. Anyway, he follows the instructions, and up on the screen before him comes the word "SEARCH" with an oblong box next to it – and in it George types the magic words "George Eliot". A few seconds elapse, then up comes a massive torrent of entries and references, all buzzing like over-anxious flies around those numinous words "George Eliot". This is quite overwhelming for our George. He has always known there is a lot of interest in his heroine, but to think that his private world is about to be invaded by, in fact is already shared with, all these hundreds, possibly thousands, of fellow aficionados is near terrifying. Looking down the list, there are (predictably) large numbers of Americans and amongst all the professors and would-be biographers and no doubt cranks and nuts, one name just catches his eye: Professor Robert Lush-Evans, of the University of Artemisia, Artemisia, Georgia, with an e-mail address attached. The learned professor has published a couple of books on Eliot and numerous articles, but it is something about his name that appeals to George. *Yes*, he thinks. To try this out he will send this unknown professor a message through the ether asking him some question about their heroine and see if some reply is returned. So, he clicks on "write e-mail" and, without premeditation, types in:

Dear Professor,

Why doesn't Gwendolen marry Deronda at the end of DD? Doesn't her plight leave the reader understandably dissatisfied? I'd be grateful for your views.

Then he clicks on "send". He goes off to the kitchen to make coffee and sits down there to listen to the news. Coming back into his little study about twenty minutes later he is astonished to see that he has been sent his first e-mail! What excitement! It can only, he presumes, be from the mad American professor, and so it is. Excitedly he opens it and reads:

Gwendolen gets the man she deserves, that is Grandcourt. Deronda needs Myra as his helpmeet in the land of Zion; how would the spoiled Gwendolen fare in such a circumstance? All this should be clear from a lively reading of the novel. The reader requiring a fairy tale ending must read fairy tales, not serious novels.

George feels a little nonplussed; the style, the tone of voice, is certainly not what he is expecting from an obscure

American professor, but then what does he know of the University of Artemisia and its scholars? Undoubtedly, Professor Lush-Evans has given him something to say to his young student Daniel, provided George sees him, as he hopes, before the end of term.

IX

In England Ben is just another young American – considered quite interesting, fairly attractive (if, for conventional tastes, overweight). Nothing special. But here in the States and in particular in a hot political atmosphere like this – due to his father's spectacular party-switch and subsequent (consequent?) upgrade the previous year from the House to the Senate where he now jointly represents the "moonshine state" – he is surprised to find himself received like a young aristocrat, the near-relative of a very VIP. And Ben, standing around nonchalantly holding his glass of Dom Perignon and being mildly lionised, decides the guests are definitely A list: the great Kathryn Graham and lesser media moguls, various White House counsel and their partners (some same sex), several congressmen/women, one of whom – Representative Winnie Bago, Democrat of Wisconsin, a smart tall woman with an aquiline face – comes over to Ben.

"Hi there, Ben. How's your handsome father? Everybody's talking about 2000 now, of course. The GOP aren't ready for a woman – unless they could get Maggie Thatcher, of course. They'd lick dog poo off her thigh-length leather boots any day – and even *they* wouldn't be stupid enough to go for either of the Bush babes. Dad was ultimately a washout and like father etc. No, the man for them is definitely McCain – such a charmer, with a brain too. He'll be hard to beat; by us I mean."

"Well…" says Ben, "I don't—"

"Absolutely," says Winnie who once launched can't be stopped, "The veep will be our candidate, of course, and with the economy still looking so good, stoopid – I didn't mean *you, Benjamin!* – he's ultimately unconquerable. And, lo and behold, my dear, if you wish to witness an American sage, turn and feast your eyes on the veep's most famous cousin: Gore Vidal."

In a niche of the great elegant salon, an elderly clearly distinguished man, face heavily lined but still handsome (once evidently more than handsome: beautiful) is holding court to an admiring circle. Ben approaches – happy to escape Winnie – and is drawn into the group. A young woman, plump with an eager look and big dark hair, is saying admiringly, "I really loved *Palimpsest*, sir. Is there gonna be a sequel?"

"That depends on a lot of factors, Miss… what was your name?"

"Monica," she breathes.

"Monica," the great man continues in his smooth, patrician tones.

Is that the accent of statesmen of past centuries, thinks Ben, *soaking up history?*

"My health, my age, the size of my publisher's next advance… you know the kind of thing. Youth and beauty don't last forever, Monica, which would of necessity be the plangent theme of a second volume."

It is clear to Ben that the master's irony is lost on the young woman.

"You're still a very attractive man, sir."

"Thank you, Monica. I prefer young people who state the obvious. And what career do you intend to follow, now that matrimony has become more than a career and less than a game?"

"Maybe politics, sir. I'm an intern at the White House at the present time."

"Really, Monica? Internal manipulations are often the most effective. You never know how far your peculiar abilities may take you or what degree of havoc your special brand of naivety may cause. You might bring down an empire – or save the world."

The master sips his champagne as Monica – and the whole group – continue to gaze at him admiringly.

"Now, who was it that told me Stephen Sondheim was in the room? We never appear in public together. People might talk. You will excuse me."

America's biographer and greatest novelist moves majestically on, followed by two or three attractive young men from his coterie. *I'm seeing history tonight*, thinks Ben. *No, I'm part of it. First the Clintons at Dad's wedding, then this. What have I been missing living in dull old London with dull old… No, that's not fair. And here I'm only trading on Dad's name. Mind you, that audition tomorrow could lead to something.*

Across the room Ben sees two rather handsome men in smart pinstripe suits, a kind of dark, bearish version of Gilbert and George, at least one of whom is clearly Jewish. Ben has always been attracted to small dark bearded Jewish men (how else to explain his linkage to Jonathan?) but these two have a peculiarly twin-ish – or at least dual – quality which intrigues him, and the intense rabbinic twin is certainly staring at him. As if drawn together they meet halfway across the room.

"I think we've seen you in London. You're not a New Yorker, are you? Are you Jewish?"

This barrage of questions confirms the eccentricity already apparent to Ben, but he's American and confident enough not to be fazed by it.

"You may have, though I haven't, and no and no as Mr Vidal might say."

The rabbinic bear smiles. His teeth are very white and his lips surrounded by that luxuriant beard do appear quite luscious to Ben. He has a sense of humour after all.

"I'm sorry to be so forward. But in my hometown I revert to New York manners. I'm Zachary and that's my partner Armando. We live most of the year in London now. You're evidently an American though, not a New Yorker."

Ben is warming to him.

"I'm Ben and I am American. I can't deny it. Though in England I've sometimes wanted to. They can be so bitchy, can't they? I've been living in London the past few years – my God, seven, I can't believe it – and no, I'm not Jewish but coincidentally my partner who's British is. Got that?"

"Sure. We've seen you with him. A nice-looking man. Isn't he here?"

"No, he's at home. I've been visiting my family in Washington; my dad's in politics. And what's got *you* into this party?"

"Well, my family have given a few million to the Democratic Party over the years and I'm working hard to keep Giuliani out of the Senate. What does your daddy do? Does he work for the administration?"

"Au contraire. He's in the Senate, representing the moonshine state, you know."

The big brown eyes widen.

"Senator Ben Schlesinger, of course. A fine man, your father. Especially since he came across to *us*. Handsome. Very handsome. Is he gay?"

"No," replies Ben vehemently, thinking some people really go too far.

"OK, don't be offended. I can't help finding distinguished older men attractive, can I? And what do you do?"

"I'm a musician, a singer. And you two?"

"Actually, I have *semicha* – you understand me?"

This man is so irritating.

"I presume it means you're a rabbi?"

"You got it. Though actually I don't practise for a living. But I attend a very orthodox little *shtiebl* not far from here and we are completely accepted as a couple. Completely. Armando is a monk, by the way. Of the Dominican Order. Isn't he handsome?"

Actually, the partner, standing by his side, does look tall, dark, silent and handsome but Ben is not about to say so.

"You *are* an unusual couple."

Zachary smirks then goes off to get drinks.

"It works," the unhabited (uninhibited?) monk suddenly says in a quiet, cultured voice. "We have a lot in common, being both of the cloth. And we're both of royal blood as well. Zac's descended from King David and my family are the royal house of Naples, who were also once kings of Jerusalem, of course. So much in common."

Ben thinks, *Yes-sir, complete loony-tunes. Still, dear old Francis would have been amused by the genealogy thing.* But before Ben can wholly assimilate this latest wave of eccentricity, Zac returns.

"You must come and see us some time. For dinner. Mandy, isn't that Geraldine Ferraro over there? I was wondering whatever happened to her. Let's go see."

Completely mad, thinks Ben. *But quite attractive. And sort of fascinating, in a crazy kind of way. But how annoying when people invite you for dinner and don't give you their card. So false. Not that I would have wanted to go anyway.*

X

And what has been happening to our old (well, not so old; though she often feels it) and very dear friend Celia in these weeks of high, hot summer, since we last saw her, chatting away with highly strung Harold and renouncing men for ever? It's early August and a hot and humid one it is turning out to be, which is always a difficult time of year with autumn ahead but especially for the terminally middle-aged (who permanently have autumn ahead). It's the end of a long day teaching at the Academy, which Celia has resorted to for her daily bread as she is only playing one major role at the Whippo this coming season – and that the role of an eponymous madwoman immortalised by the extraordinary Dame Joan, whom how can she hope to rival?

Essentially, Celia feels vindicated to have kept their lovely three-storey family house in one of the more exclusive squares in Islington, but it does sometimes seem lonely and a little empty these days. She looks at her image in the glass in her hallway. *A woman at fifty can still be beautiful, but Christ it's hard work*, she thinks. She sees a face etched with the lines of fifty *interesting* years and a long (too long) marriage to a wayward, brilliant, alcoholic bisexual; looking eerily into her own hazel eyes – slightly almond-shaped so that when younger she was often asked as a chat-up line whether she was of Oriental descent – she knows she will rise to this as to all her other challenges – *unlike,* she thinks, *my wimp of a husband.* She brushes her quite luscious hair vigorously – something she liked Pip to do when in one of his more communicative, tactile moods – thinking, *Why doesn't that agent of mine get me some adverts for hair products for the mature woman? The woman whose hair is strong, sensuous and seasoned like her, as advertised by world-famous opera singer Celia Greyfield. Doesn't he realise I'm an actress not just a clapped-out singer?*

She goes through into her sitting room, having swept up the letters on her mat, and pours herself a very large whisky with a drop of soda. She sits down in a comfortable chair, puts her feet up and takes a few large gulps. The day begins to come into focus; her life begins to come into focus. It's all a dream anyway as some Greek or Roman philosopher said. It's all over in about a minute, a millisecond of eternal time; why worry so much? *Don't take yourself so seriously, darling*, she advises, becoming her own best friend, her own, and very inexpensive, counsellor. Things will resolve themselves one way or another – with Pip, with Harold, with her career, with Adelina. For certainly Adelina has attracted her, interested her; though in what way, she can't work out. But a) Adelina has a girlfriend, a partner in fact, the very present and self-possessed Tallulah, and b) a small fact she has appeared to have forgotten: she, Celia, is not a lesbian. But then need sexuality be so schematic, so categorised? Just the previous afternoon, browsing in her local Waterstones, she had come across a large book of photographs by a lesbian (she assumed) photographer showing a wide and eye-opening range of fascinating and often beautiful lesbian women, some clothed, some unclothed, some cross-dressed, always women of character and dignity and therefore of beauty.

And she found them wonderful: strong, independent, and… without need of men. But was it a kind of beauty she found *sexual*? That was the unanswered question.

The first two letters are bills and another three are evidently circulars, one inviting her to subscribe for tickets to the Whippo including her own performances. Brilliant. The next letter looks more interesting, though as a singer well known for many years she is always aware that "interesting" letters often turn out to be from stalkers or other demanding fans. She opens it. This is headed "GLOW" and then below "Gay Light Opera Works" – inviting her patronage perhaps?

"You may have heard of our work…" *No, I haven't, why should I?*

She skims further down. "We are seeking a 'glowing' diva for the role of Lucia and, knowing of your prominence in this field…"

So, this is the slippery slope, is it? she thinks. To go from playing Lucia at the Whippo this autumn to playing her in the spring with a gay, and more importantly, amateur light opera group? *Forget it! How dare they?*

"The role of Miss Mapp we hope will be amply filled by Ms Barbara McTavish, that seasoned trouper opposite whom I know you have performed before…"

"Oh, *that* Lucia!" she says aloud. "That could be fun."

And she begins to laugh silently at first then out loud at the thought of confusing the two roles. Maybe she should encourage these enthusiastic amateurs – and after all she did usually get along awfully well with queers and poufters as Harold would call them. *Is there any mention of a fee?* She is just looking over the letter again to ascertain an answer to that and to who the musical director will be when the door buzzes.

Celia feels nonplussed and unsure whether she wants to answer it. Anyone could buzz you at six o'clock in the evening, including a complete stranger, and why should she see them? But then it could be Adelina – which might be intriguing – or Harold back surprisingly fast from the States, which would be fun, but it also might be Pip which would just be a bore and a nuisance, especially at this time of the evening. She almost wishes she lived in a flat because then she would have an intercom. As it is, she sidles to the window and looks askance past the edge of the velvet curtain. Of course, the visitor is standing annoyingly on the porch and so cannot be seen except for a suggestion of a back which looks decidedly masculine, quite tall and pretty erect – so not unappealing. *Of course,* thinks Celia, *I do feel a little vulnerable being alone here, but then it's broad, still sunny daylight and I can use the chain. Anyway, I've never been a coward and nothing ventured…*

She goes to the door and doesn't even put the chain on. She is surprised to see a young man standing there, very attractive, definitely familiar. His green eyes smile at her though his lips seemed serious, if sensuous.

"Hello, Jeb," she says. "What is it this time? An interview for *American Vogue* perhaps? Or maybe a photo shoot for Channel 5?"

His expression is a mélange of sheepish and roguish.

"I just wanted to say sorry for what happened last time; the misunderstanding…" The word brings out his brogue more than the others. "Me coming to see you and all…"

That smile is practically irresistible, thinks Celia. *What chutzpah.*

"Was that it?"

They are still standing at the door.

"And I brought you this by way of a small apology."

He presents her with a box of chocolates: Bendicks mints – her favourites.

"Oh, thank you. That's nice."

A slight pause while she struggles with the temptation to invite him in.

"So, I'll let you go now. Sorry to have bothered you. I'll write and explain. There are reasons."

He smiles and turns away.

She shuts the door, comes back in and, as the old queens used to say, refreshes her drink.

"There are *reasons*? What the fuck…?"

XI

Ben's audition for the Met was not quite the life-changing epoch he had envisioned, but nor was it a complete flop. (And anyway, did he want it to be life-changing? Did he want to move to New York, which would mean leaving Jonathan at least for the forthcoming season? But then Jon had left him to go off to Bruges for that earlier year, and they were both entitled to careers, weren't they?) The man who auditioned him was, he supposes, Jon's opposite number in the great opera company and was also, annoyingly, the biggest queen Ben had ever met, or perhaps confronted would be the better word. He was also, evidently, not a queen who liked his men *costaud*; in plain English, he didn't like bears. Ben arrived with an aria by Mozart and another by Verdi, his two favourite composers. He knew them both well, but he had the music with him because he was, understandably, extremely nervous. He had done a warm-up at his guesthouse in a pleasant road just off Christopher Street (didn't I mention it before? I'm sorry, but where else to stay in New York? He had been there previously and, though expensive, had found it ideal and, after all, his dad was, as usual, paying all his expenses in the States, so why not enjoy the elegant bedroom with four-poster bed, charming sitting room and well-stocked galley kitchen? Not that he used it much, as he'd enjoyed brunch in a handsome eatery in Christopher Street; Ben was never too nervous to eat.)

Having been ushered into the rehearsal room Ben faced his auditioner.

"Charles?" said the tall slim man in a nasal New York voice.

"No, Ben. Ben Schlesinger. You should have my résumé."

"Yes, I'm sure I have. Ben what?"

This was not a good start.

"Ben Schlesinger." He was tempted to say, as he had in so many similar situations this past week, "My father's the…" but he didn't.

"OK. Sing."

Ben had expected a little more preface than this.

"Shall I start with Mozart or Verdi?"

"Nothing more contemporary?"

Ben was about to lose his cool completely which he knew would be disastrous for his voice. He took a deep breath.

"No. Just those."

"Mozart then."

He gave his music to the accompanist, a grizzled older man who gave him a very reassuring smile, and he felt better.

He knew he was giving a reasonably worthwhile rendition of *Don Giovanni*'s mandolin love song when nasal voice interrupted with, "Thank you."

The pianist stopped – he was evidently used to this – and Ben, hiding or attempting to hide his exasperation, said, "Some of the Verdi? It's from—"

"That won't be needed, Mr… um… Ben. Pressure of time. Sorry. Thank you."

Had he come all this way for two pages of *Don Giovanni* (apart from his father's wedding, of course, but that wasn't uppermost in his mind)?

"Mr… um… I don't know your name."

The camp gentleman looked at him. Was there a little more respect in his eyes?

"I'm Joe. Joe St. Louis."

"Well, Mr St. Louis. I hope I'll be hearing from you. Soon please. I have to go back to London shortly."

"Sure." He paused as if weighing up how much to say. "You have good timbre and promising musicianship. The voice needs to develop more. We can't use you this season, but we'll keep you on our books. It might be worth trying next season. I'll mail you a fuller report. Thanks for coming in."

There was a momentary flash of a smile and then he was dismissed. But he had at least been heard, put down his marker for the future. It hadn't been a waste of time; Joe St. Louis was more than the camp queen he so obviously appeared.

All the same, Ben is now bathed in sweat, and not just because it is an intensely humid August afternoon. He will definitely need diversion that evening. He had heard all about the "dry" sex clubs that had largely replaced the old bathhouses of New York, and in fact, of America and he had decided it was time to try one.

New York was then probably the most vibrant city in the world in those pre-9/11 days the most self-confident and, therefore, in a sense the most sexual. True it was no longer the maelstrom of homoerotic excitement it had been in the late seventies when Francis or Jeremy, our friends' mentors, had visited and found it so much more wild and intense than

London or anywhere in Europe. The AIDS epidemic had hit New York almost as hard as it hit San Francisco and that changed the character of the great city's sexuality. At the same time, the mayor that our democratic friends were so keen to keep out of the Senate had cleaned up those mean streets of their violence and maybe purged them of some of their colour and character, but safety combined with vibrancy is extremely appealing and Ben, like most visitors, is certainly enjoying the town. So, the New York of '97 is no longer the city of sleaze and risk and sheer animal power of twenty years before, but it is the city of *Sex and the City*, of Rudy Giuliani, of enormous economic power and a still unblemished architectural skyline. It had come through the first tragedy, of AIDS; the second tragedy – more sudden, equally devastating – was yet to come. It was a great city then, at the end of the twentieth century, with huge hopes like the rest of us, in a period of remission.

As for the gay community, it had regained much of its confidence, if less of its gloriously outrageous sleaze. Nonetheless, Ben had heard through the grapevine while still in London, and then seen advertised in the gay press in New York, that not far from where he is staying – in the famous old meat-packing district appropriately enough – is a club, only a few years old but already internationally infamous, called Deep Throats. It was clearly not for the fainthearted or those who found it hard to swallow. Ever since arriving in town Ben had toyed with the idea of going there and seeing what was on offer. The fact is he has never been totally easy about his sexuality in front of Jonathan. Yes, they had had delightful, warm, loving sex together when they had first met, and still did – occasionally. Sex after all was not the most important thing that bound them together in their relationship; music, humour, shared tastes, habit and above all close companionship held them together far more closely. So far, so unremarkable; many gay couples, especially those honest and confident enough to be non-monogamous, were, are, exactly thus. But most of them negotiate this by a growing, a shared, communal sexuality based on the chase, the hunt for men whom they both desire. And this joint hunt, which might culminate in a threesome in the matrimonial bed, or in intense backroom sex in a club, is a very effective form of gay male bonding. Of course, there had been occasions when they had done this; how else, in fact, had they first picked up Grant, the tattooed lover boy himself? But in general Ben preferred to keep his sexuality individual; it was some kind of inhibition within him which he had always feared might spell danger for the relationship. But then, dear reader, we cannot help our own personalities, or can we?

Ben phones his other half this afternoon and is glad to find him at home in London's evening. The conversation is a little longer and more forthcoming than the previous one and he is glad to hear that Jonathan has decided to take on the musical directorship of GLOW, providing all works out at his meeting with its eccentric-sounding president. Of course he asks Jon if he's been out on the scene, met anyone, had any fun, adding that (of course) he didn't mind at all if he had.

Jon says that, no, he hasn't, as it happens, apart from bumping into Grant in the pub and having a grope with him for old times' sake, who (of course) had asked after Ben and been very complimentary about him. And had Ben been out yet in the Big Apple?

Well, he had been out for his audition, which he then proceeds to tell Jonathan about in great detail, adding that he needs to stay on in New York another week or so in order to get a fuller response and because it is just possible that he might get the recall to the Met he longs for. Oh yes, and he had "bumped into" a rather eccentric couple who seemed to recognise him – and Jon too – from London: a Jesuit and a rabbi, but he doesn't think that Jon would remember them. Not important anyhow. As for this evening, he might go out for a drink in the Christopher Street area; it would be a shame not to. Oh, and if he bumps into Grant again he should (of course) give him one for Ben. A nice juicy one right up the ass.

After the phone call Ben feels almost like wanking; it was the nearest they'd come to phone sex and had been predictably brought on by the image of a past shared threesome. *And what's wrong with that?* Ben asks himself. Nothing, except that it requires a fuller consummation than a quick hand job. There was nothing for it but to gird up his loins – and their appurtenances – and take the whole lot off to Deep Throats for what the adverts described as "the best blowjobs with the hottest men in town".

Predictably, Deep Throats was not easy to find. Ben feels uncomfortable about giving a taxi driver such an address and anyway he gathers from the little map in his gay guide that it is virtually round the corner from where he is staying. But "round the corner" turns out to be a fifty-minute walk – partly because Ben had taken a wrong tuning and had to retrace his steps – and because you wouldn't expect a sleazy sex club to advertise itself in neon lights now, would you? Even when Ben locates the appropriate block on a very dingy road in the old meat-packing district it takes him several walks to and fro to be sure that the unmarked metal double doors that look locked must be the place. Approaching closer he gingerly pushes one of the doors and virtually falls into a lobby with preternaturally bright lights as if to compensate for the murkiness to come. Ben is embarrassed – he is always embarrassed where sex is on the menu – and incredibly excited. He has made it to the forbidden planet; he needs to meet and greet the aliens. After all, this is what it means to be a gay man, and much as he genuinely loves Jonathan, he needs this other, personal, almost secret side of his sexual life to express himself emotionally. All that he wants now is to let go, indulge his desires and not see anyone he knows. Which seems pretty likely as he knows so few people in New York.

Ben is in a fairly short line of men in the usual casual clubbing gear – not trendy young things but mostly mature men, some bearded and beary – signing in and paying up at a table to the right. As he gets to the table a brightly cheery, youngish man showing his hairless chest beneath a leather waistcoat says, "Have you been before?"

"Uh, nope."

"You need membership. Could you sign here… and here? It's ten dollars membership, ten to come in. Just read through the rules first."

There is a page of rules, which Ben skims. Footwear must be worn… members can be otherwise naked or clothed… no anal sex allowed… condoms available but optional for oral sex… members must show respect for each other's wishes at all times…

"OK." Ben signs twice as "Ben Sherman". (What if the club is raided? It doesn't matter to him, of course, but it would look pretty bad for his dad, even now he is a Democrat. And anyway, giving a false name made it all just that little bit more secretive, dangerous and therefore exciting.)

Hairless chest, showing unexpected wit, says, "Love your shirts."

Ben looks momentarily nonplussed, not amused.

"Yea, funny."

Hairless gives him an old-fashioned look and hands him a small card with only his name, a number and the initials DT.

Then he is through an arched doorway and into the main foyer of the club. Here the light is already a little more subdued. At one side is a long counter serving as coat-check. Despite the heat Ben is wearing a check shirt over his plain blue T-shirt and decides to hand that in. The slim rather unattractive man ahead of him – why is it always the unattractive ones who do it? – is taking off all his clothes, apart from his trainers, and putting them into a large black bag prior to handing it over.

As it comes to his turn Ben hands over his shirt and shoulder bag and says with furrowed brow, "Why do people do that?"

"You does what you please here, honey, so long as you keep to the rules," says the coat-check attendant sagely.

Straight ahead is the first room; to the left are toilets, which Ben goes into. To his left is a big wash basin, and next to it a hose, the kind you might use to wash down a car or possibly a horse, as there are rivulets of water running away along the floor into a couple of sunken channels. Ben surmises this is for use by clients to hose themselves down after a particularly dirty session. On a table to the right of it are two big plastic bottles of a dark liquid and above them on the wall a sign advising that this particular mouthwash, if taken within half an hour of swallowing cum, can kill off traces of the HIV virus.

"Yea and burn out your stomach," says Ben to no one in particular. *Still*, he thinks, *could be handy.*

But there is also, on the other side of the room, a toilet, but no ordinary one, because this toilet simply stands in the room without any cubicle around it. *A bit basic*, thinks Ben. *More than basic, obscene.* And then, *Obscene and maybe, in the right circumstances, arousing*, as a kind of permitted violation of privacy, a kind of regression into infantilism. There is something intimate, exciting and disturbing about those latrines all at once; he leaves them quickly and walks along the corridor into the club proper, or improper.

On his right, through some vertical slats, is a big darkened room with three rows of banked benches. In one corner is a TV showing fairly predictable porn movies, in another is a coffee machine with plastic cups. A few men are lounging about on the benches and there is a couple in a dark corner having some kind of sex but otherwise not a lot is going on. Ben continues. He passes through a dark corridor and makes out a man tied up in a chair with leather thongs while another man bends over his crotch to perform the dominant ritual of the club. The corridor has a faint but unmistakable odour of sweat and semen. Ben is feeling slightly nauseated.

Then he comes through to a big central room which is much busier. It is on two levels. On the lower level men mostly in T-shirts and jeans but some wholly or largely unclothed and others in bits and pieces of leather are milling around and here and there applying their mouths to holes in a partition which goes all round the room on the higher level just a few feet above the ground. And through these glory-holes, as tradition decrees they should be called, are poking a whole line of cocks of many sizes and shapes, and in all possible states of flaccidity and arousal. You can't easily see whom each member belongs to as the wooden partition is high enough to hide the rest of most average-sized men. Ben is half horrified, half fascinated – and if possible, half amused. He feels like giggling; he has never seen anything quite as crass as this before. But this is nineties New York sexuality; a post-AIDS construction that is direct, sets boundaries and fulfils a need.

He walks up the short flight of steps to the upper level and feels a bit more at ease there. Here are the dicks rather than the mouths; he finds it easier to identify with them. He feels himself becoming aroused; the whole place is redolent of maleness, sexuality and release. As he walks along between the line of men pressed against the partition and the wall he pushes gently against the beautifully rounded buttocks of a chunky man with very black hair. He suspects you aren't supposed to but he can't resist caressing them just a little with his hand. Where there are rules and rituals a little transgression is usually necessary to arouse desire. The man's head turns. He is bearded and certainly handsome, and as he smiles, Ben realises it is Zac, the rabbi he had met at the party.

Zac says, "I've been wanting you," and withdraws his cock from whatever orifice it had been nestling in.

Ben puts his hand on it; it is certainly engorged, circumcised, of course, and with a substantial head, wet with spittle, which Ben begins to manipulate. Zac's hand goes down to Ben's ample tummy, caresses it with voluptuous sensuality, then eases down the zip of his jeans and puts his hand inside.

They begin to kiss, Zac stabbing his tongue into Ben's mouth while Ben sucks in the short, damp black hairs around Zac's very sensuous lips. But, as they are getting into this, people are trying to get passed and pushing them against the wooden partition. Zac withdraws his tongue, then quickly stabs it into Ben's mouth again with a gobbet of thick spittle, then withdraws it again. He pulls out Ben's now three-quarters erect dick and looks down at it. He smiles.

"Nice and fat and sexy. Like the man himself."

He drops a dollop of spit from his lips onto the fat cock and rubs like a genie working a miraculous lamp.

Ben begins to think, *This man is intensely erotic. I want more.*

Zac says, "Stay right here."

He disappears and Ben suspects a not uncommon case of game-playing and literal cock-teasing.

But, a moment later, he feels a hand coming through the glory-hole in front of him and peering over the partition sees Zac's face, leering suggestively.

OK, thinks Ben, *I can play this game.*

He places his dick through the hole and at once feels it encompassed, enclosed by the cave-like warmth of Zac's mouth; at least he assumes it is Zac's mouth, but now does it really matter?

And then he feels arms coming around him from behind, which he does not welcome. Looking round – cock still firmly held in the sucking mouth below – he sees it is another familiar face; that of the Dominican partner.

"I see you two have joined up. Like a third?"

He opens his lips to kiss, but Ben doesn't wish to play. He feels imposed upon, interrupted for reasons of jealousy. And anyway, there is something unappealing about Armando. He smiles coldly with his mouth firmly shut. He can feel Armando's cock hardening against his own arse but it doesn't help. He withdraws his dick with a swift motion from the mouth below creating an audible sound of suction.

He says to Zac over the partition, "I need a piss."

Ben quickly moves along thinking, *Well, if that causes a problem between them, that's just fine by me. I ain't gonna be dragooned into no threesome I don't wanna be in.*

Moving on, now both physically and metaphorically lubricated, Ben is certainly ready for more action. *I knew I didn't want to meet anyone I know,* he thinks irritably. *Now it's time for some handsome, powerful and seductive stranger.* He walks on through a kind of maze in which there are, predictably, a series of cubicles, most of them apparently occupied by couples, while one or two have their doors open with an expectant man within, cruising passers-by with his eyes.

Then there is another doorway and Ben finds himself going through it with surprise into the hot open air of an inner courtyard. A man with a reddish goatee and a superb, shapely bearish physique is lounging on a seat to the right of the path amongst potted plants, thick auburn chest hair bursting between the buttons of his open denim shirt, and his big, dark eyes seem to be resting on Ben. But when Ben gives him a heavily cruisy look he turns coldly away. *Don't give me such attitude,* thinks Ben. *You're just another fat guy like me, who goes to the gym a bit more often.* And while at home in England Ben might have felt deflated, here he has the self-confidence to say: *you win some, you lose some. Bring on the next.*

There is tropical greenery in the courtyard and another outdoor maze. As he walks through, eyes turning this way and that, he glimpses a man in the bushes – rather plain and pasty-faced, so probably English – wearing a leather harness and a jock strap, who looks somehow familiar. So, he turns back to escape and, retracing his steps, finds himself in the first room with the tiers of benches. This is still quiet, apart from two or three men getting themselves coffee at the machine. But lying on one of the benches, looking up at the screen opposite him which is now showing bear porn – in fact a famous flick starring several Californian glamour-bears – is a big voluptuous man wearing shiny shorts which are pulled down as he slowly and sensuously strokes and caresses his gradually hardening dick.

Ben walks over. The man is – unusually for that time and place – unbearded but with a little stubble and a sweet baby-faced expression. His head is balding with a dark brown hirsute border, and this is something Ben often finds appealing, as a guarantee of masculinity and maturity. His ample chest is downed with light brown hair above a gently bulging belly. Ben reaches out daringly and gently tweaks the man's dark left nipple. His eyes languorously turn towards Ben, for a moment coldly, then a seductive warmth comes into them and they narrow, piercingly. He smiles gently but leaves the running to Ben who now leans over and with his tongue begins to lick and play with the brown right nipple while still manipulating the other one. The man lets out a gentle, erotic moan and Ben, excited by his partner's clear enjoyment in giving himself over to be played upon, goes further by bringing his wet tongue slowly and caressingly down the line of brown fur, already damp with a sour-sweet-tasting sweat, guiding him from the centre of the man's chest over the curve of his belly (which Ben finds intensely erotic, having been awakened to the sensuality of other fat men by Jonathan's hypnotic attraction to them, including himself) and along down to the richly darker, thicker fur around his crotch. Here the scent of testosterone is heavier, thicker and he is just about to place his lips over the medium-sized, bluish uncircumcised cock when hands come around his head and guide it up towards the man's lips where they begin to kiss at first gently then more deeply, more longingly. The man's hands pull up Ben's T-shirt which he then quickly pulls back over his head leaving his shoulders in the sleeves, but his fleshy chest exposed. The hands begin to gently play with his tits, then again come around his head and guide him back to the dick now straining out of the lips of his thick, pale foreskin. (*The guy's clearly not American,* thinks Ben.) And now he goes to it with a vengeance in very active mode, deeply excited by the feeling of this man's dick filling his mouth. (Yet is sucking an active or a passive mode? Perhaps the latter as an activity conventionally thought of as feminine; yet it's the suckee who languidly lies back and thinks of England or whatever is the home country of this bulky, and very relaxed stranger.) Then suddenly Ben thinks, *What am I getting out of this? Am I being used? There's not much reciprocation and, despite the presence of that killer mouthwash, I'd rather not imbibe.* So, he stops, draws back and looks up. But the handsome stranger – as Ben sees him to be – is quite unfazed and, his eyes partially dilated, continues to manipulate his dick with expert autoeroticism while undoing Ben's fly and bringing out his semi-erect cock. Ben reverts to playing teasingly with the man's now rigid nipples while he begins to breathe more and more deeply, his strokes getting stronger and faster. Ben, hypnotised, spits onto the engorged dick and this gives the stranger the final spurt. He rubs the flecked spittle into his straining cock and as he lets out a huge groan – several groans in fact – his cock brims over with a cupful of bubbly, white juice. And then gradually subsides. Ben has not come but has enjoyed the other man's orgasm vicariously.

The man speaks. He has an educated Irish accent.

"Thank you so much. That was lovely."

"Yea, it was good. Are you a visitor?"

"Abso-fuckin-lutely. From Dublin. Just here for a few days. You're a New Yorker?"

"No. I actually live in England, though I'm originally American, as you can hear. I'm Ben."

"Hello, Ben," says the man, pulling up his satin pants and resuming the more polite, respectable mode – as one does, must, after the sudden intensity of sex, especially really good sex, with a stranger.

"I'm Tony." He reaches out his hand, very big and masculine, withdraws it a moment to wipe it on a tissue, then takes Ben's hand in a very warm, strong grip.

Ben begins to feel turned on again.

"Hi. What's your work, Tony?" *Why*, thinks Ben, *do I always ask people what they do at work? Why does it matter? Is it because I'm a snob and want to know if he's suitable as a friend or even a partner – although, of course, I've got one of those already.*

"I'm a lawyer. But I'm here for pleasure – mainly. And you?"

"I'm a singer. Here to audition, and see family."

"Great. Lovely. You staying in the Village?"

"Yea, near Christopher Street."

"So am I. Maybe we'll meet up for brunch or something."

"That would be good. Would you like a coffee now?"

"Not at the moment. I think I need the loos and maybe even that bloody great hose. See ya a bit later."

And he is gone. *And why not*, thinks Ben. *Who gives a fuck.* Though for some reason he does.

But Ben's night isn't over yet. This, he is sure, has just been an hors d'oeuvre. He gets himself a coffee and is just enjoying it when he hears a cultivated, camp British voice behind him.

"I'd recognise that arse anywhere. All right, Ben?"

Ben turns round, very reluctant to engage in banter with anyone from home. It is the man wearing a harness he had half recognised in the garden. Yes, it is the incorrigible Harold.

"Hi there," Ben says with a perfunctory smile. "You on vacation?"

"Sort of. But you know me, always networking. Did you enjoy that party the other night? I saw you in the crush around Gore. The genius I mean, not the veep. Did you get to speak to him?"

How can this man be so impossibly irritating? thinks Ben. "Did *you*?"

"Unfortunately not, sweetie, but I've had some great sex this evening. But then look at *you*. I've had my eye on that big buck Irish beauty all night. Well done."

Oh, fuck off, thinks Ben. *Why must you always show off?*

"Yes. He was a fabulous shag. See ya." *Wouldn't wanna be ya,* he thinks, quickly moving away. *What's the time? Around 2 a.m. Time for one last session, maybe.* Ben knows that, covered in sweat and already heavily sexed, he is in just the right mood and shape to attract that final shag of the night in such a club.

He moves back into the central room, walks up the steps to the upper tier and lounges. *Sod it,* he thinks, *why not go the whole hog.* He opens his zip to push his rapidly expanding cock through the glory-hole which is, by some miracle (or is it just the time of night?), at exactly the right angle in front of him. Immediately, he sees a tall fair leatherman, big and handsome in a heavily studded harness and Muir cap (*a bit dated,* thinks Ben, *but why worry?*) glowering towards him from across the room at floor level. Ben glowers back at him, darkly, sensuously as if to say, "Bring it on, big guy, I'll take you right now." And he does. The tall blondish hunk strides over holding Ben's eyes with his own, applies first his tongue, then his expert lips, to Ben's increasingly expansive cock and sucks on it with the dedicated suction of a porn actor enjoying his day off.

So, this is why I came to New York, he thinks while experiencing a hugely satisfying orgasm and then staring deliciously, stupidly, down at the big blue eyes staring up at him just above where his penis is gradually receding from the full-blown lips.

"Thank you," says Ben, not sure if he really wants – or needs – to say anything.

"That's a pleasure," replies blondie in a voice that is just a bit disappointingly nasal. "Are you a native New Yorker?"

"Not exactly. I live in England." This always brings him cachet in the States.

"Oh fabulous. I'm from San Diego."

That explains the blond beach boy looks, thinks Ben.

"That's nice."

"Do you know it?"

This is beginning to spoil a perfectly shallow experience, thinks Ben.

"Well, I went to school there."

"Do you still know folks there?"

Ben, thinking of his mentor Francis, the charming eccentric, deceased Englishman who had befriended his brother, doesn't want to go into details.

"Not anymore. Thanks."

And then he is walking away, satisfied. *That's the way to do it,* he thinks, moving towards the toilets. He decides just to pick up a quick coffee before leaving and ambles into the side room with the porn video. It is now showing something distinctly more S and M and Ben, fixing his coffee, makes out a huddle of men closely intent on sex at the other corner of the room. Reader, at the end of a pleasant self-indulgent evening, once your own pleasure is complete and you simply want to enjoy a quiet coffee, do you really wish to have group sex performed by strangers in front of you? I think not. Ben looks askance, then realises they are not strangers. The once attractive Irishman, now looking merely fat and greasy, is splayed over a bench with the pasty Englishman – yes, Harold – now doubly in harness, ploughing him hard and savagely, while Armando is on the floor sucking the Irishman's dick and Zac is standing behind Harold, rubbing his cock up against the crack of the Englishman's arse and tweaking his nipples. As a final touch, there is the handsome red bear from the courtyard sweating profusely and wanking himself off over the Irishman's broad back. It is a tableau vivant from a Victorian molly house or a scene of hell from Hieronymus Bosch.

"What a fucking tableau, or tableau of fucking!" Ben mutters, leaving his unfinished coffee and almost gasping for air.

That hose isn't big enough to wash off the smell of this place, he thinks – a little hypocritically perhaps? He leaves quickly and breathes in deeply the warm but fresher night air. It doesn't take long to pick up a cab. Once in it, with his puritan guilt subsiding he thinks, *Well, it wouldn't be so bad for a second visit, and it makes a change to do this sort of thing without Jon constantly looking on. Not that I don't love him, of course, but freedom – ah freedom. It's indivisible. Even if a bit lonely at times. But another week or two of it won't hurt.*

Back in his comfortable hotel room, Ben hardly has energy to pull off his stale clothes before falling onto the big, warm double bed.

The tall, distinguished grey-haired man, looking much younger than when Ben last saw him, looks teasingly up at him like a boy in a porn shoot.

"You're being awfully naughty, dear boy, but you know that. Have you been to see your brother? I think not! Anyway, I saw him yesterday. He's fine."

Francis gives him an old-fashioned look; very amused, a little cynical, very loving. He seems to be leaning against an elegant mantelpiece and wearing a 1920s blazer, which suits him.

"It can get a little boring here at times; perfection can be dull, you know. And I really am fed up with literature. I'm devoting myself to music now. You get the best here; it's heavenly."

He is suddenly seated at a grand piano, playing a Chopin ballade (number 2 in A flat) divinely.

"I played the piano as a child, you see. Jeremy would be proud of me. If he ever bothered to think of me at all." He looks up rather wistfully. "You can tell him that Tennessee Williams is just as charming in the flesh as he might have imagined. Well, not in the flesh exactly."

Now he is lounging on a deep, rich, luxurious chaise longue. He looks at Ben seriously. "You were terrific, splendid, my dear. To me, I mean. Just like family; better. I apologise about the will."

Everything begins to go muzzy and faint.

"Damn. I wanted to tell you," says Francis, a bit distantly. "Go back to your boyfriend. He's getting restless and that would never do – some Irish Canadian lad. Preserve your companionship – it works, darling."

And when Ben awakes with the heat of the midday sun beating into the room, he remembers only that he has had some kind of visitation. And that it is time to go home.

XI

"Darling."

"What, honey?"

"Aren't you in court today?"

"It's Saturday, Ade."

"Fantastic."

"I've got to look at some houses today."

"Oh… really?"

This is not a subject Adelina likes to pursue. She doesn't want her girlfriend moving out. She changes the subject.

"And *I've* got a rehearsal later."

"But not yet."

"Not yet, my little marsupial."

Sleepily, Adelina stretches out a hand and caresses Tallulah's dark chocolate legs with her long fingers. They are lying in what is colloquially termed the spoons position and she has no intention of checking the time just yet.

"Have to look in on baby."

"Yep, but Cleo will already have done that. No point in paying a nanny if you're going to do it all yourself. And the monitor's next to the bed."

"True."

Adelina stretches and is just starting to doze off again when she feels a gentle whispering touch on her clitoris.

"Well, Lord Chancellor?"

"The Lord Chancellor requires her pussy to be well and truly licked out or she ain't givin' no judgments today."

"Yes, madam," says Adelina going down ever so gently on her girlfriend and beginning to lick the lips of her vagina.

"Sweet honey from the rock," she murmurs in between licks, adding playfully, "And better than any cock!"

"The LC might be moving chambers, you know."

"As Her Ladyship," Some slurping here. "Pleases."

"Mm, it certainly pleases. Yea, well, you know I want to specialise more; international corporate – ooh yes, honey – affairs and some human rights as well. Well, there's talk of a new set of very prestigious chambers."

"Wow," says Adelina, coming up for air and breasting the sheets to kiss Tallulah's neck. "Involving the first lady herself?"

"Could be. Now she's taken silk. Yea, get down there, girlfriend, and suck that clit. I want to call it Clitoral Chambers." Gurgling here from down below. "But they're thinking of calling it…"

"Orgasm?" suggests Adelina as her girlfriend moans out her first of the day.

"Oh, darling, you do that sooo well. The name is Mutatrix – like female mutation or something I suppose. Mind you, honey, I did Latin A level and I never heard the word."

"But you'll hear this one," says Adelina as she eases two of her long fingers deep into Tallulah's honeypot while devouring one big pink nipple with her lips and caressing the other with her remaining hand.

"Oh baby, baby, Addy…"

But Tallulah's crescendo is interrupted by a loud clear ring on the doorbell.

"Ignore it, baby. Come for Mummy, come for Mummy…"

But the ring is heard again, louder and suddenly Adelina stops plunging.

"Shit, I brought that rehearsal forward. I fucking forgot. Sorry, honey."

Adelina gets out of bed and peers out of the window. In the Islington street below a smart middle-aged woman is looking up and smiles seeing Adelina naked – and rangily beautiful – at the window. She smiles and waves back, cheerily.

"It's Celia. She looks good for her age."

"So what?" says Tallulah from the bed testily. "What the hell does *she* want?"

Adelina is already getting into her "sisters are doin' it for each other" T-shirt and pale blue jeans and starting to comb her short dark hair briskly.

"I'd forgotten she said she would come over and pick me up this morning and we'd have a coffee and a chat about her part before going in."

"Yea, and what part is that precisely?"

"Come on, love, we do work together," she says, rubbing a bit too much Brylcreem into her hair.

"Sure, and she assumed when you told her I was in court that I was on a charge. Typical racist assumption."

"Oh, I'm sure she's not a racist, sweetie. Just a pussy-envious straight."

"Same thing," mutters Tallulah as Adelina, pulling on her summer jacket, runs downstairs to open the door.

"Come in, big girl, come in. Great to see ya. I completely forgot, of course. You know me. Hence the rush."

"No problem, darling. I was…"

Celia can hear something from upstairs, starting low but getting louder. It sounds like a contralto doing some weird vocal warm-up and then changes into a rich, loud, powerful howl of pain, or possibly pleasure? She knows she shouldn't have stopped mid-sentence, but it is too late to retrieve that now. The ululation is continuing with abandon.

Adelina looks at her with amusement.

"Once I've started her off, Celie-love, she just has to finish. Can't blame her, can you?"

Celia smiles and says nothing but thinks, *I wouldn't mind some of that*, feeling, like a gay man as she often seems to, intensely jealous of the lesbian capacity for infinite orgasms, almost as if she isn't a woman at all. And truly, dear reader, women – and most particularly women of the Sapphic persuasion – are blessed with an endless capacity for pleasure as Tiresias the great hermaphrodite seer informed us so many centuries ago, nine times out-distancing the equivalent powers of men. Oh, lucky ladies, who drink at Sappho's well, of loneliness no longer, but now of infinite joy! While we mere men enjoy just our sudden shafts of pleasure in ways that are inevitably nasty, brutish and short. And so we leave our tribadite girls, while Tallulah, our future first black/female Lord Chancellor sinks back into a delicious sleep, secure in the knowledge that she has hugely embarrassed Celia (but not in fact half as much as she thinks), and the conductor and soprano walk out arm in arm to the nearest coffee bar. While, just up the road, Jonathan is meeting Peter Hore-Commodore and his sidekick to settle terms for his new post in the warm bosom of GLOW.

<h1 style="text-align:center">XIII</h1>

The heat is intense and Jon decides to change from his T-shirt, which is already getting sweaty, to a looser and smarter short-sleeved shirt. After all, it is important to look reasonably cool for his first encounter with the president of GLOW. He needs a job and this offer seems entertaining if nothing else. But he is a bit early for the lunchtime meeting and lingers in the local newsagent. All the papers sport on their front page a huge photograph of Diana, in a saint-like posture, cradling a very sick-looking Indian child. The princess looks intensely, if pallidly, beautiful, almost like a medieval woodcut of a royal saint. Though he is primarily thinking of his forthcoming "interview", he can't help thinking there is something odd about the picture, something a little over the top; after all, she is primarily a gorgeously elegant society woman rather than a saint: Marilyn Monroe and Jacqueline Kennedy rolled into one for the nineties. Except – unlike Marilyn and in a more existential sense Jackie – Diana's story, though troubled, is *not* to have an unhappy ending. That is one of the reasons Jon and Ben have always liked her: she is a feminist princess for the end of the century, at home with everyone, adored by gay men. She is a survivor. It is also odd that the last photo he had seen of her, just a few weeks before in this mad, hot summer ("scorchio, scorchio" as they said on *The Fast Show*), showed a blur that looked like Diana in a swimsuit on a speedboat kissing a darkly handsome man, her most recent paramour, as reported by the paparazzi, a good-looking young Egyptian millionaire. She was clearly having a lively summer! But, as an admirer, Jonathan briefly worries if maybe in the madness of summer, Diana has somehow, as Ben might put it, "lost it". Was she suffering from a confusion of roles, or was it we, her stalkers, devouring her and imposing too many roles for any individual to bear? Anyway, Jon buys *The Times* and just takes the photo for granted. She may be divorced, even deprived of her title (and how nasty *that* was) but the old girl still sells papers. *And always will*, he thinks.

He moves more swiftly on and arrives at the trendy, gay-ish local brasserie where he is to meet Hore-Commodore and a colleague. He is suddenly seized with a kind of panic. *I've been deputy director of the BNO, one of the most promising stars on the operatic horizon*, he thinks, *and now has it come to this? On the cusp of forty and reduced to grovelling for a job – a* part-time *job, mark you – with an amateur gay-run music group?* And Jonathan sees with a sharp sudden insight – and a sense of déjà vu – that life is not an ever-ascending staircase but rather a spiral with a constantly amazing series of twists and turns, advances and retreats, more a surreal pattern than an architect's design. *Go with the flow, keep a sense of humour and remember all the other wise clichés, and get into that café, the café of life.* So, he does.

Just a few tables back is a tall, conventionally good-looking man of about thirty, slightly greying at the temples, and wearing a very fashionable pale blue shirt which probably cost him about £70 at Red or Dead or some such house of couture, and next to him sits – and seeing this Jonathan does a double-take, feels faint (was it the heat?) and holds onto the nearest table to steady himself – a tallish, well-built muscular young man with dreamy blue eyes, the man with the cheeky Irish-Canadian accent whom he had pursued unsuccessfully to Traffic and now collided with in a different sort of traffic: Jeb. *Why is this man haunting me?* thinks Jon. *Is he my bête noire or my destiny?* And doesn't know whether to be pleased or annoyed. He certainly feels wrong-footed.

Keep your cool and don't show it, Jonathan tells himself, feeling exactly the opposite. Peter HC, temperamentally cool, with his pencil-like figure, stands up, smiles charmingly and extends his hand for a soft, quasi-royal, handshake.

"Terrific to meet at last," he says in an appealing, expressive, lower baritone voice. "I'm *so* looking forward to working with you. Do sit down. Will you have a coffee, Danish, a sandwich?"

"Cappuccino would be lovely. And it's great to meet you, Peter. I think this must be the first time I've been head-hunted," Jonathan replies, trying, but failing, not to look at Jeb sitting opposite him as radiant as ever, and wondering how they will negotiate their meeting. Should they admit they had met before? *Leave it to Jeb to work his way through it.*

"And this is my colleague on the board – he's a great chum of Mummy's actually – Jeb Walters."

"Hi, Jon," murmurs Jeb playing it ice-cool, predictably.

"Hello," says Jon knowing he is looking too long and too deep into those cool mid-blue eyes but still attracted by them, by the soft voice, by the finely shaped head and shoulders. He pulls his attention away, as Peter is speaking to him.

"I forgot to you send you any literature about GLOW," he says handing over a magnificently shiny promotional leaflet, with photos of gaily smiling faces on the cover. "We've grown from a tiny nucleus – I wasn't there at the start actually – seven years ago to our huge present success; we had a half-page article in *The Times* last month. There's even talk of us performing in a millennium extravaganza – we're developing some links with New Labour. So, although we're technically an amateur group we have very high standards and we *need* someone at your level – a very *high* level of artistic quality – to take us up to the next stage."

Peter had a way of stressing certain words unexpectedly which was slightly distracting but he was clearly a strong character, determined to make GLOW a success, at a higher level. *And what is Jeb's role in this? Mysterious and secretive as ever.*

"I don't expect you to commit yourself yet, but will you come along and meet the company?"

"Of course, I'm looking forward to it," he lies. But he knows he needs the job. "And we'll have to discuss salary, of course."

"I don't anticipate *that* will be a problem, will it, Jeb?"

"I don't think so."

"Jeb's a kind of unofficial treasurer, you see, but don't worry, your contract won't be unofficial, far from it. And we think we can go up to £15,000 for what's approximately point five of a full-time appointment. Is that reasonable?"

Jonathan thinks it not so much reasonable as desirable for a musician in *his* position, but he knows he mustn't appear over-eager.

"I'm sure we can negotiate salary precisely once I've met the team. What are your plans for the new season?"

Peter and Jeb glance at each other like schoolboys about to reveal a very naughty secret.

"Go on," says Jeb, as sensuously as always. "Let the cat out of the bag, Pete."

"Well, the thing is, we're planning to do a light comedy piece based on the Mapp and Lucia stories – do you know your E. F. Benson? My great grandmother knew him *awfully* well apparently. And we've invited – oh, go on *you* tell him, dear, I'm too excited."

Jeb laughs quietly, with his thin lips curling seductively up to the left, and murmurs, "We've invited a lady you know rather well – a friend you might say – to sing Lucia. It's—"

"It's the greatest Ellen Orford ever, Jonathan, the finest mezzo of her generation…"

"A very beautiful and special lady," purrs Jeb waxing unexpectedly lyrical.

"Miss Celia Greyfield. Mrs Pip Travers, as she also is, or should I say, *was.*"

Jon isn't sure if he likes the name of his heroine and much-respected friend taken in vain in this way, but he will be delighted to be working with her again as he had, before that brash Aussie dyke had taken his place.

"I believe she's still Mrs Philip Travers," he says puritanically, "And if there's money available, why not commission a new opera from *him*…?"

Peter and Jeb exchange meaningful glances; perhaps the thought had already crossed their minds.

"But anyway, it would be splendid to work with her though I doubt if she'd be available this season." Meaning he doesn't think Celia will condescend to work with an amateur operatic company for quite a few years yet. But then if there really is a lot of money awash…

As if reading his mind Peter cuts in. "Mummy can be awfully generous when it comes to commissions and hiring big names, and she's not our only benefactor, is she, Jeb?"

"Not at all, Pete, not at all."

Are they going to name any other names? There is an eight-month pregnant pause. Peter can't resist.

"There's a certain Labour peer – a very *New* Labour peer in two senses – who's young, and rich—"

"And gay," Jeb throws in.

"And brown, who's also intimated there's money available. So, for future productions the sky's the limit. And this can only help your career, while you will be helping us, of course, immensely."

Peter evidently realises that Jonathan's career needs helping, so the cards aren't entirely in his hand. Settling the deal seems increasingly desirable, but if all that money is available, shouldn't he be aiming to be paid more of it?

"It all sounds very… exciting. When can I come to meet the company?"

"We have a rehearsal booked for next Wednesday, 7 p.m. in the rehearsal room at the Squarehouse in Tufnell Park. Can you make it?"

"I shall make sure I can," says Jon. "Now I must be getting to the Whippo for an early afternoon session."

"Can I give you a lift?" asks Peter.

"No, that's fine. I have some things to do on the way."

Peter gives him a peck on each cheek; Jeb kisses him lightly on the mouth.

"If I need to contact you…" says Jonathan vaguely looking towards Jeb, as if having forgotten that he has already corresponded with Peter.

"Well, here's my mobile number," says Jeb, scribbling it down.

Jonathan's heart misses a very guilty beat; he feels elated.

"Thanks," he says coolly. "See you both on Wednesday evening."

Jonathan leaves first, pretending to be in a rush; he isn't and has no appointment at the Whippo that day or anywhere else, but he needs to get away to think and definitely call Celia, whom he hasn't seen for several weeks, and still regards with some awe. And as he walks down the street towards home, the long series of numbers is burning hot in his pocket. Next to his balls.

When he gets home, contemplating lunch, there is an envelope on the mat. He takes it through to the kitchen, puts the kettle on and opens the letter. It is two tickets to the Reading Festival, which is on the next weekend, marked "Privilege/Complementary" which sounds auspicious. With them is a note:

Jonathan dear,

These tickets came to me from some admirer or other who thought I might be interested. Of course, I'm not, but wondered if a pop festival might appeal to you.

They say the hospitality's pretty good at these things even if the music's crap. Take a friend – or an enemy!

Lots of love,

Jeremy

About as gracious as you would expect from that two-faced creep, he thinks. But he has nothing else arranged and it will be a healthy change from cruising the bars in this renewed single life. And maybe he can use this ticket as bait to catch that elusive and beautiful man? Feeling there is no time to lose, he fishes Jeb's mobile number out of his pocket – thinking, *Now I've got you, my beauty* – and dials it. *Maybe,* he thinks, *we'll have to stay the night in Reading, perhaps in a hotel…*

The door buzzes. *Damn, who can that be?* he thinks irritably. He picks up the phone – the call has gone through but without any answer – and walks to the door. *I hope this is something important.*

A rather fat young man with a light brown beard is standing there, with a couple of cases by him and looking extremely tired.

At that moment he hears an Irish Canadian voice on the phone line. "Hello, who is this?"

Jon disconnects the call.

"Hello, darling, what a lovely surprise. Come in. I'll take the cases."

He drops the phone, helps Ben in with the cases and they kiss and hug for a full three minutes.

"I've missed you a lot," he tells Ben and is surprised that he means it.

XIV

"Two opera queens walking to a rockfest, just 'cause they got free tickets. Clever, right?" says Ben.

They are making their way, mid-afternoon on a Saturday, quite slowly and wearily, after nearly an hour of walking in the late summer heat, in a crowd of people heading through Reading for the festival, not really knowing where or how far they still have to go.

"We've seen signs for it. It can't be far now. Don't look a gift horse in the mouth, babe," says Jonathan, thinking Ben is sounding irritatingly American since his trip.

Half an hour later, they arrive, and see through barbed wire a huge field apparently filled with muddy, grungy heterosexual student types.

"I wanna go home," says Ben disconsolately.

"You've been home for the last three weeks. Now you're back in England. Get used to it."

"I meant *our* home, baby."

"Look there's *our* entrance."

It is the entrance for guests with special passes like theirs. Having been given cardboard wristlets which they are told not to remove for the weekend ("It's like parole," mutters Ben) they find themselves in a spacious enclosure, away from the crowd.

"Do you think they changed the air here?" says Ben in a different tone.

"We're on a different planet, baby. And like all the best things in life, it's free and unsolicited."

They find comfortable seats in the marquee and eat delicious food served from heavily laden side tables with drinks using some of their generous stock of tokens while watching the bands on a huge screen.

"Now this is the life, eh? Stick with me, kid. It's like being in the royal enclosure."

And sure enough at that point rock royalty passes as a diminutive female figure with blond hair enters the enclosure surrounded by bodyguards and admirers.

"Kylie!" The word goes round as the sophisticates pretend not to be impressed, while Jon and Ben crane their necks.

The pop princess – not yet at the height of her fame – is chatting to another couple of celebrities one of whom they recognise as a TV newsreader. (Sitting next to him briefly a bit later, they ask about her: "She's got a great arse, but she'll never make that comeback," he sighs wistfully.)

Being based amongst the *cognoscenti* gives our two boys a sense of importance, of status that licenses them to wander freely outside the enclosure of privilege amongst those less fortunate than themselves, and enjoy that too. They explore more widely during the late afternoon while some band they have never heard of is playing – though its admirers have come from far and wide across the country to hear it. They meander freely around the enormous and muddy site, smell the greasy food – which makes them feel distinctly superior – and mingle amongst the thousands of young and not so young people, for whom these events are almost religious festivals, marking regular milestones of the year like medieval pilgrimages. A middle-aged couple sit on the grass – he with grey hair and bushy beard, she in a kind of woolly bonnet, both in caftans, as she hands him boiled eggs and they dig into a bowl of salad, evidently totally at ease and content in each other's company, a couple, an entity, in every sense. *And*, thinks Jonathan, *is this how Ben and I appear to other people, or will appear when we are in our fifties like these two ageing hippies. Is that how we ever appear now?* And while he knows that a year ago he would have had no hesitation, now the canker of doubt has crept into his mind along with the intriguing image of a tall, well-shaped Irish-Canadian, the not-bear, who keeps appearing and re-appearing in his life like Tchaikovsky's fate motif. Is this the infamous seven-year itch, an itch that has to be scratched and will bleed and tear open the flesh of their hitherto cosy relationship? And how unfair is all this to his unsuspecting partner, who is, he knows (unlike him) essentially monogamous, direct, warmly almost naively American, and so much more trusting than *he* is? Surely he can never hurt this supremely loveable man by telling him he needs something – even worse, someone – else?

And as they wander comfortably around, their arms touching, heading towards the "comedy tent", Ben is thinking of New York and his new step-mother, Dorothea, whom he wants to spend more time with, and the oddly ambiguous audition at the Met, and the almost nauseous excitement of Deep Throats and the fascinating, infuriating rabbinic/Dominican couple, and the voluptuously sexy Irish lawyer (was he getting more attracted to bears like himself and less to sleek "otters" like Jonathan?) and he mentally luxuriates in the idea of how exciting America had been, how much he had missed it, and whether that is where his future lies.

"You OK, babe?" says Jon.

"Sure," says Ben, "Do you wanna look in the comedy tent?"

"Let's."

The comedy tent is not very large – it is after all an *alternative* comedy tent – with maybe a couple of hundred mostly young people standing, watching a plain-looking middle-aged man doing a routine about a plain-looking middle-aged man who writes atrocious songs and sings and plays them badly on a small organ. He is going down surprisingly well, with the audience – or parts of the audience – in gales of laughter. Jon and Ben watch for ten minutes or so, look at each other, shake their heads and walk out.

It is beginning to get dark now, but it is still very hot and lights are beginning to come on, giving the untidy site a more romantic appeal.

"Shall we go back to the enclosure and watch on the screen?" says Ben.

"Well, let's go back and eat something – something tasty. It's such good food we've got to enjoy it. And then come back out and watch some of the bands. There's going to be some good ones on later. Ones you'll have heard of."

"You're sure of that?" says Ben, looking sceptical and a bit pained.

"Definitely. You've heard of Suede. Don't pretend you haven't. Look, if I can like opera *and* rock, so can you."

"I like pop music, some of it. Wham, for instance. Because it's tuneful and it doesn't pretend to be something it isn't. But some of the stuff here…"

"I agree. The Warbling Dizzyheads earlier were a load of utter crap but the top bands on later are different. It's good music. And you only get the atmosphere out here. It's nice in there, but a bit too cosy."

"Well, I like it."

By now they are back at the quasi-royal enclosure where a gang of groupies and glitterati is gathered admiringly round the TV newsreader's table, ignoring the band on screen and the food but taking full advantage of the free drinks. Ben and Jon take a table and are helped to chicken and salads by a kind black lady presiding over the foods.

"Now, shall we get out there for an hour or so and see a few bands? Otherwise, it wasn't really worth coming."

Jonathan has really got into the spirit of the thing and is determined to force Ben to do the same.

"I think it was worth coming just for the catering. Thanks, ma'am," he adds turning to the serving lady who nods back graciously. "But you're right, I guess. It has got a unique atmosphere out there, babes. Otherwise, we might as well just be watching TV at home, a fucking big TV, granted. Let's do it."

So, they go out onto the field and in the twinkling lights and the heat of a late summer's evening watch some talented and very professional rock bands. And Ben begins to get into the spirit of it, an almost sixties spirit of camaraderie and laidback friendliness and easy, slovenly, peace-loving hippiedom. He begins to feel a warmth for these students and their camp followers, some of whom, despite their untidiness, are young, male, hunky and increasingly appealing now that darkness is descending. He looks warmly at Jonathan, who smiles back, almost for the first time since their reunion that morning, and their arms go round each other's shoulders feeling once again the warmth that had originally brought them together and sustained them despite so many distractions, separations and differences. It is a balmy evening, and increasingly romantic, as they watch the performers on stage – or more clearly on two huge screens on either side of the stage – and feel they are gradually, and for the first time since Ben has unexpectedly arrived, returning to each other, re-establishing their relationship.

For, dear reader, no relationship in our world is easy to sustain or re-establish after even a fairly short gap. All the pressures, all the influences, are to split. To go your separate ways and give up on what is one of the hardest things to achieve: togetherness with another human being. And you must have noticed, dear persistent reader, you who have already come with me so far, that almost every other person (except your closest friends and sometimes even they) are intent on putting every obstacle in your path, to make this hardest of unities impossible. In the three weeks our boys have been apart they have been re-exposed to the temptations of freedom, and in the gay world such temptations are particularly intoxicating. And think how easy it is to drift apart and to dwell on the delights that the single life, the untrammelled, self-expressing, self-fulfilling life can, once again, reveal. Jon and Ben have drifted, have been tempted, have dabbled, and sweet it felt, but will they re-establish the warmth they have known? Listening to Suede singing their song of the cover girl who's – ambiguously – *in fashion*, they find, momentarily at least, the previous fashion of their love, and as they stand in the twinkling lights, arms around each other, oblivious to the strangers encircling them, we can soar above like a receding movie camera, and leave them beneath us sharing warmth and the familiarity of what has been their love.

"Sorry, babe," says Jonathan, waking from their shared reverie, "But I suppose we'd better think about getting back."

Ben looks round from the stage blinking as if wanting to re-direct his gaze right back. "Is it late?"

"About ten thirty. And remember we've got to walk back into town, then get the train, then get buses home. Did you forget how difficult transport is here while you were back home?"

"Shit," says Ben. "I guess you're right, hon. How about a final snack in the royal enclosure?"

The food has gone but there are still drinks to be had. The black lady is clearing up.

"You two boys back tomorrow?"

"I expect so," says Jon.

"So, remember to keep your bracelets on. You probably used to handcuffs in bed." She giggles. "No, no, I only jokin'. Come tomorrow. I save you some special curried chicken."

"Thanks. See you then. Bye."

"She's great, isn't she? Definitely back tomorrow. What day is it tomorrow?" says Ben.

"You're still jet lagged, baby. It's Sunday tomorrow. See how you feel in the morning. I would like to see Suede again. And the Spice Girls."

"The Spice Girls'll be here? Fantastic. They're so cute."

"Sure. But they won't be here. Just kidding."

It is a long, slow journey home on what seems an uneventful, insignificant Saturday night in late summer. But it is a sweet, warm night and they are back together. For the moment, their ambiguities seem resolved, or at least suspended. The walk back is easier, more relaxed and then they get a train fairly quickly which stops at every station.

The final leg of the journey ("Shit, we've just gotta get a car. I'll see what my dad can come up with when I see him. Will your new job pay for it?") is slow. They have to wait forty minutes to get a night bus from Paddington.

"You haven't asked me about the new job, not once."

"I'm sorry, babe. I am jet lagged. And a bit self-obsessed. You know me. But you haven't asked me about New York."

"OK. Ditto. Let's face it. We're a pair of self-obsessed wankers. But hey, what's new? Anyway, the new job sounds kind of interesting. But I've got to meet the whole company on Wednesday before I commit myself. They seem to have plenty of money. But not a lot's coming my way."

"Do you know anyone in it?"

"Uh… no. Not really." Jonathan decides to skirt round this; honesty's not always the best policy. "The two guys I met seemed pretty eccentric."

"They're just English."

"Middle-class *southern* English, true. One of them. The other's kind of Irish."

"Is he the Irish Canadian guy?"

Jon practically jumps out of his skin.

"What?"

"Uh… Didn't you mention a guy you'd met?" Ben can't remember for the life of him where he'd heard about an Irish Canadian but he realises it wasn't from his lover. "Anyways, the audition was interesting."

"Really? What happened? I presume they didn't offer you anything or you wouldn't have come straight back."

"Well…" Ben wants to keep his options open. "They didn't commit themselves. But they might call me back. An' I really need to see my step-mom again."

"Why?"

"Because… I like her a lot. She's kinda special."

"Oh," says Jonathan thinking that might suit him too.

"But I have missed you, honey," says Ben, as if he means it.

They briefly kiss and then the bus comes.

They are finally at home in their little kitchen.

"I'll make a pot of tea," says Jon.

"Now I know I'm home. I'll have one too. Let's hear the news. It's just two o'clock."

He switches on the radio as Jonathan gets out the teabags.

The clipped tense tones of the newsreader are saying, "…that Diana, Princess of Wales, has been injured in a car crash in Paris. Early reports suggest that she was travelling with her companion Dodi Fayed and one other person. News agencies are reporting that Mr Fayed was killed outright and that the princess was badly injured. But this has not been confirmed."

"Jesus," says Ben, "That's incredible."

"I wish you hadn't put the news on so late. That's terrible."

"She may have died already, you know. They could just be saying that to prepare people."

"True," says Jon. "The hospital would have to inform the French government, then Chirac would phone the queen or whatever. There's a protocol about this kind of thing."

They sit and drink their tea. It's strange how calm and clinical people can be before a shock sinks in.

"How sad for her kids. First the divorce and then this."

"She might be OK," says Jonathan. "It might only be a minor thing." Then he remembers that was exactly what his dad had said at first news of the shooting of President Kennedy.

"I don't think so," says Ben, more realistically. "And her lover killed as well. Can't people ever just be allowed to be happy?"

He looks deeply sad, and Jon goes over and hugs him.

"We'd better go to bed, babes," says Jonathan. "And I know you liked her a lot, we both did, but she's not part of our family. She's not a relation. We mustn't get too involved."

But it feels to both of them as if she is, and that somehow they are.

PART III

Autumn – Andante lugubrioso

Harold had flown back from the States on Sunday. He read the news in the headlines – and saw it on TV monitors – at JFK. On Tuesday he is drinking coffee with Celia.

"She was a stupid girl. She didn't know what was good for her. Always flailing around. Something like this was bound to happen."

"Oh, come on, Harold, that's very harsh. She was treated rotten by Charles. He's just like most men; *all* men. What could she do? She had to have a life. I blame the paparazzi. She and Dodi just wanted to escape and it all went wrong."

"Well, the good thing is that at least Charles is free to marry Camilla now, and that dreadful embarrassment is out of the way for the royal family. Still, I do feel sorry for her boys."

"So, you're not totally heartless then."

"It must be awful to grow up without a mummy. And Wills is going to be absolutely dishy, you know."

Adelina and Tallulah are at the breakfast table on the Monday morning.

"I feel fucking awful, darling," says Addy. "Like I've lost someone really close. I don't get it. And I'm a fucking Australian."

"I know, love," says Tallulah, spreading marmalade fitfully on her toast. "It's because she was so beautiful."

"Beautiful and vulnerable. It's an irresistible combination."

"Yea. And she took on the whole establishment, the whole fucking lot of them. She had guts."

"Yea, she was the only one of the whole lot worth anything." She pauses. "Do you think they did her in?"

Tallulah looks at her. "I know *nothing*," she says in the voice of Manuel from *Faulty Towers*.

George has just got back from his holiday when he hears the news. His first thought is that it really doesn't concern him. Why should it? She was not part of any circle he belonged to – not that he belonged to any – and he has his own problems.

But gradually his consciousness is permeated by the gloom of the nation and he is gripped by the drama of the queen's decision not to come back to London from Balmoral. He is depressed by the sense of national bereavement, but excited by the drama of the royal crisis.

Out shopping one morning in that dramatic week, he sees the headline: "Where are you, ma'am? We need you here."

Picking up his groceries in the supermarket, he is intrigued to overhear two women talking.

"It's disgusting. Treating us all like they treated *her*, as if nothing mattered but their holiday. Did you see them coming out of that church up there on Sunday? Cool as cucumbers, as if nothing had happened."

"Didn't even mention her name in the service. They want to write her out of history. They can't do that."

"It's those boys I feel sorry for. Think what they're going through. Mind you, sounds as if the funeral's going to be lovely.

They think Elton John's going to sing. Are you going to go into town to see it?"

"No, I'll watch on the telly."

And George wonders what his colleagues will say about it when they reassemble next week. And how will their students react? But, of course, he isn't going to know, and he feels a coldness around his heart. Has he made a mistake, a terrible mistake, taking early retirement? Has he cut himself off, finally, altogether, from humanity? He buys himself a particularly nice dinner, goes home and switches the TV on to participate fully in the gloom of the nation.

Zac and Armando, still at their apartment in New York's Upper East Side – where they have considerable business and property interests – are in their spacious double shower and Armando is soaping Zac's dark and hairy back.

"She was a gorgeous woman, Zac, and she was royal, like us."

"True, true," Zac replies, enjoying the warmth of the suds and Armando's skilful back massage. "Though she was a little *meshuga*. I thought so ever since that weird TV interview."

"Agreed. But so beautiful. People are always envious of beauty, wealth, success. Have you seen the way people look at *us* sometimes?"

"There's so much envy in the world. But we know true beauty is deeper than that, like true happiness. It's spiritual, *chatchke*."

"Do you think they've found happiness in the next world, she and Dodi?"

"You realise it means 'darling' in Hebrew? I don't know. I doubt if they'd have enough *yichus* for that, enough…"

"I know, spiritual capital."

"Exactly. I suspect they have a long way to travel yet. But I hope they find peace eventually."

And he turns round and, with the warm water still cascading down, puts his tongue sensuously into Armando's mouth as they embrace, celebrating life.

Jonathan, working part-time at the Whippo, bumps into Jeremy there on Thursday.

"Terrible news, isn't it?"

"Sorry?" says Jeremy.

"About Diana."

"Oh, of course. I expect I shall be at the Abbey on Saturday. In some capacity or other."

Jon is a little surprised.

"Oh really? I'm glad the queen's coming back to London."

"Well, she had to come back for the funeral, didn't she? It's all very sad, of course, but let's hope it doesn't affect our takings for the opening weeks of the season."

Jonathan looks at him with evident horror.

"Life has to go on, dear. Get real. Otherwise, you'll always be nobody."

Ben decides to phone his step-mother at home.

"Hi, Dots. It's Ben."

"Who else? I knew you'd call."

"How are you and Dad?"

"We're fine. Things must be kinda strange in England this week."

"Kinda weird. All very sad an' all. What do you think about it?"

"It's such a waste. She was so beautiful and so young. But I don't think she'd really grown up yet. I don't think she'd really found herself. Some people don't, you know, until they're forty-five or fifty or whatever."

Ben suddenly thinks of Jonathan, and himself.

"Maybe they're the most interesting people."

"Maybe we are," says Dorothea and laughs like a young girl.

Francis leans back on his elegant chaise longue.

"I'm sure they'll be a fascinating couple to meet. Once they've re-adjusted, of course."

"Some people never do," says Oscar. "They just go on... *living*. It's so sad."

"What do you think of it all, Mrs Cross?"

"A sad story, Professor, but they were people of immaturity who reached an immature end. The Almighty is still at work on the novel; we must not anticipate the catastrophe."

"I fear that was the catastrophe, dear lady," murmurs Francis. "Why am I always in nineteenth century company?" he says to himself, sighing. "There's such a waiting list to meet Kit Marlowe; not to mention the great Will."

On the Thursday evening – the Thursday of that week that seemed to last a month or a year, and marked an epoch in British history – Ben suggests they go down to Kensington Gardens to judge for themselves all the flowers and wreaths and other tributes that they had seen brought there on TV. Jonathan feels a little odd about it; he wants to show his respects but – and here his Jewish background kicks in – at the same time is wary of participating in something that might seem idolatrous.

But they decide to go and find the experience strangely moving. They are swept out of Kensington tube station in a river of mourners who have come like them to pay their respects and who move, quietly and calmly, across the road and along the pavement in a remarkably dignified, unhysterical way.

There are countless little tributes stuck onto or between the railings: dolls, candles, poems, bouquets, all in honour of the couple who, like Romeo and Juliet, had died after their one brief moment of bliss. There before them is a vast, richly fragranced ocean of flowers. The Gardens are packed with people as if this is some pre-arranged public ritual, some sad festival that happens every year, and most of them are moving quietly around; though Ben and Jon do see a few young women sitting on the ground weeping hysterically, being comforted by others whom they have never met before. It is like a new-fangled congregation, a special kind of cult, and Jonathan wonders whether some new religion or world-view will emerge from it. Nonetheless, they both find it an intense and unsettling experience.

On the Friday evening – the eve of the funeral – the two boys decide they need some kind of release of tension and take themselves off to spend a few hours at a south London sauna. There they watch the queen's broadcast – so hastily arranged on the monarch's enforced return to her capital – relaxing in damp towels in easy anonymity with a group of other gay men they don't (yet) know.

"She looks embarrassed," says one.

"So she should," says a big bear.

"I suppose she's doing her best in a difficult situation," says Jonathan.

"Of her own making," says the bear.

They listen to some more.

"She can't bring herself to say she *loved* Diana. Just respected her."

"That's so British," says Ben.

"Not where I come from it isn't," says the bear, who has a northern accent.

Ben looks a bit peeved. He gets up and says to Jon, "I'm gonna take a walk. See you later."

"OK," says Jonathan and looks at the bear.

When the painful speech is over, there is a palpable release of tension.

"Well, at least she said *something*," says Jon.

"Something mealy-mouthed, I call it," says the bear.

He gets up and walks heavily upstairs to the cubicles.

Five minutes later Jonathan is licking the nipples on the bear's hairy rather pendulous breasts and then going down to take his short, fat cock between his lips.

Life – and therefore sex – has to go on. Or should that be the other way round?

They decide not to go into central London on the day of the funeral.

"We'll see more on TV, babes," says Ben, which is true.

But after watching the whole event on television – the cortege with its gorgeous armorial covering and its gorgeously uniformed guard of honour, the crowded scene inside the Abbey, the strangely regal appearance of Elton John with his partner and George Michael, like a threesome of gay royalty, outranking those more formally titled, the powerful speech by Earl Spencer which momentarily shook the foundations of the Crown, and the moving, camp, rendition by Elton John of his re-written version of the pop song composed in tribute to Marilyn Monroe and sung now for another prematurely departed lady – they suddenly decide to take a bus to a point on the Finchley Road, where they know they will see the coffin pass by en cortege.

There, a group of people – mostly women – are standing, patiently waiting, as there must have been all along the route, with whom they feel somehow linked, emotionally allied, as if in wartime or some other season of national or natural disaster.

One woman says to another who happens to be standing next to her, "She was very needy, you know, and they ignored her needs."

And Ben and Jon applaud with the rest of the little assembled crowd as the polished hearse with the royal arms on the bonnet moves quite slowly past them, with fresh flowers trailing like tears onto the road beside.

The day after the funeral is Sunday. Ben is busy with a singing lesson and Jonathan decides to go into the West End. He feels faintly guilty for having watched the funeral on TV, instead of experiencing it in the flesh and bone, and wants in part to make up for that by visiting the arena where the obsequies had happened and participating in the afterglow – or aftermath.

He is taken aback by the atmosphere of central London. He has ridden the tube into the West End and finds everywhere an eerie calm combined somehow with an undertone of nervous unease, a sense of dislocation and anticipation of change. He walks down Whitehall, and sees that, around Horse Guards Parade, doors and gates are open that previously have always been closed and that he can wander through the arches, usually jealously blocked by mounted bear-skinned guardsmen, and onto the wide-open expanse of Horse Guards Parade, where as a rule only the great and the good have access. There is an eerie calm here after the passionate intensity of the day before. Had these doors been opened by the powers that be with their guard down, or had the people, in their majesty, flung them wide open in a challenge to those in authority, a challenge that could not be dismissed? Jonathan certainly feels that Britain had come nearer to revolution in that week than ever before in his lifetime, and is this merely the detumescent aftermath or the prelude to something greater and more dramatic?

The funeral had clearly been cathartic after that tense and bitter mourning week and Jon feels a kind of cooling in the still hot, late summer air. He continues down Whitehall and comes out in front of Westminster Abbey where, on a traffic island before the ancient church, lies tumbled a profusion of wreaths, hundreds of tributes of every description thrown down indiscriminately, disturbed perhaps after the procession went by. Amongst a pile of hand-written cards and tributes similar to so many he had seen at Kensington Gardens sits an odd-looking wreath tossed on the pavement, dark green, clearly quite expensive, but not he thinks in the best of taste. He goes closer to peer at the attached card. It reads: "From the king and queen of Norway." Next to it is a small bouquet of pink flowers, still wrapped in cellophane, with a card hand-painted by a child. It is clear which came from the heart.

II

George very much hopes he will see his young protégé Daniel once more before the end of term, but it doesn't happen. The student had missed his final English classes. *Perhaps he was unwell again; he looked rather delicate,* thinks George.

And then, a couple of weeks before the end of term – and the longed for end of George's collapsed career in this nightmare – he spots Daniel across what he liked to think of as "the quad" (thinking back nostalgically to his own days at Durham, the only university more Oxbridge than the original), but which everyone else referred to as the playground or square. When George had first come to this building – a good, or rather a bad, fifteen years ago – he had been attracted to this traditional academic feature, but such sentiment had long evaporated. Daniel waves – and George does not exactly wave back – thinking that would be somewhat infra dig – but sort of nods with a grimace that is the nearest he can manage at work to a smile, and makes his way through the clumps of students, expecting them in his airy way, contrary to all previous experience, to part before him like the waves of the Red Sea. But, of course, by the time he has struggled through them across the courtyard his quarry is gone. George realises, with a sigh, he will never see him again, but he will put all it behind him when that longed for consummation comes:

the day of his *release*, when with his very big cheque and his very small pension he will begin once again to find the soul of the young George who had set out on a lecturing career with such high hopes so many years before. For he will be free, and freedom is what, above all, he desires.

As the date of release approaches, his old pal Frank offers to organise a leaving party for him, as he puts it, "If you want the dosh for a leaving present, mate, you're going to have to put up with the bastards' fucking sentimentalising one lunchtime. Otherwise, Georgie boy, you'll get fuck all."

In the end, on his very last Friday, Frank and his old sparring partner Jenny and a couple of other members of the older generation of lecturers ("The old lags the fuckers haven't managed to boot out yet, with their not-so-subtle mixture of brickbats and lollipops," as Frank calls them) assemble together at their local, The Washout, with the intention of having a few drinks. After about half an hour and four pints of larger, Frank becomes sentimental and morose, much to George's amusement and everyone else's embarrassment, and makes a rambling speech telling George – telling the entire pub actually – how much he loves him and will miss him terribly and finally handing over a gift token for fifty pounds with the words, "Don't use it, love, keep it as a souvenir." He then falls into his seat weeping uncontrollably. George is more convinced than ever he has made the right decision.

The following month certainly looks fair to prove him right. August is always college holidays for George and this will be the best yet. He doesn't often go away, but he decides to be truly daring and spends ten days in the best hotel in Bournemouth – there'll be plenty of time for foreign holidays later when he's sorted out his finances and settled into a routine. It is a delightful holiday and he spends many happy hours enjoying the balmy air and exploring the local museums. He doesn't speak to many people, but he does have a daily natter with the hotel housekeeper, a big woman with muscular arms and a cheery personality, whom he finds rather appealing – and provides his ever-vivid imagination with lubricious nightly wank material. So, he is keenly looking forward to his new life of study and rest.

Within a few days of returning home, he begins to realise it isn't going to be quite like that. He rests, unpacks and thoroughly cleans the house. Then he is suddenly aware that it is two weeks from the start of term, and one week before he would normally be expected to show his face in college. Like a retired actor or a recent amputee, he begins to feel the absence in a positively painful way. Already, in the mornings, he begins to feel a tingle, a strange disturbing sense of not quite knowing what he is going to do. Or why he is going to do it. He is counting the days to the end of the holiday, as he always did, with sick anticipation of the term to come. Now there is no term to anticipate or loathe; there is nothing to hate, and that seems odd.

In the week that he knows term is actually starting, things get distinctly worse. Having set his alarm resolutely for 8.30, he wakes up on the first day of term at 7, unsure why he is awake, and then a terrible sense of loss, pain and guilt takes a grip on him, like a physical pain in his chest. He is shivering and sits up in bed wide awake, saying, "You bloody fool, you've made the most dreadful mistake." And immediately the whole thing is reversed like a photograph in negative, and all his longing for freedom is transformed into a longing to be back in bondage. He suddenly misses everything and everyone: Frank, Jenny, Daniel, his other students, the quad, the learning centres, the CEO, even Dr bloody Death. He had, it is absolutely true, hated them with a vengeance, but at least they had given him something to hate, something to respond to, fight against, *feel* about. Why should he bother to get up, or get dressed or do anything? He feels that within him and in front of him is nothing but a void.

Actually, things improve a little when he gets up and begins to make breakfast and potter around, and even more as he anticipates starting work now on his project to write the definitive study of his heroine: the great George Elliot.

The next evening the phone rings and George rushes to answer it.

"Hello, old love," says Frank's dry tones, "How's it going, you lucky old sod?"

Never has George been so pleased, so excited to hear another person's voice.

"Oh, it's… OK, Frank. It's OK. How are *you* doing?"

"You sound a bit off, old man. You can't be bored already. Christ, I wish I was in your position."

"It's great not having to get up early," he lies. "But, well, it's a bit like leaving prison, you know, Frank. We've been institutionalised in that dump and it's not that easy to de-institutionalise. Not after twenty-five years. Don't get me wrong, I've no regrets. Hell no. But… it's not that easy."

"You mustn't let it get to you, old mate. After a while I'm positive you'll get over that. You could even come back and do some part-time work, if you're feeling bored. Shall I ask around the departments for you?"

"Oh no," says George and his old hatred floods back renewed, fortified by his huge, overweening pride. "No, I'm not that desperate. Never coming back there. I swore it and I meant it. And I've got a lot to do: redecorating the house, reading all those books I've been accumulating and writing that book I've always wanted to do. And after all I don't need the money."

"Well, that's good to hear. Mind you, you do realise you can claim the dole, unemployment benefit, whatever the hell they call it nowadays, as of right. I know *I* would. You've paid enough bloody taxes over the years – you might as well get some of it back for the next six months."

"Erm, I'll think about that one, Frank. Maybe I will."

"Course you should, mate. Look, enjoy it. The world's your oyster. Anyway, we should meet up for a drink in two or three weeks' time. When the worst of the rush is over at the fucking dump. I'll have to go, mate. Got a load a marking to do. Shit work that is. You're well out of it. See ya, George. And George?"

"What, Frank?"

"Keep your pecker up, mate."

Marking, thinks George, *I always quite enjoyed marking. It was something useful you could do without having to talk to people and you could do it any time and place you liked.* And sometimes – just occasionally of recent years – there was a really interesting essay to mark, like the one he'd got from Daniel which, he suddenly realises, he had never even marked, let alone given back. No wonder the poor boy had waved at him pretty frantically in the – the playground. *Oh well, that's in the past. Like the rest of my life,* he thinks with intense, almost pleasurable self-pity.

Maybe it would be worth going to the dole office to investigate, he thinks. *I've never done it before and at least it would give me something to do.* And he goes back to his cold supper, thinking enviously of Frank with his pile of marking, his wife nagging from the kitchen and his teenage kids running noisily up and down the stairs and playing their CDs so loud he can't concentrate. *At least he's experiencing life,* he thinks, learning the somewhat painful but fundamental lesson that we often deceive ourselves as to what we want and that getting what we want may be a punishment as much as a gift. And, of course, once we have what we want, what more is there to long for? Above all, dear gentle and sympathetic reader, getting what we've prayed for is always a test; one which, George, in his middle-aged angst, is in dire danger of failing, with potentially catastrophic results.

For George, Diana's death is something to think about, something to distract him from the queer empty round of his days. Oh, there were things he did: one bright autumn day he joined the British Library, and went back there once or twice a week ostensibly to pursue his research into Miss Eliot but essentially just to get out of the house. For his home, which had been for many years his refuge from the horrors of work, has become his prison; the sanctuary has become a trap. His retirement has turned out to be a sentence of house arrest. And if he feels like going out – which he does practically all the time – he questions himself: why is he going out, and can he afford it? Whereas previously, for as long as he can remember, he had purchased a monthly travel pass, now such a regular expense seems an unnecessary extravagance and therefore the cost of every journey has to be weighed up and justified. And each day

has the same rhythm, moving from emptiness in the morning –
and a painful inability to answer the question: why am I getting
up? – through a morning of desperately trying to find things to
do, and gladly forgetting his ennui only in the mundane tasks
of housework and shopping which he begins to love – through
the dullness of an afternoon reading and making more notes on
George Eliot – whom, even as she remains his hero, he begins
to hate – to the quietude of the late winter afternoon when he
can switch on the TV, draw the curtains and lose himself in the
restfulness of evening. The evenings are not too bad; though
he spends hours watching far too much TV and then reading
himself into oblivion when time comes for bed. But what is the
point of it all? He can answer that question even less readily
than he ever had before, and constantly he feels himself to be
just on the edge of despair.

Then the hand washing starts.

George had always been a clean person, perhaps over-
clean by most people's standards, but now cleanliness,
especially of the hands, becomes an obsession. It isn't enough
to wash his hands just when they are dirty; he begins to feel
he has to wash them just when they might get dirty or he has
touched something which might have touched something else
which might be dirty. And where can you be sure such a chain
will end? In the morning he would wash his hands several
times before he could sit down for breakfast, and then on the
way down the stairs to the kitchen he thought he might have
touched the walls – which evidently could not be clean – so he
would have to go back to the bathroom to wash them again.
When at last he got into the kitchen he might find that he
had to open a new carton of milk, which would necessitate

handling and – heaven forefend – *tearing* some cardboard, which could leave a residue of paper or muck on George's hand. So, that would require another wash. Of course, the kitchen contained an ample sink, but the taps were not somehow clean enough for George's liking – nor ever in cleaning them could he get them clean enough – so he would have to go upstairs to the bathroom to use the only sink he could trust. But then that sink itself began to cause problems. Because he was using it so often – and using so much soap each time – it began to clog up with scum and thus fill up after several washes with water, and not the cleanest water.

While trying to come to terms with this, the next step occurs. Looking at things which are, or might be, dirty, becomes a dirty act and requires another ritual wash. Thus as he is leaving the bathroom he would catch sight of the loo out of the corner of his eye and – whoops! – that would require another handwash. So, actually negotiating his way out of the bathroom becomes a very delicate and skilful procedure requiring him to shut his eyes at certain points whilst being very careful when doing so not to touch anything – even the wall or the door – which might in any way be soiled and therefore necessitate another wash. The complexities are endless and, George is well aware, completely ridiculous and redundant. But somehow it has all become an unavoidable maze from which he can't escape and, he muses self-pityingly, at least it gives him something to do.

Not that it is all darkness, neurosis and despair. For one thing, there is TV and certain particular programmes which George will look forward to eagerly like the return of a loved one. One example is *Watchdog*, which George loves for its magnificent moody inquisitor, Anne Robinson, whom he has watched but hardly been aware of previously in her more thoughtful and kindly guise on *Points of View*. But now she emerges as a grand and powerful interrogator, the new dominatrix of his dreams. The red hair, the snarling lip, the sarcastic turn of phrase: all combine to make her the new mistress of his waking – and sometimes sleeping – dreams. *If only*, he thinks, *someone could invent a programme that would fully exploit her full sadistic potential, dress her in flowing black and give her a whip hand over a group of cowering, masochistic contestants; that would be a masterpiece.* And George plays around with various ideas, having as we have seen, always fancied himself in his dreams as a game show presenter, but the right idea always evades him. Still, it gives him something much richer than the rest of his day to look forward to between the less powerful escapism of reading and the sweet longed for oblivion of sleep.

III

For some reason he doesn't understand, Jonathan is very nervous about his first rehearsal with GLOW. It isn't something he is looking forward to. But he needs the money, he needs the experience, he needs the job. What is there to be nervous about? Peter Hore-Commodore is certainly odd, but probably harmless and certainly influential. And as for Jeb… he is certainly attractive and definitely not harmless. But Ben is now back and things between them seem to be on a more even keel than they had been for a long time. Maybe there isn't the excitement in the relationship that Jonathan still craves, but there is a soothing companionship and a reassurance in the mornings when he wakes up to see Ben's broad warm back and in the evenings when he returns home from the Whippo or from teaching to Ben's singing and cooking. But Jeb will be at GLOW and that will make the glow brighter and more dangerous.

The first rehearsal has been postponed twice; once due to Diana's death and then to illness amongst the group, but finally in the third week of September Jonathan goes along to the Squarehouse to meet his new flock.

"Jonathan dear, how super to see you," says Peter Hore-Commodore with a warmth that is almost convincing.

They are all assembling, the mass ranks of GLOW, in a big rehearsal room beneath the massive rotunda of the

Squarehouse. Jon has only been here once before for rehearsals of Jeremy and Pip's ill-fated operatic version of *Streetcar Named Desire*. He had found that very exciting – the rehearsals in this venue, that is – because the Squarehouse, as an ex-Victorian engineering foundry, had a quality of bulky, butch realness and innovation sadly remote from the stodgy theatricality of the dear old Whippo. The show itself had *not* been exciting and was perfect proof of the adage that a clever librettist, a fine composer and solid financial backing (the ideal ingredients of first-class musical theatre) sometimes equal crap. *No, crap's too harsh,* thinks our new MD, nervously making his way down the steps at the side of the rotunda into the submerged rehearsal space. It had had some lovely moments – especially the card game scene which, as Dorothy Tench noted in *The Times*, "was worthy in its subtle thematic inter-weavings of middle-period Verdi" – and had a solidly constructed book (surprisingly well-built as it was Jeremy's first). It simply lacked the punch and the poetry of Williams' play. Harold had even remarked at the first night party held in this very room that it had lacked the flair even of *The Simpsons'* version, but that was a characteristically cruel view. The general reaction was that the writers had had nothing to add and, as the *FT* commented, "quite a lot to subtract" from the original. But that was six years ago; Pip had moved on (and out as far as Celia was concerned), Jeremy had moved inexorably up, and Jon, well, ineluctably down?

He is quite sure that Peter is one queen who, like Jeremy, moves ever onward and upward.

"Peter, we get together at last. I've been looking forward to it. Is everyone here yet?"

"Well, we don't do a roll-call as such, but it looks like a pretty full house. They're all agog to meet our new MD – strictly speaking on trial, of course, but in practice… Oh, my sidekick Jeb sends his apologies, got a bad cold; you remember him?"

What do you mean sidekick? thinks Jonathan, feeling irrationally possessive about the only person he had been hoping to see here. And then realises it is probably for the best as Ben is at home and they are getting on so well again.

"Are you going to introduce me? Because I'd like to start with a warm-up and then – well, I've brought some music I've borrowed from the Whippo, erm, the BNO as we haven't had a chance to liaise yet about the coming season. But, of course, if I am to take over I shall have to give approval to your choices for the new programme." Jonathan thinks it is about time he shows some leadership skills.

Peter looks impressed or pleased or just self-satisfied; it is impossible to know which. Anyway, he smiles. "Splendid. Except to make it less taxing for you, I've asked Flora McDougal our acting assistant MD to take our usual warm-up, and then you just take over. I'll say a few words first."

Jonathan feels control slipping away from him but as he hasn't yet been officially appointed he feels powerless to object. Peter, tall and self-composed, goes up onto the stage at one end of the room.

"OK, boys and girls, let's quieten down."

The enormous racket falls to a hush remarkably fast.

"Welcome back, dears, after our summer break. As most of you know, this evening we're going to meet Jonathan Gordon, a very distinguished conductor often seen on the podium of the Western Hippodrome." *Often* used *to be seen there,* thinks Jon. "Who's considering whether to take up the post of our new MD." *That's a diplomatic way of putting it.* "A daunting prospect for even the most experienced musician I can assure you." Titters all round. "But first I shall hand you over to Flora to get us warmed up after our long spell of cold turkey."

Flora climbs onto the stage. She is a big woman with large breasts, about thirty-ish, and moves, as Jonathan has often noted before about big people, extremely gracefully. She has an open friendly face and is wearing a bright embroidered waistcoat. *If she was a man,* he thinks, *I'd fancy her.*

She gets the whole group doing stretches and breathing exercises and then starts them on a few scales. That gives Jonathan a chance to take a good look round and he begins to feel grateful to Peter for it. There are about sixty people present, two-thirds men, and though there is a pretty full age range there is definitely a preponderance of men under thirty – which gives the whole group a sort of preppy, smart, camp-aggressive ethos which he isn't sure he likes. There are some good-lookers undoubtedly, though mostly too slim, young and blond to be of interest to him. But who is now coming in? A rather handsome man, late twenties, well-built with glasses, which gives him an appealing rather scholarly look. He is carrying a briefcase and, going confidently over to the piano, places it by the piano stool.

By now Flora is leading the group in a hearty rendition of a practice ditty which goes: "We may all have come on different ships, but we're all in the same boat now," and shouting out, "No, we didn't come eating *chips,* we arrived on different *ships,*" when Peter comes over with his arm on the newcomer's shoulder.

"Jonathan, this is our pianist Charles. Charles, this is—"

"Of course, it's the famous Jonathan Gordon. I'm sure you're going to do wonders for this opera group." Charles smiles, radiating charm.

"How kind. It's a pleasure to meet you too," says Jon, meaning it. Evidently Jeb won't be the only attraction here.

"Charles is also our co-assistant MD when he isn't required at the piano", adds Peter.

Jonathan begins to wonder whether there might not be an excess of musical talent – or ambition – in the musical team already.

Flora gives him a significant look and he realises it is his turn. He suddenly feels very queasy.

Then, without knowing how he got there, he is up on stage with sixty curious, lively and sharp-eyed strangers in front of him.

"Good evening, friends. I'm Jonathan and I'm your pilot for this evening's flight. I'm sure you're all a little nervous but as your pilot I can never admit that I'm pretty nervous too. So, fasten your seat belts, while I pass round some music."

There is quiet laughter and smiles appear on most people's faces; there is a palpable easing of tension and Jon feels he has made a reasonable start. He personally takes over the accompanist's copy of the piece to Charles who is now perched coolly at the small battered grand on the edge of the stage.

"I thought we'd start with something quite straightforward, that we can just belt out," he says conspiratorially to the pianist.

"*Les Miz*. Yea, right. Not my favourite show but whatever."

Ignoring this first barb, Jon takes up the baton and leads them gently through their paces. The rest of the rehearsal goes pretty well without being particularly interesting. The after-rehearsal drinks in the upstairs bar, however, are a different matter.

Peter takes him to a corner table and brings him a drink.

"That went brilliantly, Jonathan, at least from my point of view. What did you think?"

"I think this company has tremendous potential. It's an exciting challenge."

"Fab. Mummy will be thrilled; she's longing to meet you. Well. Let's stop beating about the bush. The committee have authorised me to offer you a three-year contract for a minimum of sixteen hours a week at a salary of fifteen grand per annum. Obviously I'll put it in writing but – what's your feeling?"

Three grand more than he'd offered before, thinks our boy. *I can't say no. With my seven or eight a year as a repetiteur at the Whippo that makes a decent salary for the first time in years, especially with a bit of teaching added in. Committee, my arse; you and Mummy run everything around here. But play it cool.*

"Sounds fine. I'd expect a proper contract, of course, which I can run past a lawyer friend [*run past – where do I pick up these phrases?*], but in principle I'm sure we can work together. And who would be my deputy, Peter?"

"I'm thrilled you've said yes. Wonderful. And as for a deputy – that's entirely your choice. See you a bit later."

As he gets up, Jon spots Flora behind, standing at the bar with two other women. He waves and she smiles back. He is about to go over to join her when Charles comes up with a seductive smile.

"Anyone sitting here?"

"*You* are."

A sprig of black hair pushes up over the top of his white T-shirt and under the words "Who are you kidding?" Jonathan sees the curvature of his breast. Not exactly a muscle bear but shapely; he obviously works out.

"Nice rehearsal."

"Thanks."

"I assume you're taking the job."

"It looks like it."

Charles is silent for a moment.

"I must show you the score of my new opera."

"You're a composer?"

"Absolutely. You see Jim over there." He points to a tall, sleek young man with tousled, almost white hair. "He's my librettist. A published poet too. It's based on the Arthurian legends, but with jokes. You might want to give it a try-out with the company."

Jon thinks this is going a bit too fast. Charles' arm is on the table; he feels its warmth touching his.

"Flora's great. Have you had a chance to speak to her yet?"

"No, but I'm looking forward to it. She's got charisma."

"Definitely. But she misses the north. I think she'll go back up to Yorkshire as soon as she gets the chance."

"Really?"

"And she can be too nice. With the guys, I mean. This company needs discipline. You and I could impose that. She's a bit weak in that department."

Jonathan thinks he has seen no sign of it. He is more interested in Charles' too short T-shirt which is riding up to reveal a slightly fatter stomach than he had imagined and a thick line of black hair curving downwards into his blue jeans.

"I'll just go and have a word with Jim." Charles stands up and squeezes Jonathan's right shoulder warmly.

He watches the pianist's tightly jeaned buttocks walking away and thinks, *Can't you think of anything but sex?* Before he can answer himself, Peter stalks past.

"Enjoying yourself?"

"Absolutely. And making some new friends."

Peter smirks. "You know what Mummy says? There are no friends at GLOW; just enemies you haven't met yet."

Flora comes over.

Jon is feeling shell-shocked. "Come and join me. Let me get you a drink."

"No, no, let me. You're the newcomer."

As she is getting the drinks, he hears an Irish voice saying, "So, there's our new MD."

He turns, gasps, then smiles at Jeb hesitantly.

"Glad you're joining us," he says and winks.

Jonathan is so embarrassed that he can hear his heartbeats, loudly. He wants to ask Jeb to sit down but it doesn't feel right.

Flora comes up breezily with the drinks and another woman, slimmer and pretty with crinkly blond hair.

"This is my girlfriend, Sophie. She's one of the best sopranos on the team and a bloody good actress. Which is what she actually does professionally."

"Fantastic. And what about you, Flora? You have to be a professional musician."

"Thanks. I teach music and drama to kids with special needs. I love it. I also love conducting this mob. Though they can be a serious pain in the arse, as you'll soon discover."

I already have, he thinks.

"Which opera company isn't? Amateur or pro."

"You know more about the pros than I do. It must be fantastic conducting Wagner at the BNO."

"It was. But you know this profession. Very… unstable. One minute you're on the podium at the Whippo…"

"Next minute you're conducting a load o' clowns."

"I didn't mean…"

Flora and Sophie are both laughing.

"Of course not. I'm kidding. We're going to have some fun here, mate."

"I think we are," says Jonathan, feeling the third Scotch go pleasantly to his head.

IV

George is submerging more and more into the world of TV – not transvestism, though that too appears occasionally in gaudy guises in his ever-lengthening late-night fantasies – but telly, the phantasmagorical box, the magic lantern that sits as focus in the sitting rooms of the embourgeoised world and seeps inexorably into every pore and orifice of our culturally impoverished lives. At least that was how George had regarded television while he was a lecturer: a stain on our literary culture and a snare from which students needed to be rescued. But now, marooned like a prisoner, released from the trap of work he has grown to hate into the trap of a home he could not escape, the TV becomes a means of release, the box that holds all the secrets of the outside world, his only means of contact with the rest of humanity. And he tends to watch those programmes that he looked down upon before; not only Anne Robinson's stuff but light game shows and comedies, anything that might, and often briefly does, lift him out of his misery. He even decides to go out and investigate the options of purchasing cable or a satellite dish – ugly eyesores as he had always thought them to be, and even though it would stretch his meagre resources – because of his desperate need to be entertained, to be removed from himself and his solitary circumstances.

George has also become very lazy. For that reason, he has hardly sat at his computer recently, and also because he has been a little disturbed, frightened even, by the odd reply he had received from his transatlantic correspondent, Professor Lush-Evans. But a day arrives in mid-autumn when he wakes up feeling inexplicably lighter and more cheerful than he has for ages; there is a weak but pleasant sun in the sky and, after a bigger breakfast than usual, George decides to go out while it is sunny to do his shopping, and then after lunch at home, gets down to some more work on his computer. And tomorrow, why, he might even go back to the British Library, where he had taken out membership some weeks ago, and get down to doing some of that research into Miss Eliot which was supposed to be his whole post-redundancy *raison d'être*.

And, true to his intention, with lunch over, he settles down at his computer screen to search for other sources of information on his chosen subject. He even discovers that the entire resources of the British Library are in fact "on the web", so he can begin excitedly to assemble a list of texts that will be useful for his work there. And it occurs to him that at some point in the near future, scholars – and mere dabblers like himself – will be able to sit at home (or anywhere else they liked) in front of their own computer screen and call up the entire resources of all the libraries of the world before them. Remarkable, wonderful and, at the same time, dreadful, as it will complete the process of atomisation, of de-communalisation of work and enquiry as researchers work away like snails in their solitary shells never meeting for discussion or even seeing each other across the desks of the traditional, non-virtual, library.

And wouldn't that take away the joy of travel, the thrill of encountering the new and making fresh connections?

And immediately, sitting in front of his bright white screen with black letters, George's mind drifts off to that wonderful scene in *Middlemarch* (not his favourite amongst Miss Eliot's novels but the *weightiest* and the one for understandable reasons most highly prized by scholars) where Dorothea, in Rome, that dream city of history, to support her dry-as-dust elderly husband Casaubon in his historical (and in his case often hysterical) research, leafing through some tomes in the lovely and non-virtual Vatican library is suddenly confronted by a young and deeply handsome journalist from home whom, of course unforeseen by any of them, she will, after her husband's death, finally fall passionately in love with and marry. And George also ponders that, in the biographies of his heroine, it is speculated that this scene was inspired by the chance encounter she and her "common law husband" Mr George Henry Lewes had with their friends the Cross family in similar circumstances. At the time John Cross was merely a shy though charming youth and she a middle-aged blue-stocking novelist with her long-term partner. And stranger still, even when she wrote the scene up a few years later, she was still apparently happily married to George Henry and John was still a very young man. Had she somehow been vouchsafed a vision of the future in which as an elderly widow she would, contrary to all sane expectations, be asked to marry him by that very young man now become a successful and even more handsome stockbroker, and thus move from having been a scarlet woman, the long-time mistress of a famously ugly little jack-of-all-trades to being, for the first time in her life, the respectable wife of a professional man, though twenty years her junior? Or was it all simply coincidence? And was it life reflecting art, or art reflecting life?

At that point in the late afternoon George needs some contact with a fellow Eliotian whom he can engage with intellectually, so he plucks up his courage, locates the e-mail he had received from Professor Lush-Evans, clicks on "Reply" and types in:

Professor,

I sent you a query once before and you sent me a most stimulating reply. I was contemplating how sad it is that the use of computers and e-mail etc. has made travel to foreign libraries unnecessary. This reminded me of George Eliot's famous visit to the Vatican libraries in Rome where she and her "husband" Mr Lewes bumped into the youthful John Cross and his family. Doesn't it seem extraordinary that – when she wrote up this scene in Middlemarch *of course substituting Dorothea and Casaubon for herself and husband – she cannot have known that much later she would marry the young Cross, just as – in her almost "fairytale" ending – Dorothea marries the handsome Will Ladislaw?*

Your fellow "Eliotian"

GHD

George clicks on "Send" and feels empowered by this act of postage. Somehow, in an electronic medium he cannot comprehend, that message is flying across the Atlantic Ocean and will appear on the computer of his correspondent – whatever he actually looks like, indeed whoever he really is – almost immediately. He turns away and spends a few minutes delving first into his copy of *Middlemarch*, where he eventually finds the scene, and then looking at one of his favourites amongst the many recent biographies of Eliot which tells the story of her *real* encounter. *Yes, he seems to have got it right, roughly.* He looks out of his window – it is six o'clock and still light and remarkably sunny. Will he work at home again tomorrow or risk a chance encounter in the British Library?

He goes back to the computer screen, and there already is his reply. *Has this man nothing better to do*, he thinks, *than reply to random e-mails from people he doesn't know?* Then he opens the reply and it reads:

> *Chance governs all and often fact follows fiction. To be a wife, to be legitimate, is not an ignoble aim. Nor is it, to be a scholar or author – even if, like Mr Casaubon – one fails. Do not assume that Casaubon is George Henry, or Dorothea Mary Anne, or even that Ladislaw is John Cross. Life and art are separate spheres. But remember the dictum: it's never too late to be what you might have been.*

As with the previous e-mail, this Delphic utterance is unsigned. *What a strange man*, thinks George and begins to speculate on whether his correspondent is actually hiding behind a nom-de-screen. But one thing is certain: he feels emboldened to go out the next day to pursue his studies and take his chances in the great library of life; at least the one that resides, squat and post-modern, next to St. Pancras Station.

The next afternoon, a young man with a dark beard and a yarmulke on his head stands gingerly outside George's house and rings the bell. He feels uncomfortable about coming to his ex-teacher's home on the pretext of recovering his marked essay about *Daniel Deronda*, especially as he has copied down the address from a computer screen when the departmental secretary was briefly out of her office. It wasn't quite the thing for an orthodox boy to do, but Daniel is no ordinary orthodox boy. He genuinely needs to have his essay back to get the necessary credits for his exam – a system with which Mr Darkside evidently has little empathy, and understandably so, now he has left. But also, Daniel has an intuition that *somebody* should go and see Mr Darkside, if just to keep in touch, and that intention eliminates any feeling of guilt he may have had about his method of finding the address. However, after five minutes – no, almost ten – of ringing the bell he has to accept there is no one at home. He has a momentary, horrible vision of his ex-teacher collapsed dead within and slowly disintegrating, but dismisses it as melodramatic. *Next time I'll call first,* he thinks, having acquired the phone number by the same method.

About two hours later, George arrives home. He feels much better physically than he has for ages, as he had done what almost amounted to a day's work. He has copious notes from a new book about the lady and has begun reading her last work, the extraordinary *Impressions of Theophrastus Such* which he finds fascinating. He had also enjoyed taking his lunch and tea in the library's elegant cafés and had relished a rare bout of people-watching. He had even not minded missing one of his favourite late afternoon TV programmes. Of course, he had had no encounter with a young man, handsome or otherwise; that pleasure had been reserved for Dorothea/Marian (though he must remember they were not the same person). But, he smiles to himself, he would continue to live in hope.

Going in, he finds there is a rare message on his answerphone. Excitedly, he plays it: "George, you old bugger, it's Frank here. Where are ya, you lucky old devil? Off on the Cote D'Azur with some young bird you've picked up? Hope you're well. You've got to call me to arrange that drink and get all the dirt on the old place. There's loads of it, I can tell you. Keep smiling, mate. Call me back."

George chuckles; it is nice to be remembered. He may even return the call; one of these days.

V

Mid-September. Celia is at home one afternoon – the same sunny afternoon when George, whom she has never heard of, goes to the British Library – being single and beautiful, and feeling at a loose end. She has the opening of *Maria Stuarda* tomorrow evening, which will be exciting, nerve-wracking in fact. Her first-night nerves have never left her; indeed, they have become rather worse than they used to be. She has done her vocal warm-up this morning and there is no rehearsal. She *could* do some housework, but most of it has been done by her home help and anyway she never liked housework, even when bored. Her "treasure" seems practically the only other person to cross this threshold now. And then feels annoyed at her self-pity. But at times like this she does miss Pip, his humour, his charm, his salty body smell, even his clothes left untidily around the bedroom, and above all his presence working at the computer and the piano, giving her the inestimable and irreplaceable sense of human company. But she knows that is also to delude herself. The company had grated on both of them; as a relationship it was no longer working. While there is still a chance of a future, she wants to be open to it.

And unlike Pip she has never been able to have relationships "on the side"; he was comfortable with that concept on the basis, conveniently, that they were relationships with men, therefore gay and therefore something else, not embraced by the concept of marital fidelity. Had *she* started a relationship with a man, all hell would have broken loose. Pip had even been jealous of her stalker, Stephan, whom he was now apparently dating. More than once Pip had asked why she didn't try a relationship with a woman, though it had never happened – yet. But a single life, while more open, also required constant planning and attention; her single friends were used to that. She, after twenty years of marriage, was not. Perhaps she had made a major mistake. Perhaps she should not have left her cosy, long-standing marriage until she had something better in mind. Perhaps a relationship was like a job and it was much easier to get one if you had one. Perhaps she should ring Harold for some consolation, for after years of offering other people consolation she now needs some herself, and ask him out for dinner. The phone rings.

"Darling."

"Harold. I was just thinking about you."

"You shouldn't have masturbatory fantasies in the afternoon, dear. It'll wear you out. The only opening *you* should be thinking about is your big one tomorrow."

"Yes, darling, and I'm a bit nervous. But in a very good way. Shall I leave your tickets on the door? Who are you bringing?"

"Oh, we'll see," he says vaguely. "Or you can bring them round tonight. I'm planning a delicious chicken casserole. And I've got a cheeky little Montrachet to wash it down. Unless you're planning to wash those dirty fingers in some nice wet pussy?"

"Harold!" Celia always enjoys being genuinely shocked by Harold's imagery even after years of it.

"No? What a waste. Then you need what I need: cock. Actually…" His voice suddenly becomes warm and confidential. "I met a rather nice man in New York, one of my political contacts, a cute chubby Irishman called Tony, so I plan to see him next week."

"He's coming here?"

"No, I'm going there. For a wedding and a bit of business. But I'll tell you more later."

The doorbell rings.

"That could be your pussy, dear. See you here at, say, 7.30?"

"I'll look forward to it. Bye."

Celia is intrigued by the bell; she thinks, *Not Jeb again*, though half-hoping it is. Perhaps he can be her new stalker.

It is Adelina. She looks dishevelled, hot and sweaty having just got off her bicycle. She also looks beautiful.

She smiles, like a cute teenage boy delivering the milk.

"I wanted to see where you live and talk over a couple of things for tomorrow night. I've even brought the score," she says, fishing it out of her pannier.

Is she pursuing me? thinks Celia, as she admires the breezy, perspiring woman before her, standing there like an advert for dykes on (pedal) bikes.

"Don't just stand there. The neighbours'll talk."

"They must lead depressingly boring lives."

"This side is a judge and the other is a Formula One driver."

"Proves my point," says Adelina, almost falling through the doorway. She seems slightly breathless.

"The judge probably knows your girlfriend. Or if not, I could introduce them."

"Maybe," says Adelina who doesn't seem to want to talk about her partner.

"It's too early for alcohol…"

"Except a nice cold beer…"

"Except I haven't got any. So, it's tea or coffee."

"Coffee would be perfect, Celia."

She goes through to the kitchen. It's a big, rather old-fashioned, "living" kitchen and Adelina goes through and watches her as she puts on the percolator.

"Does anyone ever tell you what a beautiful, full-breasted woman you are, Miss Greyfield?"

"People are telling me all the time, till I get tired of it." She half-turns slyly.

"Well, now I'm telling you, woman. And it's true."

She comes up behind Celia and puts her hands very, very gently on her breasts.

Celia turns, the warmth of Adelina's hands melting her resistance, not quite sure what either of them is going to do.

"Your eyes are almost grey. Like your name."

She gazes into them and Celia is hypnotised.

Then they kiss.

Celia will remember this as the longest, tenderest, most intrusive kiss she has ever experienced. It has a woman's intense sensuality. It is like being fucked. No, it is better than being fucked and certainly more personal. This dark, powerful, Australian-Catalan woman is kissing *her* – not, like her husband's kisses (in those early days when they used to kiss), some imaginary male lover. Her lips are softly sensuous and her mouth tastes like a chilled Australian chardonnay.

When their mouths eventually become unstuck, Celia is about to say, "Should we be doing this? You've got a girlfriend, we work together, and I'm supposed to be straight."

But Adelina who is at least three inches taller than Celia – and Celia's not short, having been described as statuesque on stage – takes her firmly round the waist and pulls her gently but incontrovertibly into the elegant Queen Anne-style living room. She starts kissing Celia's eyes, her face, her neck, especially her neck, and as she does so she pulls her down onto the thick beige carpet. Celia wants to say, "Why don't we go upstairs?" But as she slides onto her own carpet – she's often reclined there but never to have sex – she almost loses all sense of herself. Adelina tears open Celia's shirt and deftly removes her bra.

"Glorious nipples, fabulous."

And Celia knows they are, and senses adrenaline and all the other aphrodisiac juices flowing through her as after years of neglect she feels appreciated, admired, worshipped somewhere other than on stage. What exactly Adelina is doing with her lips and teeth to Celia's huge roseate nipples she doesn't know but it feels intoxicating, rejuvenating. Who needs a man, music or anything, except this life-enhancing, overwhelming pleasure?

And the pleasure is spreading downwards now like a river of molten joy or golden light flooding the sky. Adelina, most of her own clothes somehow thrown off revealing smaller but shapely brown breasts with small very dark nipples and a deliciously dimpled belly button, is beginning to work magic with her fingers between Celia's labia, which open and contract like an insect-consuming flower. She is panting now, and in a moment Adelina goes down and is inserting that long, sensuous tongue between another pair of lips. She is licking, sucking, biting – using on a lesbian virgin all the techniques of a Sapphic adept. Drifting out of herself and into ecstasy, Celia comes. She reaches down and pulls the other woman up and they embrace with passionate intensity. Then she goes down again and Celia – astonished by what the human mouth can achieve – is rising, rising to yet another bigger climax.

And the doorbell chimes.

Adelina doesn't miss a beat; she just keeps on working that sweet and juicy vagina. And suddenly, as the door rings again, Celia, liberated, hears her own voice crying out, each time higher, "Fuck off, fuck off," and then, coming, "FUCK OFF!"

Five minutes later they are lying there in a totally comfortable silence, an enclosed and deeply satisfied peace. Celia reaches out to hold Adelina's hand.

"Thank you *so* much. That was… unbelievable."

"Thank *you*."

"You didn't come."

"I came with you. Vicariously. *That* was unbelievable for me."

"Whoever was at the door obviously fucked off."

"Feeling pretty fucked off I should think."

"I hope it was my husband."

"I hope it *wasn't* my girlfriend."

This jars a bit on Celia. But she ignores it.

"Let's keep this as a lovely and unique experience. I don't want to cause problems between you and Tallulah."

"No problem, Celia. She and I have an understanding. Life is meant to be lived and occasionally…" She leans over and starts to caress Celia's breasts, "You just can't help yourself."

"I think we should have that coffee now," Celia says, beginning to get up.

VI

"So, darling, who was your scrumptious visitor when I called you today?"

Harold is just serving his superb Moroccan-style chicken casserole with its wonderful tangy fragrance. As Celia well knows, Harold is an excellent cook, far more adept than she. Which is why visiting him was the better idea. Nonetheless, knowing Harold's huge appetite for *information* – anything he can store in that massive political compendium of a brain – she is not lulled into a false sense of security, though the light and fruity wine is taking her in that direction.

She is cautious.

"Why do you say scrumptious? The truly scrumptious thing is this casserole. And I'm hungry."

"Precisely, my dear. You arrive here late – not like you when dinner's in the offing – as flushed and rosy as Queen Vic after a heavy ride on John Brown and hungry as all hell. Now what, Doctor Watson, am I supposed to deduce?"

Celia is already tucking in.

Between mouthfuls, she says, "Nothing at all, dear. It was that silly Jeb calling again. What the hell is that boy after?"

"Jeb?" says Harold vaguely, also with a full mouth.

"Isn't he part of your spy network or something?"

"Darling, what do you think I do? Run the KGB?"

"I didn't think they were called that anymore. But you certainly love to have information."

"Doesn't everybody?"

"And Jeb is one of your contacts."

"He's some kind of journalist, I believe. But we were talking about you."

"*I* want to hear about New York."

"Have some more wine first. The Montrachet goes well with this, doesn't it?"

"Absolutely. What are you going back for?"

"I told you. Some friends of mine are getting married. I'm going to be an usher."

"Oh, how lovely."

"It's an inter-faith union. There'll be a famous rabbi and a cardinal – well, they're hoping for the cardinal anyway – as celebrants. All very camp."

"Sounds very you."

"It will be. And I'll be getting together with this Irish lawyer Tony, he knows several important US congressmen – so *there's* the political connection – and he's a fucking good fuck. I'm so glad rimming's coming back now…"

Celia stops chewing a slightly thick chunk of yellow pepper.

"Harold, we're eating."

"With a dental damn, of course."

Celia removes the yellow chunk with her fingers, and takes a healthy swig from her wine glass.

"But I don't need to tell an experienced lezza like you about those."

"Sweetie, as you well know, my entire sexual experience would fill a postage stamp, while *you* could write an encyclopaedia."

"Have you never thought of singing at the Met? You like New York, don't you?"

"Like New York? *Love* New York – though it's a few years since I was there." She sighs. "Pip and I went over for the premiere of *Lady Macbeth of Stepney*. My God, we were lionised. That was at Lincoln Centre."

"Ah, New York State Opera. What about working with *them*? A change of location would do you the world of good. I have some good contacts there, you know."

"I think it's a bit late in my career for that, love. But I'm open to offers."

"Except to offers from GLOW it seems?"

"Darling, since you evidently know everything why bother to ask?"

"I don't blame you there. They're pretty insignificant. Save them for your retirement. Ready for pudding?"

"Why not? What is it?"

Harold disappears through into the small kitchen where he works such wonders and Celia follows with the dishes.

"Go back, go back. I'm coming through."

Celia obeys, and re-fills their glasses to finish the bottle. She remembers she shouldn't be drinking so much on the eve of an opening night and decides not to finish hers. But then it has turned out an altogether surprising kind of day. Very satisfying, if a little worrying for the future. Tomorrow her professional relationship with Adelina will have to resume exactly as before.

It is also satisfying in that she has so far avoided Harold's prying questions. Some things she is entitled to keep private.

Harold comes in with a tray and on it two crepes aflame with a heady aroma of cognac. He serves one to Celia with a flourish.

"And, of course, if you did go to New York, you could continue dabbling with Adelina because they've made her an offer to do some work over there next season. But she must have told you that."

"She hasn't told me anything about that," says Celia, feeling a bit peeved at, as Harold would put it, being outside the loop.

"Not even when she was visiting you this afternoon, dear?"

"Harold, what are you talking about?"

"Darling, if you weren't shagging Adelina, why did you tell your poor husband to fuck off, when he could see her bicycle on the front steps?"

VII

Monday morning. Ben and Jon are sitting at breakfast. Jon is reading *The Guardian*.

"Nice review here from James Agate. 'Exquisite vocal control from Miss Greyfield, proving she is still at the top of her form. Her performance as the power-crazed Virgin Queen confirms that her acting skills are equal to her musical brilliance.' She'll like that. It was a fabulous performance. A lot of tension. Fireworks between her and Jane."

"Actually, now I think about it, when I went backstage, there was a good deal of tension between Celia and Adelina. You could cut the atmosphere with a baton."

"Do you think something's going on between those two?"

"Of course not. Adelina's with Tallulah. And Celia's straight."

"You sure about both of those facts?"

He looks up from his third pain au chocolat to see Jonathan looking intensely pensive. It irritates him when his lover gets into these moods. Retrospection will get him nowhere. It was so… *British.*

Ben stares at him quizzically.

"A penny for them."

"I was just thinking that a few years ago…"

"Are you definitely taking on the GLOW job, babes?"

"Yea, I think so. I need it. And it could be interesting. Are you coming to a rehearsal soon? What about Thursday?"

"Oh…" He sounds suddenly vague, remote. "I won't be here Thursday."

"No? Where will you be?"

"I'll be flying back to the States on Wednesday. Just for a couple o' weeks."

Jon is choking on all the questions in his mind.

"Why? And why didn't you tell me before?"

"I just got a letter yesterday. I've been called back to the Met. And I really want to see my step-mom again. You should meet her. And then this morning, I just got this."

He holds up a stiff card, embossed with two regal coats of arms.

"What the fuck is that?"

Ben looks a bit hurt.

"It's a wedding invitation."

"Not another one."

Ben sighs. "It's an invite to 'the celebration of life-partnership of Zac and Armando.' Two guys I met over there."

"Where?"

"Um?"

"*Where* did you meet them over there?"

"Oh… some club."

"You said you didn't go to any clubs."

"Oh, it was nothing. You'd like them. They're cute. And you're invited. Officially this time. Look."

"You think I'm going to drop everything when I'm just starting a new job to go to New York on two days' notice for some weird pseudo wedding ceremony of two men I don't even know who you've obviously had a session with without even telling me. Which is anyhow just a pretext for you to do a second pointless audition with the Met and spend a load more of your family's money?"

Silence.

Jonathan knows that he's said too much but he is very angry and he can't take it back now.

"And you deliberately kept all this secret till the last minute!"

Silence.

They look at each other. Ben tries to speak, and can't.

VII

The constant buzz of the engine; it never recedes on a flight, does it? Always that dull, electronic, mechanical sound; a heavy, monotonous, late twentieth century drone of speed, ambition, adventure and anxiety, while the passengers – or do they call them "customers" now, as if all the excitement of travel has been overtaken by the dreary exigencies of the market? – sit in relative degrees of cramped and unhealthy discomfort, musing on what their destination has to offer them in terms of opportunities for business – or fun.

Ben sits there on this autumnal Thursday morning, feeling physically rather comfortable with his first glass of champagne in hand – thanks to the business class ticket sent him by his step-mother, Dorothea – but emotionally less so. He knows he has mishandled the situation with Jon, but what *was* that situation? Were they still in love, did they still regard each other as life partners, or was their seven-year relationship approaching its natural term? That thought brings up a pang, a queasiness that proves his feelings for Jonathan are not dead. But why then this restlessness, this constant desire to get away, and specifically to get "home" to the US, a home he had left behind seven years ago? He is very aware that this is the first time they have ever parted after a quarrel without a proper reconciliation. True, they had patched something up in the two intervening days but the bitterness his sudden announcement had evoked was evidently still simmering beneath the surface. Ben knows he needs time out of the relationship, time to take stock – *and probably*, he comforts himself, *Jon needs the same* – but whether it will still be there when he gets back only time will show.

There is something about partnership – *their* partnership in particular – that he reveres and needs and loves, but there is also something he yearns for in freedom, individuality and flight. In a long-term relationship you give up your individuality or at any rate pool it with your partner. It is like the whole thorny question of Britain in Europe – a question that, as an American, Ben finds unbelievably repetitive and boring, but nonetheless parallel: in going in, you lost your sovereignty, and the question was, the question that had bothered and bedevilled British politicians for so many years: did you gain something better, by becoming part of something greater? Some people just seemed to fall easily into relationships as the Dutch or the Belgians slipped into European mode – no worries, no soul-searching – and actually that was how it had been for Ben at first. He had never really questioned the way it had happened because it had happened so gently and easily and, of course, it was always contingent on his staying in Britain, with flight to the USA – like today – as an escape clause. On the contrary it was always Jonathan who was the more introspective partner, the one who worried too much and thought too hard, and who had gone off first to Amsterdam and then for a longer time to Bruges to help him make up his mind. And now both their minds seemed unmade. Yet distance is already beginning to lend enchantment and Ben is looking back on their joint trip to the Reading Festival and their few weeks together as a kind of halcyon summer he would be loath never to repeat.

Meanwhile, several rows further back, Harold is looking at the dinner menu and considering his options. *Well,* he thinks, *the chicken's appealing – and so is that rather nice hunk on the aisle seat three rows forward. Bloody hell, it's that operatic wannabe that lives with Jonathan. What a nice opportunity to have my wicked way with the nice cuddly boy. Why should Jonathan have all the luck? In fact, I don't think they even get on anymore, and I could certainly give him some very useful contacts in the Big Apple.*

About twenty minutes later Ben is just getting into the new Armistead Maupin and looking forward to lunch, when he feels a crotch brushing, or rather insinuating itself, past him in the aisle. He looks up to see his least favourite English queen smiling ingratiatingly. He pretends not to recognise him.

"It's Ben, isn't it?"

"I'm sorry?"

"Aren't you Ben, the very talented tenor? You don't remember me. I'm Harold. I'm an intimate friend of Celia Greyfield's."

It's a cunning tack; Ben has always had a huge admiration for Celia. Then he remembers the last time he saw Harold, and the scene from Hieronymus Bosch.

"Of course… how are you?"

"Fine. And what are you doing in New York? Auditioning for the Met?"

How did he guess that? thinks Ben. *He's cunning.*

"That kind of thing," says Ben.

"Well," says Harold, his face coming in uncomfortably close and speaking more intimately, "Should the Met be foolish enough not to recognise your quality I can put you in touch with the MD of the NY State Opera; Frank's a *huge* buddy of mine."

A queue of people are now trying to get past Harold so, much to Ben's relief, he moves off, with a great glittering smile.

I suppose he could be a useful contact, thinks Ben, *and he has a certain charm.*

A couple of hours later, a surprisingly fine lunch has been served with a nice half-bottle of wine, and Ben, before settling down to watch a few classic English comedies on his TV-on-a-stalk, gets up to go to the loo. *Even the toilets are bigger and more comfy in business class*, he thinks, settling himself down on the loo. *How many more hours? Long flights can be lonely without company, but then you can have adventures. I must have a wander round the compartment a bit later. Someone is rattling the door. Am I taking too long?* He pulls up his trousers and washes his hands.

"OK," he says aloud as the rattling continues intermittently. Some people are so impatient.

He opens the door – it will only move a little – and sees Harold staring lasciviously.

Ben starts. *Oh no*, he thinks, *definitely not.*

"If you'll stand back, Harold…"

"I could always join you," says Harold in a quiet, seductive voice.

"If you'll *stand back*… thanks," says Ben, as Harold with evident reluctance, does so.

"I know these aren't the best places for it," says Harold unabashed as Ben squeezes past him, unavoidably feeling Harold's very firm erection.

Ben gives him a perfunctory grin, as Harold throws his Parthian shot.

"See you at Zac and Armando's wedding, my dear. It should be divine."

Shit, shall I never escape him? thinks Ben, walking away, desperate to get back to his seat and a few hours *alone*.

VIII

Thursday, and Jonathan is alone in London. Ben has gone back to New York. They are superficially reconciled but both know that while going to New York once unannounced may be a misfortune, twice is downright carelessness. Something significant has happened; they have parted without a proper coming together for the first time in their seven-year relationship. That is clearly significant; whether it is also irrecoverable remains to be seen.

For Jon, it is time for GLOW, and GLOW means work, GLOW means salary, GLOW means Jeb. And now that there has been a certain clearing of the decks with Ben, our boy feels free to… live a little.

Around 10 p.m. the rehearsal is over and Jonathan is having drinks at the bar in the Squarehouse, feeling pretty pleased with his first official meeting with GLOW. Peter had started the evening by introducing him formally as the new MD to huge acclaim; *they're an enthusiastic lot here*, he thinks, *or at least, they pretend to be.* The committee hadn't met so far to draw up a musical plan for the coming year, but Sondheim was definitely on the agenda for both Peter and Jon so he had taken the group through several of the master's songs, in particular "Not a Day Goes By" and "Attend the Tale of Sweeney Todd". As Jonathan is musing on this, waiting at the bar, Charles comes up, his sculpted chest looking particularly appealing under a granddad-style T-shirt.

"Great rehearsal. What are you having?" asks Charles in his mellifluous but slightly over-cultured baritone.

Jonathan remembers that his first big decision will be between Charles and Flora for assistant MD. Someone is bound to get deeply offended.

"Let me get them in."

They squeeze their way through the crowd, receiving plaudits and pats on the back on all sides, till they find a small table.

"They responded well to *Sweeney,*" says Jon. "I'm thinking of recommending that to the committee for this season. Are you on it?"

"The committee?" Charles laughs; *his teeth look a bit brown and knackered,* thinks Jon, which is somehow attractive. "Only if I'm your deputy."

"Oh right," says Jon, embarrassed. "I thought probably as pianist—"

"No, that's a different thing altogether."

"You sure you'd want both jobs?"

"Sure, no problem in doing both. But if you're not happy with that I've got a mate who's a brill pianist and could take over straight off."

Naturally you would have, thinks Jonathan, thinking how much simpler it is in a professional company.

A couple of guys he had noticed earlier come up with drinks in their hands.

"Hey, Rob, Phil, sit down, join us. Jon, you've got to meet these guys. They're a lot of fun."

Rob and Phil exchange glances.

"We always give Charles a lot of fun anyway," Rob says, a touch superciliously. He is tall, rather well-shaped with a slight lisp.

"Jonathan, this is Rob and Phil, two good mates of mine. Rob's studying voice with me. And Phil kind of joins in, when I'm over there."

Phil is shorter and fatter, much fatter; both look immensely self-satisfied, but Jonathan is realising that is the house look. He notices Flora and Sophie both looking over from a short distance where they are standing with their pints, clearly watching out for signs of favouritism. *Hell, this is going to be difficult.*

"You should seriously think about *Assassins*. There's some great numbers in there," Rob puts in. "You should hear me do the big John Wilkes Booth number some time."

"Yea, you must come over and see us one afternoon, when Charles is with us," says Phil, smirking. "The four of us can make some great music together."

There is a look of complicity between the three of them that makes Jon suddenly feel a little queasy. Has he just been invited to make up a foursome? He has to admit they are almost attractive, if somehow not quite the real thing.

"That sounds terrific. Hi, Flora, how are you?"

She is just coming over.

"A really good session," she says. "Glad to see you've met some of the lads."

"Yea, I want to meet everyone in time. Look, next week," says Jonathan, having a possible inspiration, "Why don't you and Charles divide the first half between you, half an hour each, take whatever you like, and we'll get someone in on piano. Give you both a chance to work with the group before we've got anything set in stone." *And me a chance to see you both in action,* he thinks.

"Great idea," says Flora.

"Fine by me," says Charles.

At that moment an Irish Canadian voice says, "Gettin' down to business, are we?"

Jeb walks up to the table. Jon feels himself blushing.

"Have you two met?" says Charles.

"Sure," says Jeb. "Who doesn't know Jonathan?"

"Enough said," lisps Rob knowingly.

"And who doesn't know *you,* darling?" says Charles to Jeb, *a tad jealously*, thinks Jon, flattered if a bit unnerved by the attention. But then the attention is less for him than for his position in the company.

"Maybe," says Jeb, "We should have a chat about a few details, when it suits you, Jonathan?"

"Sure, why not now?" he replies, happy to be extricated from a potentially embarrassing situation. But at that moment Flora and Sophie approach again and begin talking about the advantages of performing various Sondheim shows. Charles then chimes in with more information on his Arthurian opera, by which time Jeb has annoyingly disappeared.

Nearly an hour of bonhomie later, Jonathan is beginning to realise that most members of the company – or at least of those who stayed behind to socialise – are much heavier drinkers than he is. But through the haze produced by several Scotches he begins to feel a great warmth for this crowd, which is evidently shared by Charles and Flora who are now sitting alongside him having a drinking competition while Rob keeps score and Phil talks ceaselessly at Sophie. Peter ambles up smiling broadly.

"Jonathan, my dear, you are *terrific*. We've made the right choice. And I'm really looking forward to getting down to choosing this season's programme. Week on Tuesday at my place, right? Mummy's got some fabulous ideas and she's absolutely gagging to meet you. I'll call you. Bye!"

Peter turns to Jeb, as usual bobbing about in his wake, to say, "And I'll call you too, darling. Must have an early night. Got that business meeting in the morning. Bye!" He gives Jeb a big kiss on the lips.

Just as Jonathan is wondering what precisely the nature of their relationship is, Jeb comes and sits down opposite him. He looks radiant and, unlike everyone else, composed. His green eyes, looking into Jonathan's, have a certain intensity.

"I think it's about time we got together," he says.

"Uh, yes?" says Jon suddenly breathing more shallowly.

"To talk over a few arrangements."

"Ah, yes."

"Shall we do that here, or shall we go somewhere quieter?"

Jonathan gulps. Why does he feel like a seventeen-year-old on their first date?

"My flat?" he says almost inaudibly.

"Sure."

And that is it. Of course, it means they are seen leaving together, but if Jeb doesn't mind, why should he?

It turns out Jeb has a nifty little Nissan Micra outside so they drive back to Jonathan's flat. There is so much he wants to know about Jeb – what was his relationship with Peter? How did he make a living? What made him, the non-bear, so sexual? – but he feels he will learn more by asking less. He is also a tad uncomfortable about taking Jeb back to the home he shares with his absent lover, but hell, why be bourgeois about this?

Halfway through the so far silent journey, Jeb suddenly says, "I really wanna write an opera based on *Middlemarch*. I've already made a start on the book. I just love that Dorothea woman. Would you like to collaborate on it?"

Jonathan, his thoughts mainly in his groin, is taken totally by surprise.

"Why not? It sounds interesting. I used to compose."

"Peter's in on it as well, of course. His mum can provide a lot o' dosh." He turns slightly. "Fuck, I'm looking forward to sucking your cock."

There is something in the way he says "cock" – something about the Irish vowel – that gives Jon just about the hardest hard-on of his life. He puts his hand on Jeb's left thigh, strokes it, moves into his crotch and gently squeezes.

"Oo," says Jeb.

Jonathan wants to open Jeb's fly right there but thinks it will be just a bit risky.

"Here we are. Just park there."

As he takes the ignition keys out Jeb turns and places his mouth firmly on Jonathan's. The suction is intense and deeply pleasurable.

Jeb looks at him with an amused glance.

"So, d'ya want me to *come* in?"

"You'd better."

As they go through the door Jeb grabs Jonathan and embraces him from behind, his long thin cock moving up and down between his buttocks. Then he turns him round and they kiss; Jon feels as if his tongue will be sucked right out of his mouth. Jeb gently picks him up and carries him over to the couch, where he begins removing Jonathan's clothes. Having got down to briefs he starts to remove his own but Jonathan says, "My turn," and begins to unbutton Jeb's shirt. But he starts to get held up by the buttons.

Jeb laughs and says, "You silly little fucker." He pulls it off over his head, rips off Jon's briefs and takes his whole cock deep into his throat. Jonathan has to hold tight not to come straight away.

Jeb gets up to take off his jeans – he isn't wearing underpants – and then sits astride Jonathan, alternately playing delicately with his nipples and rubbing their two cocks together. Jon appreciates the beauty of his body: long and fairly slim with broad shoulders and superbly shaped pecs. His nipples are lusciously pink and Jon sits up to lick and suck them.

"Hang on there, you fucker," says Jeb.

Jonathan notes his penchant for dirty talk. It is certainly erotic.

And there is an intensity about the way Jeb has sex, which is stronger than anything he has experienced for a long time and reminds him why he has pursued the man so determinedly. He has sex as if nothing else matters in the world; as if he really means it. It is not – like so much sex – just sex; it is *desire*.

He digs a tube of cream out of his bag and begins applying it to Jonathan's chest, nipples and finally cock. They embrace for one more long, lingering tongue-sucking kiss and then Jeb rubs and squeezes their twin cocks with passionate abandon.

Jon looks at him and says, "You're fucking gorgeous."

Jeb starts to reply with, "You too, you fuckin'…" but at that moment they both shoot with a huge, throbbing, deeply satisfying orgasm. Jeb falls on top of him and they cling together for what seems like an age. They doze awhile, their skin sticking to each other with a mixture of cream, cum and sweat.

Eventually, Jeb says, "Do you think that's the sweet smell of excess?"

"I guess so," says Jonathan.

"You're lovely," says Jeb kissing him tenderly, sounding very Irish.

"Thank you." Jon is really grateful for that. "Are you Irish or American?"

"I'd better be going. I've got a busy day tomorrow. You don't mind?"

For a second, Jonathan does, intensely, then he feels relieved, as it will reduce his guilty feelings at bringing this very sexy man back to the matrimonial home.

"No, that's fine. It's been… something else. Truly, something else."

"Something else than what?" Jeb's face comes up close to his. Jon thinks his eyes look incredibly alive, shining.

"Oh, I don't know," he replies, smiling. "Other than the usual crap, that's for sure. You really enjoy sex, that's the point."

"And so do you, as far as I can tell."

Before Jonathan can decide whether to say, "Shall I call you?" or "We must do it again" Jeb is fully clothed and at the door.

"It was a pleasure. See you soon, gorgeous."

They kiss again at the door. Then he is gone.

Jonathan comes back into the room. He is floating. He feels like a big juicy marshmallow, filled with cream. He doesn't know what has happened. And he doesn't care.

When they had moved into this flat, four years before, friends had warned him against it because of the noise of traffic. But Jon has always enjoyed the noise of the city as long as it is not too loud. It provides a gentle hum which reminds him of the aphrodisiac sound of the sea. Lulled to sleep by the urban equivalent of the ocean, he dreams of dolphins and bears and a solid, shapely, unknowable man with green eyes and a soft Irish voice.

IX

Jonathan wakes as the yellow-grey autumnal light streams in through the slats of his Venetian blinds, which in his happy haze of the night before he had forgotten to close. He feels thick-headed and thinks, *What the hell happened last night? What am I doing, a forty-year-old professional musician, conducting this weird band of queens? And why am I alone? I want my big warm boyfriend with me.* Then he squirms because he remembers there's some problem about that. The problem being that he's had – is having? – a fling with the desirable not-bear. Which makes him feel very, very guilty. And absolutely delicious.

Several hours later – and at roughly the same time – in Tony's spacious rented apartment in Greenwich Village, Harold is also stirring. His head feels heavy and confused. He is still jet lagged, very, but, with his usual iron self-discipline, he knows he must get up to be ready for his luncheon meeting at Bloomingdale's.

He staggers to the bathroom, but finds himself in the kitchen. He hasn't quite sorted out his left from his right this morning. Finally, in the bathroom, he looks in the mirror.

"Shit."

His mother's face glares gloomily back at him – lined, middle-aged, Jewish, plain. Harold knows, has always known, that without that twinkle of chutzpah and ambition – currently lacking from his unanimated visage – he is decidedly and irredeemably unattractive. Not ugly – ugly can be interesting, even exciting – but very, very plain. At school and at Cambridge he was always jealous of the pretty boys who could attract interest, attention and sympathy without even trying. But that simply hardened Harold's rock-solid determination to be cleverer and do better than all the pretty boys put together. With his brains and his drill-like ambition he would succeed, he would come out on top whether it was in the field of money, career, social life or the pursuit of men. The pretty could afford to be self-indulgent. Harold's steely self-discipline would always protect him from that trap and feed his endless – and so far highly successful – ambition.

That steely self-discipline propels him forward, through the fog of jet lag and exhaustion, under a long cool shower and through several strong black coffees. He forces himself to eat breakfast and gradually, gradually, feels his accustomed zest for life revive. For, make no mistake, Harold vastly enjoys life; more perhaps, dear reader, than any other of the characters in this novel. For by denying himself the indulgence of introspection and focusing unashamedly on the pursuit of wealth, success and fun, Harold gives himself no room for doubt and enormous room for satisfaction.

Accordingly, as this is potentially a very important meeting, he dresses with extreme care in his best suit – black, classic made-to-measure by Oswald Boateng with a Harrods silk tie – and looking this time in the hall mirror before leaving, gets a much better impression. Yes, this man may not be handsome, but he is clearly important and – and this practically gives Harold an erection – definitely powerful.

Power is the biggest aphrodisiac known to man. Especially to the man known as Harold Rosen.

Lexington Avenue. The penthouse restaurant of an exclusive department store. High camp and high politics. Three men and two women are sitting round the table, the remains of their lunch before them. Harold is holding forth in his best modulated, most business-like but charming, Cambridge-inflected voice.

"So, to sum up so far. We are to set up a new political consultancy forming a London/Dublin/New York/Washington axis…"

"I demur from the term 'axis'; I find it fascistic. Can we say 'link-up'?" says one of the women, an elegant platinum blond in her thirties. "I feel the bank would prefer it."

"Whatever the bank wants, it surely gets," says Harold winsomely. "And this linkage will be known and incorporated as Rosen, Mackinley, Starr…"

"Starr, Rosen, Mackinley…" says the red-haired American man, a rather handsome very self-appreciative muscular bear, who sits wearing a dark brown suit and polo neck facing Harold. He is one of Washington's top political consultants already, but he needs an influential British connection.

"Why not Rosen, Starr, Mackinley?" says Harold. "Unless Tony objects?"

"You know me," says Tony, in his cool brogue. "I never object to anything. Within reason. But shouldn't we be thinking of a more generic name. Something with a ring to it?"

"Like Insignia?" says the other woman, tall slender with long blond hair and a richly seductive voice.

"Well, Solange, what do you think the White House would approve of?"

"Oh, the White House neither approves nor disapproves. I'm just here with a watching brief. But personally..." She pauses significantly, her voice becoming even more richly contralto. "I suggest Billary would feel comfortable with anything that carries a third or middle way connotation."

"Brilliant suggestion, Solange. And most helpful. What about Third Way Consultancy?"

"I feel the bank would consider that a tad too... um, *political.*"

"Well, this is a political consultancy, Deborah, but I take your point. It's a bit... obvious."

"How about MidCon?" says Tony. "It's nice, it's short, it's got warm connotations, and it doesn't mean very much. What could be better than that?"

"I like it," says Harold. "Solange?"

"Fabulous."

"Jon?"

"I can live with that."

"And the goals of this consultancy?" asks the banking woman.

"In the deeds of incorporation," says Tony, "The aims will be expressed as the provision of political and business information and representation for a wide range of commercial and other organisations in the USA and Europe."

"And the real goals?" purrs Solange.

"Quite simply to solidify the Clinton/Blair axis, sorry, link-up," says Harold, "Solve the Irish question – I jest, of course – and ensure the hegemony of Third Way politics – and politicians, of course…" He smiles at Solange, "Well into the twenty-first century. And to make us all millionaires by the end of this one."

"Those of us who aren't already," says Jon Starr, smiling. Harold is beginning to wonder whether bringing him in had been such a good idea. But then his contacts in Washington will be invaluable.

"And, of course, we're planning to bring Zac Bronstein and Armando Soave on board as sleeping partners."

"With what purpose?" asks the bank lady.

At that moment the waitress comes up.

"Can I get anyone dessert?" she says in a loud voice.

"Not right now, thank you," says Harold.

"Are you speaking for everyone at this table?" she says. "Because there are five of you, right? And up to four might actually be requiring dessert *right now.*"

Harold smiles broadly.

"Will you be requiring dessert *right now*, Solange? Deborah? Tony? Jon? Then in that case…"

"I would love to see the dessert trolley, thank you," says Jon.

The waitress glares at Harold triumphantly.

"My pleasure, sir."

She withdraws, temporarily, to fetch the trolley.

"Where were we?" says Harold. "Ah yes. We are bringing them in because they have extremely valuable contacts in the stock market and also amongst the royal houses of Europe. Priceless. And considerable cash to invest."

"You're sure, Harold, it isn't just a mixture of snobbism and sex appeal that's clouding your judgement on this one?" says Jon. "I mean that in the kindest possible way, of course."

"Of course," says Harold, whose Achilles' heel is acute embarrassment at mention of his sexuality in front of ladies (Celia, of course, not counting as a lady for these purposes). He blushes a bright purple.

Tony intervenes. "You're a live wire, Jon. I would trust Harold on this one. But I suggest we hold back on it if you're at all concerned until after the… er… wedding when we can re-examine the question."

"If there are doubts that seems a sensible course," says Solange.

The waitress returns with a hugely heaped dessert tray.

"And here's a much *less* sensible course," says Harold.

"Excuse me?" says Solange, who understood but did not appreciate Harold's sometimes puerile wit.

"Let's all have a scrumptious dessert," says Tony. "I'm guessing you shan't be going to the wedding on Sunday, Jon."

"Of course I'll be going, Tony. I shall be an usher."

Harold flushes with envy. Jon Starr has stolen yet another march on him. But he will have his revenge.

X

What am I doing here? thinks Ben as he enters the magnificent, pillared portals of the Central Park Odeon, just over the other side of the park from the plaza, which the elite of New York society abandoned in favour of its even plusher sister that autumn – and, as we now know, that autumn only. (But that's very New York, of course.) It is a slightly smaller, older hotel founded, it is claimed, in 1763 and re-built to its present gorgeous plan about a century later. It is one of the very few public buildings in New York City built in adoring imitation of French Second Empire style, by a passionate admirer of the Bonapartes, Mrs Josephine Van Duys (who was actually named after – or as our American cousins say "for" – the first Napoleon's first empress by her equally Bonapartist mother, who was one of the Rohan de Valois clan, but enough of them). It was Madam Josephine's four times great grandson, Theodosius Van Duys IV (one of whose intervening ancestors had been a descendant of the Byzantine dynasty) who had, on coming into his substantial inheritance in 1995, resolved to totally refurbish, re-gild and re-dignify the sadly declined and decrepit family-owned hotel, then abased as a huge, seedy bingo hall come strip joint. Theo IV, who had a degree in design from one of the best New York art schools, was no slouch and had studied the original architect's drawings with great attention to detail.

The result was a magnificent confection which immediately drew rapt attention from New York society and within a year had recouped Theo's enormous expenditure.

And here stands Theo on this bright chilly October Sunday afternoon – handsome, darkly bearded, thirty-five, a personal friend of Zac and Armando, of course (who, being anybody in New York society, is *not* a friend of theirs?) – at the head of the lush, magnificent Napoleonic staircase, welcoming the guests as they mount the steps on behalf of the soon-to-be-married couple.

Ben is impressed; not so much by the hotel and staircase – he's seen this kind of thing too many times before and is quite jaded in his tastes – but more by the good-looking Theo himself who is wearing a very debonair white tuxedo and purple bow tie. He has always liked smallish men with a Mediterranean look (wasn't that what first attracted him to Jon?) but Theo is not so much small as compact and, Ben guesses, muscly. He obviously works out and Ben regrets that it's months since his last languid visit to the gym. As he approaches Theo, who has just shaken hands with the previously announced guests, an elderly straight couple who simply drip money and prestige, the footman, in an elegant deep blue livery, hands him a card at which he glances before smiling at Ben and saying, "Mr Ben Schlesinger? Welcome to my hotel."

"Hello," says Ben in his richest tenor.

"I'm Theodosius Van Duys. The partnership ceremony is in the Napoleon III room to your right. Guests are assembling in the King of Rome anteroom. By the way, are you related to…?"

"He's my father."

"Patrick Schlesinger, the hunky slalom champion, is your father?"

Ben feels slightly embarrassed at having anticipated the question.

"No, actually he's a cousin, a pretty distant one. Senator Ben Schlesinger is my dad. Though as he's left the GOP…"

"I'm not concerned with party politics. Just with issues. But I trust we'll meet up later, Ben?"

Becoming aware that he is clearly holding up the long line of guests behind him, Ben moves right into the King of Rome room, hoping to discover later what are the issues so important to his cool and luminously handsome host.

Ben sees that this large anteroom is already packed with an extraordinary mixture of people drawn from several strands of New York society that rarely if ever meet: Chassidim with long, dark locks over their ears and finely cut eighteenth century frock coats; New York matrons, frighteningly overdressed, almost indistinguishable from equally ostentatious drag queens in gorgeous wedding attire and vertiginously high heels; large numbers of highly groomed, bearish gay men in singles, couples and larger groups looking round confidently as if to claim the territory as their own; several quiet, dignified and clearly immensely rich older couples, looking just a little uncomfortable; a clique of power-dykes with big hair and big glasses coolly holding hands and holding court; some well-dressed straight couples with noisy, over-dressed kids, presumably family of the grooms, who are going to grow up with the wonderful knowledge that gay couples can love and marry just like straight ones; Sisters of Perpetual Effulgence with big white wimples and short black habits; several priests in robes of superb if indeterminate origin; and, just entering, a small cadre of men in leather, whips, boots, chains and not much else, one of whom leers at Ben, cracking his whip and winking.

Our friend feels highly amused and a little honoured to be amongst this weird conglomeration of New York's elite. There is a heavy buzz of conversation almost drowning out the very lively and skilful klezmer band in the corner of the room. Just as Ben is wondering if there is anyone here he knows, a well-built auburn-haired man with a fine beard and elegant morning coat approaches him and says, "Come this way please."

Just as Ben is about to admire his guide he remembers where he has seen him before: he is the arrogant bear from Deep Throats who is part of the Zac/Armando clique. *Hardly surprising to find him here*, thinks Ben as he is led through by his coldly smiling companion into the Napoleon III room, which is a large splendid chamber set out as a place of worship of a non-denominational kind. A huge mellifluous organ is being played in one corner; *a mixture of Wagner and Yiddish melodies*, thinks Ben. He is led down the aisle, as other guests are being brought in, and shown to a row surprisingly near the front (*maybe this guy ushering me isn't so bad after all*, he thinks) where he takes the aisle seat.

A few seconds later he hears a familiar sensuously soft voice behind him. "Isn't it the lovely Ben? Did you enjoy our flight?"

Harold, looking it must be said quite superb in his maroon tuxedo, is coming up fast with another familiar face behind him, expecting Ben to move along the row. But deftly Ben moves aside as if politely to allow them both through, with the result that he gets the big Irishman beside him instead.

"We have met, haven't we?" says his neighbour smoothly, "In slightly less salubrious circumstances. Tony."

"I remember. Though I'm not convinced yet that they were less salubrious."

Harold leans over to butt in. "I realise you boys have already had the pleasure. Judging from the guests, I'm sure there'll be a lot more of that to be had later."

Before Ben can summon up a deflating reply, he is startled by the sound of trumpets blaring a grand fanfare from the big double doors behind them. The guests are now assembled and a palpable hush descends. There is certainly an atmosphere of electric anticipation.

Jon Starr's stentorian tones announce, "The congregation will stand."

They do. The trumpets sound again. The trumpeters are dressed as medieval heralds in tabards bearing various royal coats of arms, *to which*, thinks Ben sarcastically, *no doubt the happy couple have extensive claims*. Nonetheless they do look impressive and Ben is undecided as to whether to expect high camp or real style. He doesn't have long to wait as the wedding procession begins its magnificently baroque entrance into the hall.

First come the clergy; a sort of interdenominational colloquy in miniature. Two acolytes precede – pretty youths in pink cassocks carrying three-foot high lit candles – followed by two monks swinging censors and then the bigwigs: a Catholic prelate of considerable distinction in rich dark blue robes with a big white hood thrown back to reveal a fine tonsured head. ("He's the prior of the Order of Saint Francis of Bordello," Harold leans over to whisper, loudly. "Handsome devil, isn't he?") He is closely followed by a large rabbinic figure in full

Chassidic rig and a huge tasselled multi-coloured prayer shawl, like the coat of many colours, topped by a noble head with masses of grey hair and a very long grey beard ("That's the famous Leftover Rebbe; he's risking a *herem* for this, you know, excommunication; love the tallit, don't you?"), and behind him two Buddhist monks, one scattering rose petals and the other chanting hypnotically.

And then there is a gasp from even this crowd who believe they have seen everything, as the groom and groom come into the hall. They are walking under a canopy.

"Jesus," says Harold, then, "Sorry. But I've never seen a couple bringing the *chuppa* in with them before."

"I've never seen anything *like* this before," mutters Tony.

"Not even in your dreams," adds Ben.

The canopy is plush-fringed purple velvet and is held up on poles by four hunky men.

"So, that's why the royals call them supporters," says Harold.

"Shush!" says Ben, irritated.

The front two are a muscle Mary (or beary) of impressive proportions wearing a leather harness, a rubber kilt and calf length boots, and a slimmer, well-built man in full highland dress including a hugely magnificent sporran. ("The hunky muscleman is Zac's ex, and the fucking – sorry – gorgeous Scotsman lived with Armando for three years. Now they're like one big happy family.") The two supporters behind them are a huge Dominican monk in a vast white habit with a black hood over his head and a Chassid with locks and a beard in an elaborately embroidered black silk gabardine. But if the onlookers think these are eye-catching, they haven't yet looked upon mine hosts, the about-to-be-united ones, who walk imperiously and calmly beneath the canopy. Zac looks coolly elegant – quite understated in fact – in a beautifully cut pearl grey morning coat with black trousers, a small but fine silk prayer shawl over it, and – his one touch of extravagance – a heavy ruby-encrusted gold Star of David hanging from a gold chain onto his chest; while his partner, Zac, appears equally handsome in a purple velvet suit with a large silver crucifix hanging on *his* breast. As they proceed in stately fashion up the aisle the organ plays Mendelssohn's "Wedding March", which Ben finds surprisingly appropriate. The eyes of the entire congregation – for so they have become – move slowly with the procession as they glide up to their place at the front, transfixed. It is camp, high, low and every level in between, and combines vulgarity with an extraordinary amalgam of religious traditions and sexual styles. And yet as the prior and the Rebbe begin the weirdly interfaith service, Ben feels a little droplet in each eye.

When the grooms hold hands and take their vows – in Hebrew, Latin and English – Harold says, "Ah." Tony wipes away a tear and Ben is surprised by a sob rising in his throat.

"There's something moving about love," whispers Harold, loudly, and several people nearby turn and smile. And Ben wonders whether this is what he and the partner he has left behind in England should really be doing, right now.

"'I marry thee according to the law that the Almighty has put into our hearts.' Wasn't that lovely?" says Harold holding a glass of pink champagne in one hand and trying to lodge the other firmly on Ben's buttocks. "As distinct from the usual 'according to the laws of Moses…'"

"And of Israel," says Ben. "Yea, I've been to a few Jewish weddings. It was sweet," he adds, jumping smartly away. "I'm gonna watch the dancing."

"Yes, let's," says Harold, following a bit disconsolately; he has developed a real crush on Ben which is evidently not reciprocated.

It's been an hour since the ceremony and the two grooms were being "chaired" – carried around the great banqueting hall (the Empress Josephine room) on gilt thrones – by a whole crowd of their friends, relatives and exes (mostly exes in fact) dancing with abandon, and singing with fervour "Hava Nagila", "Hevenu Shalom Aleichem", and a series of celebratory songs in Hebrew, Yiddish and other languages.

"What language are they singing in now? Any idea?" asks Ben, between mouthfuls of delicious smoked salmon canapés, ambrosia-flavoured Pringles, and the most delicious Bollinger he has ever sipped.

He is speaking to Theo whom he just happens to find himself standing next to, having at last escaped from Harold's advances.

"I'll tell you one thing, dear boy, it certainly ain't Greek!" He speaks with an almost British upper-class accent, presumably due to his three years at Winchester before going to art school. He smiles. His teeth are flawless. Absolutely flawless. So is his smile.

"You're Ben, aren't you? Actually, I think it's Ladino. It has that kind of Hispanic medieval timbre, don't you think? But we'd have to ask Armando to be sure. He's the linguist. Are you an old friend of theirs?"

"Hardly. I met them a few weeks ago at Deep Throats and I guess Zac took a liking to me."

Sometimes, thinks Ben, *shock tactics can work real well.*

"I don't think I've ever been there."

And sometimes they don't.

"But it sounds fun."

"I must take you sometime," says Ben, with deliberate provocation. For a moment their eyes link, cruised, challenged. Ben feels something leap in his solar plexus.

Theo smiles.

"I should circulate. Make sure you stay for the disco."

Zac and Armando are standing together regally beneath the vast central chandelier giving audience to various assorted guests when Harold comes up with Jon Starr.

"It's a wonderful party," says Harold. "A thousand *mazel tovs.*"

"We wanted it to be a real amalgam," says Zac. "A celebration of the soul of New York."

"A chance for the cross and the *mogen dovid* to come together and dance," adds Armando.

"Well… yes," says Harold, feeling a little out of his depth.

"Boys, shall I tell the caterers to bring in more canapés? We're running out over here," says Jon.

"Thank you, Jon, if you wouldn't mind. And can you ask the klezmer band to start up again? Ask them to play 'A Brievele der Maman'. I love those old Yiddish songs."

"I shall if I can pronounce it, Zachary dear."

And Jon goes off on his errands.

"That boy's been fantastic today," says Harold.

"We really love him," adds Armando. "He's like family."

"I understand that," says Harold warmly, confidentially, "Which is why I was so taken aback at our business meeting when he wanted you two excluded from the board of our new consultancy. I had proposed you, thinking he'd be the *last* to object and then he was the only person who did. Unless you'd told him you preferred not to participate?"

Zac and Armando look at each other.

"No, we'd love to be on the board, wouldn't we, dear?"

"Absolutely. After all, Harold, you know Mondy has political ambitions, in the longer term."

Jon Starr returns.

"I hope that's the right tune," he says anxiously, as the band strike up a plaintive Yiddish melody.

The very large Dominican – who, according to Harold, is some kind of monsignor – is standing nearby, stuffing his face with Belgian chocolates and smoking a hugely phallic cigar, while chatting to the Rebbe who is lighting one only slightly smaller. *He's got a very masterful, manly, handsome face,* thinks Ben of the monsignor, *but I hope I never get that fat. He's huge, gross, gargantuan… voluptuous. Voluptuous? He might appeal to Jonathan – he sometimes goes for big, impressive chubbies, but not to me. Far too big. Too much of a warning of where I'm heading if I don't get a grip. No, give me the dark, buff, bearded beauty of a Theo any day or preferably this very night…*

In one corner of the ballroom Ben spots an unexpected board on an easel and goes over to look at it, nodding to a couple of vaguely familiar faces on his way and getting his glass replenished by a liveried footman. On the easel are two printed posters. One is the wedding list, which Ben hadn't even known about, but as it includes items such as "Cadillac convertible" and "cottage in the Hamptons" – surely in jest, but then perhaps not? – he is very pleased to have sent them two annual passes for the New York Yankees; a gift from his dad which, like most gifts from his dad, he has no interest in. The other side of the notice board advertises an array of commercial endorsements: e.g. "All leather accessories supplied by Expectorations Inc. – you'll want to spit if you paid other tanners' prices" and "Smile: you're on candid camera. This celebration is being photographed by *Paint: the stuff that's in front of you*, and its sister title *Skin: the stuff that's all over you*, New York's hippest, happeningest magazines."

Christ! thinks Ben. *These people are into commercial endorsement big time. That's how to make money these days. How come Jonathan and I are so crap at it?*

Midnight. The disco's in full swing and most of the straight people have gone home tired, and stuffed, to sleep before work and the new week starting tomorrow. The gay people – like over-eager kids – are just beginning to let their hair down. At ten, a second huge and magnificent buffet had been served consisting this time of a mixture of Greek and Oriental delicacies, the specialities of the house it appears, which Ben devoured with aplomb. Now he is chatting to Tony, whom, through a haze of Bollinger, he very much likes again. But, out of the corner of his eye, he spots Theo who has changed from his elegant tux into a brilliant white tank top showing off his muscled hairy arms and black leather shorts precisely delineating the contours of his arse, and looks even more desirable. The hippest, hottest DJ in NYC has just put on the Spice Girls' "Who Do You Think You Are?"

"I want that man," thinks Ben, then realises he has actually just said it. "I'm sorry, that's really crass."

"Not at all, he's very cute. Good luck to you," replies Tony.

To hide his embarrassment Ben goes off to the loo.

The men's room is, like everything else in the hotel, large, shiny and smart with gold fittings. As he goes in, he sees the kilted ex of Armando standing at the urinal, his kilt hitched up showing off a large uncircumcised cock with a massive erection. Ben is momentarily transfixed and tempted, but is pre-empted by Harold, who is, of course, standing at a nearby urinal and, with his usual adroitness in such situations, ducks down fast and comes in low to take the huge glorious thing down in one big gulp. *Well,* thinks Ben, relieving himself in a cubicle, *that will keep him occupied for a good long while.*

When he gets back to the dance floor he watches Theo with mounting excitement mingled with jealousy as he dances sensuously with the magnificently muscled leatherman who is Zac's ex. Watching the two of them together is driving poor Ben into tortured ecstasies and he can't resist going up to join in nearby, along with Tony and Zac and other bears, leathermen and assorted beauties. He exchanges glances with Theo who then gives him a little smile and he feels that this is what he has been missing in his years in London, this free-wheeling cruisy sexuality of the old days when he was young and single and living in California.

The DJ has just put on "Vogue", which is already a classic, and at the sound of Madonna's voice all the queens go wild. Ben feels himself dancing with a clear and sensuous rhythm and is confident now that the prize – the dark and beautiful

Theo – is within his grasp. And then suddenly he is dancing opposite a big man, a magnificent Bibendum of a man; it is the Dominican, now out of his habit and also changed into T-shirt and jeans. He looks strong, manly and cool and he gazes deep into Ben's eyes and before he knows it, they are kissing very, very deeply and very excitingly. And Ben puts his arms round this massive man and feels comforted and warmed by his glorious bulk and all the pheromones rising from the men around them add to their mutual pleasure. For a moment their lips part, and their eyes meeting again clearly say, "Yes, we must spend the night together," and they do.

Ben had never had sex with a *really* fat man before. True, Grant, the tattooed lover boy, was big but essentially a well-padded hunk, whereas this man (he had said, "Call me Dom", and little else) was a great zeppelin, a huge manly powerhouse of middle-aged voluptuous flesh; very masculine, with his big blue eyes and receding nearly white hair, yet with a pair of almost female breasts and huge, gorgeously dimpled, darkly pink nipples which, contrary to his expectations, Ben found immensely pleasurable and sensuous. He found that he could lose himself in the great fleshy bulk of the other man and be enveloped by the bigger, older man's warmth. How nice it was for once to be the smaller man, cuddled and surrounded by this warm avuncular priest. And they passed a night of hugely satisfying sensual bliss, such as Ben had not experienced for several years.

XI

Ben wakes next to a mountain of flesh. It looks much less attractive than it had five or six hours ago; not attractive at all, actually. His head is throbbing, pale grey light is just discernible between heavy velvet drapes and the clock next to him reads 10 a.m. Where on earth is he? He remembers Dom, he remembers extremely sensuous sex, he remembers the party and the wedding, he remembers Theo (Oh why hadn't he woken up next to Theo?) but he can't remember where they had come to. He *does* remember it is Monday morning, and that he has an appointment he is looking forward to: lunch with Dorothea his step-mother, at Macy's at 12.30.

How can he get out of this place quickly and quietly, get back to the Village to change and then be on time for lunch? If he creeps softly out of bed… but at that moment the mountain stirs and speaks.

"Good morning, nice young man. Surely you don't have to get up yet?"

Dom has a rather lovely voice; Ben wonders if he was a singer.

"Yea, I must. Got to meet someone for lunch at Macy's and I gotta get to where I'm staying first."

Dom turns his big, rather handsome head.

"But Macy's is practically round the corner, Ben. The presbytery's next door to the cathedral, remember? We're right up town here. Don't go back to your hotel. Stay and have a shower and breakfast here."

Dom leans over. He is massive. Ben feels guiltily excited all over again. It is something to do with the attraction of transgressive desire, that heady sense of pursuing forbidden needs. He reaches out and fondles one of Dom's big, luscious nipples. He suddenly remembers calling Dom "Daddy" in the middle of their encounter during the night and is flooded by a very powerful desire. Soon they are kissing deeply and Ben feels the huge, enveloping weight of the man on top of him, covering and crushing him. It is a revelation.

After they have come, Dom gets up and opens the curtains. It is a large very elegantly furnished room; Ben feels much less like rushing back to the Village, only to turn round and rush back again.

His host re-appears draped in a voluminous, beautifully embroidered kimono.

"Come and have some breakfast, young man. Then you can take your shower and I'll direct you to Macy's".

Dom is preparing them a superb breakfast of fresh fruit juice and pancakes.

"There's maple syrup and honey on the table. Want anything else? Coffee or tea?"

"Coffee please. I'm only worried that I can't change out of that shirt I was wearing last night. It can't be very fresh by now. And it's my step-mom I'm meeting."

Dom smiles.

"I'm sure it'll smell good to me. But of course you want to change. I've got a lot of shirts from when I was your size – a few years ago now. You're welcome to have one. Same with briefs."

"Thank you."

They are a little awkward with each other, as they are basically strangers who put themselves in a position of extreme intimacy, but they get through it pleasantly enough. Ben enjoys his ablutions in the huge and luxurious bathroom and then comes out to choose an haute couture pair of underpants and a smart shirt from Dom's ample collection.

"I'll bring them back."

"You're welcome to keep them. You're also welcome to come back – with or without the clothes."

"Thank you," says Ben getting dressed. "That's a beautiful shirt hanging there, but too small for me."

"Ah yea," says Dom, without looking up from his newspaper. "That one actually belongs to Theo."

"Theo?" says Ben, feeling a bit queasy.

"That's right. He visits occasionally. He's a handsome man."

"You're damn right he is."

Ben is about ready to leave.

"It's been really good and…"

"What?"

"Thanks. I've never slept with anyone bigger than me before and, well, it was terrific. A real revelation."

"I wrote my thesis on a whole book of those. Here's my card. Turn left and then right for Macy's. Give my love to your step-mom."

They kiss, quite tenderly.

Then Ben is out of there.

Dorothea is already sitting at a table when Ben, only a few minutes late, comes into the restaurant. She is a big woman, very handsome for her fifty-six years, with a mass of dark hair loose in a kind of halo round her face. She looks at Ben as he comes in and smiles very warmly. Although he has only known her for a few months he feels very close to her, closer than to his own mother, a much colder woman, whom he rarely sees. In fact, Ben has a recollection that he has met Dorothea a couple of times in his childhood when, as the wife of one of his father's political associates – a much older Republican judge – she had visited their home. He had liked her immensely then and was embarrassed to remember that he had wished *she* was his mom instead of the remote lady who was. Now in a way his childish wish had come true. His father had done something right for once.

"Hi, Ben. How are you?"

"Great." He kisses her on both cheeks and sits down. "You look wonderful."

"You too. Glowing. You must have had a great night."

She smiles mischievously.

"How do you know that?"

"Something about your skin. And that fabulous shirt. Not your usual style. I'm delighted."

His mother would have been censorious; his father would never have noticed. Dorothea was different. He could tell her things.

"I went to a big gay wedding yesterday. At the Odeon Central Park."

"Nice. How was it?"

"Camp as all hell, but kinda touching as well. Handsome couple – very eccentric. Anyways… anyways, it was a great party and I ended up sleeping with a – you're not going to believe this – a Dominican monk. Wasn't he breaking a vow or something?"

"Well, nobody's perfect. But I get the feeling he was pretty damn good."

"And…" Now Ben has started he can't stop, but nothing seemed to faze Dorothea, "He was huge. Much bigger than me. But I enjoyed it."

"Big people can be very empowering, very *real*." Dorothea pauses and sips her water. "I'm presuming this was something on the side for you. I mean, are you happy with Jon? I wish I'd met him."

"I wish he'd met *you*. I'm not sure… if I'm happy, I mean. I used to be. I needed a break but during the service yesterday I kept thinking of him and how nice it would be for us to do that."

"I'd say take your time before you throw away a seven-year relationship. A bit more transcontinental activity might help sharpen up your taste buds. Your dad and I keep a degree of independence, you know. Always have. What would you like for lunch?"

Always have? What did that mean? They'd only been together for a few months.

"I'm hungry. Some nice fish? You choose."

The waitress comes up and Dorothea orders for them both.

"What are you busy with now?" asks Ben. Dorothea always had some interesting project.

"It's a biography of Randall Thompson. You know any of his choral music? Really beautiful. He also had a very interesting life. So, I'm researching that. And what's happening with the Met?"

"I'm not sure. I told Jon I had a second audition but actually I haven't heard from them. I've gotta check."

The food arrives.

"Do you love him?"

For a moment he thinks she means Dom.

"You mean Jonathan?"

"Yea. Who else?"

"I think so. I kinda miss him when we're apart."

"Sounds positive. But if you're really unhappy in a situation then just walk away from it."

"Absolutely."

He thinks, *At last I've got someone to come to for advice.*

"Love's a lot more important than sex, Ben. In a long-term relationship you get accustomed to someone very deeply. It's about companionship. Not desire."

"I guess so. This fish is real good."

"But good sex gives you a really wonderful appetite."

They both laugh.

"I want to meet him when we come over to England in the spring. He sounds interesting."

"He is. And talented. I know he'll like you." He pauses, takes another mouthful, then speaks. "I know *I* do."

She squeezes his hand.

"Like father like son," she replies.

XII

George's paranoia has now reached an advanced stage. His iron standards, steady through a quarter century of teaching, have begun to slip at the moment of retirement and are now sinking fast. *Then* he had risen religiously at seven – often even at weekends. In August that had moved, very sensibly, to eight, then in September – why not? – to nine, and now nine is beginning to give way to ten. Because if waking up is difficult, getting up is excruciating; not physically – though it isn't easy for this suddenly fast-ageing man – but mentally, morally. He feels a deep, dull ache each morning as the recollection duly hits him that there is no reason for him to rise, and no one will notice or care if he does or does not. And this most reclusive of men yearns not so much for company – though even that will be less unwelcome than it has ever been before – but for somebody to care where, who and what he is. At least, his first excursion to dip into the cultural capital of the British Library had been a tonic, a success, and so, to get himself out of the house he decides to repeat it once or twice a week.

Then the panic attacks start.

He had really been looking forward to getting out of his prison – his house – and giving himself the illusion of work by getting into a regular habit of going out to the library. So having got up with a huge effort earlier than usual, he leaves the house quite happily by ten thirty and marches up the road to the local tube station, which is overground. He stands on the platform thinking about the very useful research he is planning to do that day and delighting in the cool autumnal morning air – something he misses very badly, cooped up at home. A train snakes up the line and comes to rest at the platform and several passengers – not many as the rush hour has long gone – stare out inquisitively at him. And suddenly he feels he can't get on the train. He can hear his heart palpitating in his chest and he begins to lose control of his breathing. How can he get on the train? He will have to hurry and that will make breathing even harder. And, as soon as he is on, the doors will close and he will be trapped, and though here the line is overground, within a few minutes it will enter the tunnel and he will be surrounded by darkness and the terrifying possibility of being stuck underground if the train stops between stations. The doors now shut; and there he is, still standing on the platform. Christ! Is he now marooned forever in his local area or will he have to take the much longer bus journey – and can he be sure the bus won't also cause an attack of panic? He steels himself; another train glides in. He breathes deeply a few times, focuses on the *Impressions of Theophrastus Such* which he is planning to read to distract himself on the journey – one of the few works of his heroine he has not yet consumed – and forces himself to get on the train. Then he sits down, and suddenly feels normal, fine.

But coming home on the tube is a lot worse. It is about 5.30. He has established the beginnings of his research – he was looking at the very little known works of his partial namesake George Henry Lewes and fast realising why they were never read – and he decides to go home to watch some well-earned TV and have dinner. Totally oblivious of the rush hour he descends into King's Cross Station to find the platforms and the trains completely chock-a-block. If getting on the train in the morning had been a bit frightening, this situation is completely terrifying. Again the palpitations start, and the uneasy breathing and queasy nausea. He is swamped by anonymous humanity on the platform and the thought of mounting a totally jam-packed carriage to be squashed and buffeted and breathless is far too frightening to handle. But he so much wants to be home, needs the comfort and safety of his own house and things. For a moment his panic is total; his head becomes very hot and he is sure he is going to faint. Then somebody – a young man, dark, wearing a skullcap – looks at him concerned, and reminds him of that former student, the Jewish one who had been interested, genuinely interested, in George Eliot. He feels a little stronger, smiles politely back, pulls himself to his full height and walks out of the station. He decides to go back to the library, use the little coffee bar – which is still open – and read the newspapers. Common sense – reasserting itself – tells him that in an hour or two's time it will be a lot easier to make his way home. But oh, how he longs to be home right now.

Eventually, at about eight o'clock, he gets home, having missed his usual, comforting early evening programmes, and feeling utterly stressed and frazzled. As he shuts the door heavily, almost desperately behind him, he wonders if he will ever dare leave the house again. After all, now he is online he can even order his groceries over the internet. Then he notices – astonishingly, as it is the first he has received in months – a message left on his answering machine. He presses the button and hears, "Hello, Mr Darkside. I don't know if you remember me, my name's Daniel, Daniel Cohen, I was a student of yours at the college. I hope you don't mind. I got your number from the office there. I just wanted to keep in touch. Maybe I could come round to see you one afternoon? Talk about George Eliot maybe? I hope you're fine. My number is…" It is a long number, presumably a mobile.

What a fucking cheek, thinks George. *Obviously thinks I'm in need of some kind of sympathetic "support". Or maybe he just wants his essay back; I wouldn't know where it is now anyhow. Or perhaps he's some kind of nutter who's got an obsession with me; a kind of stalker of older men.* That idea rather amuses George and he thinks – somewhat surprisingly – *I really must tell Ted about that one. Not that I ever hear from Ted anymore. Or maybe this kid's dangerous and thinks I've got lots of valuables here.* He thinks that the least likely explanation. But he still erases the message quickly, thinking, *I certainly don't need him.*

He goes to bed late, doesn't even have the energy to masturbate and dream fitfully of Anne Robinson, now somewhat aged, marrying a young student called Daniel, with a skullcap and a ridiculously long beard.

After the wedding she keeps saying, "I am Mrs Cross, at last I am Mrs Cross."

To which he replies, "You may be cross, but your name is Mrs Cohen and you will have to wear a wig."

At that, a big, handsome boxer with dark brown skin comes up and demands ten rounds with Anne. Daniel starts explaining why this isn't allowed by Jewish law, but they ignore him and George Henry Lewes appears in a vulgar pink dinner jacket to act as a fairground barker and referee. The fight is very exciting and Anne is just about to land the knockout blow when the bell sounds – and sounded – becoming a ringing which drills into the dream and wakes George up.

"Damn it, I was enjoying that dream," he thinks, says out loud, actually – why not? There is no one there to object – and ignores the phone, which rings on, and then, rather sadly, stops.

He looks at the clock. "Shit, ten thirty. But who cares?"

In fact, it is a good excuse not to have to psyche himself up to go out again and face the horrors of the underground system. Maybe he will take a gentle walk locally and have a look in the neighbourhood bookshop. *How exciting*, he thinks, *I wish I was dead*. And then another voice – he doesn't know where it comes from – tells him he should get back on the internet today and consult the mad American professor in the hope of receiving another of his Delphic utterances. Now that thought *is* exciting.

So, he disconsolately scrapes together some breakfast – thinking, *I must get out shopping later, at least that's something to do* – has a long, slow shower and then gets onto the internet. He types in a message to his only friend, the distant professor:

Good morning, Professor Lush-Evans.

At least, it's morning here in England. I have no idea what time it is in Georgia. Life is a little dull here. I have been investigating the works of George Henry Lewes, and they seem very dull to me. I wonder if our heroine was happy with him? Did she, for instance, discover that he may have been unfaithful? And why was she so eager to marry John Cross, who was so much younger than she? Was she in love with him? Or was it simply that she, not ignobly, yearned for respectability at last? I wish we could ask her these questions. But what are your views?"

It is the longest, most impertinent e-mail he has written and he is nervous about the reply. But he nonetheless sends it; what has he to lose? And then settles down to sort out his notes from the day before. After lunch, he goes back to the computer and – as punctually as ever – Lush-Evans has responded. Very excited, George clicks on the message and up it comes.

Do not hasten to lift the veil. The veil itself is a mirror which reflects more than that which is beneath it. Never despair. Remember that there are books to be written, stories to be enjoyed, people to be known and loved. The adventure of life is not over. Marriage was George Eliot's final and most fulfilling act. Why should she not have happiness and peace at last? It could still be so for others.

George reads this with mounting panic, but also a sense of exhilaration. Who is Lush-Evans and how much does he know about George? The message is positive, life-affirming and he cannot reject it. As usual it does not answer the questions that George had raised but does, profoundly, answer others. And why the references to *The Lifted Veil*, one of the most terrifying stories ever written? Who, in heaven's name, is Lush-Evans? Can he be…? No. George breaks out into a cold sweat.

He rejects the idea at once as preposterous. *But either,* George thinks, *I myself am already going mad — which isn't itself such a mad idea in the circumstances — or somebody very strange and intensely perceptive is at the other end of this electronic, trans-oceanic beam of light.*

XIII

Celia is flushed with success after the critical reception of *Maria Stuarda.* She feels like a star again – a feeling she hasn't experienced for several years – and this, combined with the sheer physical exertion of performing such a demanding role four times a week, causes her to feel very fulfilled, radiant.

Unlike playing a musical instrument, dear reader, singing is a total physical experience, especially for opera singers; many a diva has given up family or childbearing in order to bring everything to her roles, and that isn't simply self-denial. No, singing with your whole body and mind is an intensely sensual form of expression, which dare I say, may substitute quite happily for the sexual life of some of its greatest exponents. Again, the exchange with the audience in a big and passionate performance has an almost sexual charge which may account for the interesting fact which, my friend, you may or may not have had the good fortune to experience or observe, that after appearing on stage a performer is radioactive with sex appeal and for actors and singers, post-performance is indubitably the best time to pick up.

But then as we well know, *cher lecteur ou lectrice,* Celia has had no need to rely on stage performances or critical acclaim, however impressive, for her sexual satisfaction. Adelina's visit the day before the premiere had given her a series of orgasms of mind-blowing proportions well beyond anything her relationship with Pip had produced in many a long year and the reverberations of these, both physical and mental, are still within her well into the second week of performances. But her relationship with the tall and lovely Adelina is still unresolved. Celia has no particular wish to enter into a continuing passionate relationship with her – working together can make things awkward and she certainly doesn't want to wreck what seems an essentially happy relationship between her and Tallulah, nor would she like at her age to take on joint responsibility for a baby, and while the occasional repetition of that delicious theme they had created – with ongoing variations – would be very appealing, Celia is mature enough to finish the thing amicably right away if that is what Adelina prefers. But saying nothing and keeping her distance: this is the worst predicament and Celia is beginning to think that the Australian, though a mature musician, is not mature enough emotionally to handle this situation.

Celia has never relished confrontation herself – why else had she allowed her unresolved marriage to drag on for over twenty years? – and knows that, before she decides how, if at all, to confront Adelina, what she really needs after two weeks of such demanding performances is an afternoon in London's most glamorous spa for women: Splashes. Which is why she is there on a Thursday afternoon in early October, enjoying her day off and wallowing in a delicious hot tub.

Through half-sleeping slitted eyes Celia sees a little group of women nearby. *Everyone here's so terribly middle class,* she thinks guiltily, *but it's such a gorgeous place, with elegant marble slabs and delicate pastel tiling. And it is so nice to get totally away from men for a day.* Did she think of herself now as a lesbian? Not really. *No,* she thinks, *I must be, like most people, more or less bisexual; ironic after all these years of being married to one and not knowing it.* Then she notices that the woman walking up to the Jacuzzi is black; almost the first black woman she has seen here today apart from the receptionist and one of the masseuses. Black and attractive and with a sharp, intelligent gaze – and Tallulah. *Shit,* thinks Celia, *just the person I wanted to meet on my day of relaxation! Is this some kind of retribution? Has she seen me? She has.*

Tallulah, elegantly draped in a big white towel tucked in at her quite ample cleavage, comes over to the whirlpool and lowers herself in. She smiles icily.

"It's Mrs Greyfield, isn't it?"

"Celia. And you're Tallulah."

"Thanks for the reminder."

Celia chuckles politely. *Shouldn't this woman be at work on a weekday like most normal people?*

"How's the bar?"

"Oh, they don't serve alcohol here," she says settling down opposite Celia.

"No, I meant the law."

"That's *very* good. I had a case in the high court that was expected to last several days but the defendant's witnesses collapsed. So, here I am."

"Really?" says Celia, feeling totally indifferent. She doesn't know what to say. Or want to say anything.

"Do you… specialise?"

"I'm starting to. Human rights and international commercial stuff."

"Sounds terribly complex."

Tallulah smiles or rather grimaces again.

"It is."

Celia closes her eyes and hopes she will go away.

"She's a beautiful woman, isn't she?"

Oh Christ, thinks Celia, *she must have guessed. I hope she doesn't try to drown me.* She opens her eyes and smiles sweetly.

"I'm guessing you mean Adelina. Yes, she's lovely… And so are you, of course."

Actually, thinks Celia, *she is. Sensuously attractive with glistering green eyes, a rich dark chocolate skin and wonderful ringleted hair.*

"Was it the first time?"

This is confusing, and irritating.

"Now you've lost me."

"I don't think so," says Tallulah.

Celia feels a hand gripping her knee, quite tightly. *Shit, she* is *going to drown me. Is it worth screaming?*

"But I can see why she fancies you." The grip has relaxed into a caress. "You have a very expressive face. And voice, of course." The caress, combining with the ripple of the Jacuzzi, is sensuous, relaxing, tender.

Celia is dumbstruck. *Go with it,* she thinks. *Why kick a gift horse in the teeth?*

"Thank you…" She clears her throat. "Have you been here before?"

The hand is gently gliding along her thigh. Then a foot is simultaneously stroking her other foot and moving ever so gently up her leg.

"Only once or twice," Tallulah replies, her voice a few tones deeper than before. "You OK?"

A couple of women walk past laughing and talking.

"I'm… fine," says Celia, adjusting her expression, and allowing her legs to gently open as a finger begins assiduously teasing her clitoris.

It is a moment frozen in time, as she feels herself drifting into a kind of sexual trance. She had never expected this in a spa, except between men. But why should they have all the fun? One of Tallulah's hands is delicately playing with her left nipple while the other continues, languorously, to tease her now very emboldened clit. How she would like to lean over and kiss this incredibly sensual woman, but the very fact that the surroundings make that impossible increase her excitement. She is just thinking that she will certainly have to tell Harold about this when, far sooner than she would have expected, a delicious orgasm begins to creep up from the base of her spine. She can barely control her breathing and has to put on as polite a smile as she can manage as the black masseuse walks past, giving her a slightly odd look. But it is extremely satisfying. Tallulah is obviously as sexually talented as her lover. Or maybe all lesbians are as sensuously expert. She lies back as the hand gently kneads her thigh.

"I'm really pleased you're having a good day, Celia," says Tallulah, withdrawing her hand. Her voice hardens. "But you realise it has to stop."

She is out of there in a moment, leaving Celia feeling distinctly *had*.

As she gets out of her cab Celia notices someone hanging around across the street. This makes her feel uneasy until, deciding to sort this out before opening her door, she realises it is the attractive but annoyingly elusive Jeb.

He comes across the road looking preoccupied.

"Are you coming in, or is this a stalking visit?"

He laughs nervously.

"Neither, Mrs Greyfield. Really sorry to bother you again. What you must think of me!"

"To quote the late Dick Emery, 'You are awful, but I like you.' What do you want *this* time?"

They are standing in front of her porch in the late afternoon twilight.

"It's just that I'm trying to get in touch with Harold, Harold Rosen. It's quite important. And we don't know where he is. His mobile doesn't seem to be working."

"Doesn't it? And what's that got to do with me?"

"It's just that we know you're a great friend of his and we wondered if you'd heard from him…"

"Who's we?"

"Oh, just friends of mine."

Celia – the consummate actress – makes a dramatic pause. She's had enough of people fucking her around today.

"OK, wise guy. Either you come in, sit down and explain what the hell's going on, or you get no information out of me, now or ever. Got it?"

Jeb smiles in spite of himself. He is quite impressed.

"Fair enough, ma'am. Give us a nice drop of the hard stuff and I'll spill all the beans."

She unlocks the door and leads him in, realising she would do well to taste just a few of those juicy beans.

Jeb is settled on Celia's couch holding a glass of single malt with one of those haunting highland names in his hand and looking a bit more relaxed. Celia sits opposite drinking hers and scrutinising him for clues.

"I have a message for Harold from someone very senior in the government…"

"The PM?"

"Not exactly."

"What does that mean?"

"Different job." His accent becomes thicker. "Same initials."

Celia thinks she understands.

"And…?"

"He's disappeared."

"That's very melodramatic. Have you tried his mobile?"

"I told you. He's not answering."

Celia sighs. "So, you think he's been abducted by the KGB or whatever they're called now?"

"Why? Does he have links with them?"

Celia feels angry.

"No, of course not. I was *joking*."

"This is too serious to joke about, Celia. We need to find him. We know he was in New York a few days ago. Has he contacted you since?"

"No. I'm assuming he'll be back in a few days' time. We're supposed to be going to see *Don Giovanni* at the Garden next week. One of my friends is playing the Don, Jaime Garcia. Harold and I both fancy him rotten."

"If you hear from him, please do call me or better get him to call me. Here's my number."

He gives her his card.

"Now you can do something for me."

"What?" He looks a little apprehensive.

Celia feels very seductive and strong enough to cope with a rejection. She decides to test out her theory about young Jeb.

"Hot in here, isn't it?" she says, removing her blouse.

Jeb is transfixed. Is it fear, or even revulsion?

She calmly unhooks the bra. She knows her breasts are looking very pert and shapely after her day at the spa, not to mention her orgasm in the pool.

"I just wondered if you found women attractive, especially an older woman?"

She can read in his eyes; it is not revulsion but fascination. She gets up, her eyes fixed on his crotch.

The doorbell rings. She can easily ignore it. Again.

But Jeb gets up. "I should be off, you know. Though you are a temptress, Mrs Greyfield."

She suddenly feels like Mrs Robinson in *The Graduate* and the part doesn't feel right; not in real life.

She puts her brassiere back on.

"I suppose I'd better answer the door. And don't worry about Harold. He can look after himself."

They go to the door, with Celia still fastening her blouse. Adelina is standing there, looking tall and boyish and flushed, holding her bike. Her face flushes a deeper, very dramatic red.

"Oh. I see," she says, in a clipped Aussie voice.

"No, you don't," says Celia. Then under her breath adds, "Not that I care."

Adelina rides off, furiously.

Celia looks at Jeb, curiously.

"You *are* a naughty girl," he says.

"I know how to enjoy myself."

"Good for you, girl. We'll keep in touch. And thanks."

Celia goes back indoors, thinking if Harold didn't re-appear soon she would be off to New York to find him.

XIV

The next morning Celia wakes and wonders if she really had tried to seduce that annoying young man the previous evening. Despite having a strong gay component there was something indefinable about him, some quality that took him outside the usual dreary categories, which is why, she tells herself, she had tried it on. And, on production of her recently overworked breasts, he certainly looked interested – or merely transfixed? As she gets up to fix breakfast, she wonders if she was simply making a complete ass of herself or if she had, as the younger members of the Whippo company would say, completely "lost it". At fifty she seems to be re-living her lost youth – when she had been fairly promiscuous though not excessively so by the standards of the sixties. Her most sixties memory was meeting John Lennon at a party in Kensington which she had been taken to by her singing teacher – whom she was occasionally sleeping with – but the great man had chosen to sleep with the Chinese girl she was talking to, rather than her. But she had never – unlike most of her friends – been to an orgy or had lesbian affairs, so perhaps she was simply making up for lost time. Clearly separation from Pip had been a sort of liberation, and she really must speak to him about plans for their divorce – or not. But what point was there in remaining married to a man who had become little more than a casual friend – even if she still missed his presence. That was simply a question of getting used to living alone which, she now knows, has advantages.

Her more pressing worry is Harold who seems to have gone off the rails since going over to "New Labour". She preferred him as the old Tory whom she had always enjoyed arguing with. But then if she was changing her preferences – or at least loosening them up – wasn't he entitled to do the same? What had happened to him in New York and why was young Jeb – and how she still lusts after him, proving that lesbianism has not taken her over with Adelina's caress – so concerned about him? She decides to test out whether Jeremy may have any information about that when she goes in to the Whippo that morning to talk to him about her upcoming role as Lady Domina in a hitherto unproduced opera of that title by Janáček. She has already spent some time looking at the score, so she is looking forward to receiving enlightenment from Jeremy, who – whatever his faults, and he has many – is a superb musician whose score-reading and interpreting abilities are far greater than hers. In recent years she and he, having been intimate friends, have grown apart; probably because, in Celia's eyes, he had taken Pip's side in the separation. Yet she is fond of Jeremy, and this production – due on stage in less than two months, premiering just before the Christmas break – will be their first collaboration in three years. She is looking forward to it, and to picking Jeremy's intricate brains on Pip's intentions and state of mind and even, possibly, Harold's whereabouts as the two men seem to have some sort of political entanglements in common.

"Jeremy, sweetie. How are you, my love? Longest time no see."

Jeremy, sitting at his imposing desk and turning to see his old friend Celia, thinks she looks older and yet healthier and more confident than when he had last seen her. He rises to embrace her.

"Darling, you look radiant and so young. I don't need to ask how *you* are."

Celia smiles broadly at Jeremy. Since Francis' death, over seven years ago, he has become harder, colder and less emotionally dependent on her. But she knows what a neurotic mess he is beneath his brilliant and brittle exterior and she isn't going to let him forget that she knows. And really, he looks more and more like a middle-aged Jewish businessman, not that Jeremy ever acknowledges his heritage.

"You wanted to talk to me about *Lady D*," she says settling down on the sofa.

"I think, darling, we had better call it *Domino* or *Domo* or people will think we're referring unreverentially to the late blessed Princess of Wales and they'll have us for *lèse majesté*."

"*Domo* at the Whippo; I like that."

"And you'll like carrying a big golden whip while your slave boys – also painted gold, just leaving a little space for their arseholes to breathe – will dance and sing and perform disgusting indignities at your command. Won't you, love?"

"Possibly, dear," Celia replies feeling slightly queasy, "But what is this opera actually *about*?"

"Have a drop of aqua vitae than I'll give you my interpretation, for what it's worth."

He brings out a bottle of very old single malt from his Louis Quinze side cabinet (the one that used to be in Francis' country cottage) and pours the drinks.

"Francis would have loved this show," he says.

"Yes, right up his alley, isn't it? Who actually discovered it?"

"*I* did of course, darling, who else? Well, I didn't actually find it, I *identified* and *verified* it when Adelina dragged it in here one day last autumn. She'd picked it up for a song – or an aria! – at some jalopy boot sale in Ruthenia, I think, when she did her tour of Mitteleuropa last year. She brought in a whole heap of junk, then threw this up and said, 'Looks interesting,' in that quaint colonial accent of hers. Believe me, dear, give her ten years and she'll be indistinguishable from Dame Edna."

"Bitchy as ever, darling. But go on."

Jeremy puts a hand to his mouth.

"But of course, I forgot."

"What?"

"Darling, don't try to deny it. We all know. How thrilling. A lesbian triangle in our very own house."

"Nonsense," says Celia, realising she is sounding a bit too vehement. "Tell me about the bloody opera."

"Now you *do* sound like Francis. Anyhoo, I know you're not a great fan of Janáček."

"Hate the long-winded old bugger."

"It didn't sound like it when you sang *Makropoulos* for us in '94."

"Playing that 337-year-old bitch practically killed me. The show seemed to drag on that long."

"This one's much shorter – two hours max. He didn't finish it, you see. He was working on it 1927/28, just before he died. So, I've just sort of finished it off for him – with a few ideas from Jonathan, funnily enough."

"So, Jonathan finished it off."

Jeremy blinks significantly. "Our collaboration – with Leoš and each other – has completed a minor classic. Don't worry, your young friend will get equal billing for it. And your role, darling, as the great Lady Domina herself… well, it's magnificent. Your near namesake will be green with envy."

"Who?"

"Cecilia B, of course."

Celia laughs. It is a nice thought.

"And who – or what – is Domina?"

"She's a Roman empress, of course, dear, in the late Byzantine very decadent period and she's officially Christian but dabbling in the old religions and she decides to get rid of her husband, Elasticos…"

"You're joking!"

"No, I'm not, you have to take this seriously, Celia, old Leoš certainly does."

"That's his bloody trouble, no sense of humour."

"Jaime Garcia will be singing Elasticos…"

"Dishy."

"Exactly, darling, and we're bringing in a brilliant young director called Peter Hore-Commodore; you'll love him."

She is trying to think where she knows the name from.

"Is he connected with that GLOW company?"

"He virtually runs it, dear."

"And you recommended Jonathan to him?"

"Something like that."

Celia sighs. "Do your manipulations never end?"

Jeremy gasps. "If you're referring to my acts of generosity, yes, they can end *very* easily." He gives Celia a stern look, then softens. "Except for you, my angel."

"Perhaps I know just that bit too much about you, dear."

He shoots her a genuinely hurt look.

"Only kidding. Let's look at these arias. I can't make out what happens at the end."

"We shoot into the twenty-first century, the third world war is in progress and Domina has become president of the US. Then she makes love to the king of the opposing superpower and peace is restored. It's a lovely ending."

"Sounds like pure bollocks to me, love. But I'm only the soprano. What's happened to Harold by the way?"

Jeremy, moving over to the Bechstein upright he keeps in his office and opening the score, is caught off guard.

"He's... I've no idea. Harold who?"

"Oh, come on, love. You know. Harold Rosen. Your fellow New Labourite. He went to the States on some mission and now he's got lost."

"Lost? Nobody gets lost nowadays. Doesn't he visit opera houses over there? He's very knowledgeable."

Celia makes a calculation. It is the only way to deal with Jeremy, who is much more calculating even than Harold.

"You tell me about Harold... and I'll tell you what's happened with Adelina. Fair exchange?"

He smiles at her. "And you say *I'm* naughty. OK, I'll go first as I know I can trust you. Harold and I are great believers in New Labour, and especially in Tony. It's a new synthesis, you see, a third way. And old-fashioned socialism's finished, darling, it really is. So, he's gone to the States to set up a new Anglo-American political consultancy, which I *might* put some money into. And that's it. Now spill the beans about our Aussie girl."

"So, why should he have disappeared?"

"Who told you he has?

"Jeb. I'm sure you know him."

"He's awfully cute, isn't he? You didn't... did you?"

"We didn't. And I don't even want to know if you did. But there's more to it. Jeb said something about the CIA..." She is improvising now, but it works.

"Not the CIA." He looks rather worried. "At least I don't think so. I believe his Irish friend Tony has a contact in naval intelligence; quite high up. And they all probably have to get security clearance or something. That must be what it's about."

He begins to play some dark, haunting chords on the Bechstein. It has a rich, resonant timbre.

"These are the opening chords of the overture. And they contain three motifs which recur throughout the opera. First, this little fellow." He plays a four-note tune which she recognises as the top notes of the chords. "They represent Domina at her most powerful and successful, then this melody which represents fate and sometimes death." He plays a quirky chromatic motif which has been hidden somewhere in the chords. "And finally this very sweet tune which actually derives from the bass part and symbolises love and romance – I'll play you the expanded version which you'll be singing in your biggest aria and your duet with Deng Hsiao Clint – he's the Asian king." It is a lyrical, self-developing melody which she is desperate to sing right away.

"My God," she says, "It's beautiful."

"I'll play you the big duet – which is half Jana and half Jonathan and me – while you give me the low-down on Ms Majorca."

"I'm sure you know it all. She just popped round one afternoon – oh, that phrase is beautiful. Is that me?"

"It's you," Jeremy half-shouts over the piano. "I know you're not warmed up, but try it."

Celia's clear limpid tones float out of her throat and onto the air of the office. The secretaries and crew in the rooms around stop work for a moment. Adelina, working with a couple of singers in her office along the corridor, hears it. Celia can still sing, arrestingly, even unwarmed-up, mid-afternoon.

"You see," says Jeremy, "It absolutely suits you. You were telling me…"

"And, I don't know how." She is almost shouting now. "It just happened, and it was lovely, fabulous in fact – who sings that?"

"Deng. Gorgeous, isn't it? Do you hear that first motif underneath there? And were you converted?"

"Only temporarily. There's a lot of great things women can do physically, but emotionally I'm not a lesbian and I'm going to have to tell her… I hope I have that phrase there. Who's singing Deng?"

"Antonio's dropped out for health reasons so we're recasting. And what exactly do you need to tell me? Before you tell the entire opera house?"

It is Adelina. She is standing at the door of the office, which they had left ajar. Her arms are crossed. Celia, her heart in her mouth, thinks she looks quite beautiful, and absolutely incandescent. *Thank heavens,* she's thinking, *I didn't mention the Tallulah episode – whatever* that *was about.*

XV

That evening Jonathan leads an excellent rehearsal at GLOW. It seems to him that the more complicated and incomprehensible his life becomes, the better he can concentrate – in fact the better he *needs* to concentrate – on his music. The music is good, as always totally absorbing, fulfilling; the life is a mess, utterly confusing. There are too many questions to sort out, to which reasoning would give no answer. And he had always thought that, as forty approached, he would by then have found maturity, serenity, success. Instead, there are just more questions, more confusion, more self-doubt and lack of direction. And it is so unfair: Celia is secure, confident and independent now that she is separated from Pip; Jeb, younger than himself, knows exactly what he is doing, even if no one else does; Adelina is secure in her long-term relationship with her very successful girlfriend; Jeremy, as ever, goes from one huge triumph to the next stepping over the bodies of his vanquished rivals; and even Ben seems happier away from him, back in his homeland, whence he may, Jonathan now suspects, never return. It reminds him of one of the many poems he had written as a young man anticipating with remarkable prescience the thoughts of oncoming middle age:

And you will have learnt to understand

The fickleness of your own heart

And of those of your lovers;

Thus you will anticipate

Much the worst that can befall you

And attain to a wistful content

At the heart of universal chaos.

What is it he feels for Jeb? The beginnings of love or just a healthy and wafer-thin lust? And what is it he feels for Ben: a cooling comradeship or an enduring passion? For some reason the two questions have become entangled; his feelings – or obsession – with Jeb obscuring the true nature of his feelings for his own lover. And if, as Jeanette Winterson has suggested, desire is a text "written on the body", just what is written on the big, voluptuous, quasi-pregnant body of his "husbear" Ben, or on the leaner, more muscular, smoother body of the not-bear, Jeb? On Ben's ample flesh – which Jonathan knows so well, too well perhaps – is written the text of their comradely relationship, in words of brotherly love. But it is not really a brotherly love unless incestuous, for it is firmly rooted in his since-childhood passion for the fleshly body, the manly body fleshed out and rounded, powerfully fattened with food – was it chance that his first great passion was for a chef? – the object of that other appetite which Jonathan experiences more fully in vicarious than in personal mode. Ben is emblematic of all those loves, those chefs, those fat boys, those men of broad shoulders and big bellies whom he has always passionately desired. Yes, dear reader, let him admit it: Jonathan is a chaser. Whereas Jeb is a new and surprisingly intense obsession, beautifully plastic, nearly hairless yet substantially built, whose enigmatic and almost casual intensity produces an equal and opposite intensity in him.

Jon has always sought the road to freedom, not the road to wealth or success; if he *had* – and he is beginning to think it may have been a better idea – he wouldn't be approaching forty with two part-time jobs and no assets. It was freedom, it was fun – and it was frightening.

Jeb had not been at the rehearsal. Jonathan has to confess to himself his disappointment but he has refused to hang around through the usual boozy haze in the hope he may appear. Peter comes up with his usual smiling, unctuously effortless confidence, to tell him that he will be joining Jon on the staff of the Whippo as director of the new Janáček opera, the one he had been offered no part in. Jon, almost rudely, takes his leave and goes home feeling very sorry for himself.

As he gets through the door, the phone rings; it is bound to be Ben, whose call from the States is several days overdue. It would be reassuring to speak to him. At least he is reliable, lovable, in his slightly dull, unadventurous way. It may be diverting to hear about the crazy gay "wedding" he must have been to by now.

But it is a lighter Irish Canadian voice on the line. Jonathan's heart jumps.

"Hi, Jonny boy, how are ya? I turned up for a drink here just to see you and you'd left."

Jonathan doesn't believe him. But he aches, hearing that voice.

"Hello, Jeb. I thought you'd left the country. You OK?" He can't think of anything worth saying other than "I want to have you again, now" and that would be too much like begging.

"Sure, sure. I was hoping to see you. We had a great night."

"We did."

"We should do it again. Unfortunately, Peter wants to talk through some stuff with me tonight, so I can't come over. That's assuming you wanted me to."

"Later in the week maybe?" says Jonathan, peeved and extremely suspicious about the "talk" with Peter.

"Sure. Great idea. Heard from your other half this week? How's he doin' in New York?"

As they hadn't discussed Ben at all, this comes as something of a surprise.

"He's doing fine. We spoke earlier today. He phones every couple of days."

"Has he seen Harold over there? Harold Rosen?"

What the fuck is this about? Is this why Jeb called?

"Harold who?"

"The PR guy. Camp, Jewish. Everybody knows him."

"Except me."

"OK. No worries. I just have a message for him from a friend. Jon?"

"What?" says Jonathan, now highly irritated.

"I'm longing to suck that gorgeous, beautiful cock again, you sexy bugger."

Jeb puts the phone down.

Jonathan goes to his bed and masturbates to an orgasm even more intensely satisfying than the one he and Jeb had shared.

XVI

After Dorothea's funeral, which was held on the second Thursday in November – it had had to be delayed by a week because Ben's father had to attend some important votes in the Senate – Ben feels totally empty, devoid of emotion. He can't allow himself to feel his emotions, which seem too deep to access. He feels betrayed and cheated. He had just started to get to know this wonderful woman, who already meant much more to him than his own mother, when she was snatched away. Why did things happen like that? And why did his father seem so cool about it all, so cold in fact? His old girlfriend Annalise Crump had come to the funeral – she was in Washington anyway, having just been appointed president of the prestigious Alexander Burr College – and already – *already* – just three weeks after his bereavement, they are obviously thinking of marriage. Ben feels like Hamlet at his father's funeral, as he stuffs the funeral-baked meats into his mouth. He knows he is over-eating, but that seems his only consolation. Apart from his short phone conversations with Jonathan, but even he, though sympathetic, seems strangely devoid of understanding. He just kept saying, "Yes that's dreadful. But remember she was your step-mother. And you'd only just got to know her. Why don't you go and see your mum in San Francisco? Or just come home?"

Home? Wherever that is.

His dad is speaking to him. "Come into my study, Ben. We need to talk."

Ben feels like saying, "Are you sure you can spare the time, Pop? Aren't there some important politicos here in the house you would rather speak to? Or maybe you could get down to business with Annalise, or one of your other ex-mistresses?" But he doesn't. He meekly follows his father up the stairs of the imposing mansion into his study. It is an elegant if austere room; his father had always had good taste, and, he thinks more kindly, generosity.

"I hope you'll enjoy those two passes I sent you for the Yankees, or give 'em to someone who will."

"I've already done that, Pop."

His father pauses and smiles. He is still a very handsome man at fifty-seven; *much more handsome than I am*, thinks Ben, suddenly feeling rather proud of him.

"I know you've felt this very deeply, Ben. She was a fantastic woman, Dorothea. I'd loved her for many years, you know."

Ben says nothing, but he believes his father.

"I love you too, Ben; though I realise I don't show it very adequately."

"And I love you, Dad. But it's hard, very hard. I thought she would bring us together. And we had so much in common, Dorothea and me. I mean, I felt she could have been my real mom."

Ben Schlesinger Senior pauses; possibly for effect.

"She was, Ben."

For a moment Ben feels as if he is in an episode of *Dallas.* Then he stands up.

He feels shaky, so he sits down again.

"Would you… explain that?"

"Dorothea was your mother, Ben. I know it's a huge shock to you and I'm sorry about that. We were hoping, she and I, to tell you quite soon actually. But she was happy with things as they were. She was particularly happy that you two got along so well together."

"I don't understand, Dad." Ben sounds extremely stressed, indeed distressed.

"Would you like a Scotch? I think you need one."

Ben gasps and shakes his head, in disbelief – at the whole thing.

"OK."

Senator Schlesinger pours two large Scotches.

"You know I've led a very… complicated life, Ben."

Ben looks at him; takes a gulp of his Scotch.

"Which is why I could never stand for president. And is also why I was never surprised that you *and* your brother… Anyway, I married your… I married Catherine for all the wrong reasons: political reasons. Still, we had quite a good political marriage until about two years ago. Way back in the early sixties I became very friendly with Judge Taylor, and Dorothea, as you know, was his wife. We started an affair. She was quite cool with that. We all were. She knew – we all knew – that, in those days, if the affair came out it would ruin my career and possibly the judge's as well, especially as he had kind of given us his blessing." The senator, sounding intensely senatorial, moves over to the window with its splendid view of the Potomac. *He should have been an actor*, thinks Ben, with the detachment that often surprises us at moments of maximum shock.

"But then she got pregnant. We decided between us that Catherine and I would bring *you* up as ours, with Dorothea keeping a… watching brief on you. It was really to get over all that that I went off and had the affair in New Orleans that produced your half-brother Beau. He would love to see you, by the way. I told him not to come here at the moment."

Ben just keeps staring.

"So, it seemed just perfect that when Catherine and I finally divorced, Dorothea and I should marry." He finishes his Scotch. "I do miss her terribly, you know, Ben. Believe me."

Ben is still staring.

"And I know you're not happy about my friendship with Annalise, but I'm very lonely and a politician needs a wife. But believe me, Ben, sincerely: your mother was the love of my life."

His dad looks and sounds very sad and very sincere, but is it real sincerity or political sincerity? He can't tell.

"I'm off, Dad. I think I'll go back to New York for a while. Then England, probably."

"Stay here a couple of nights, son. Please."

For some reason that *does* sound sincere.

"OK," says Ben. So, he does.

PART IV

Winter: Rondo vivace

"Rear Admiral Baker will see you now, Mr Rosen."

The female naval lieutenant in her smart blue uniform looks coolly at Harold as she indicates her boss' door. Harold has been sitting, waiting exasperatedly, in the rear admiral's anteroom for about an hour and a half. It is evidently just another phase of some kind of "cold turkey" treatment and he is thoroughly sick of it. How dare they hold him against his will?

It had all apparently come about simply because he had requested security clearance from the White House in the hope of meeting at least the veep and, if he was really lucky, the great Hilary herself to discuss policy matters and liaison with New Labour. He had presented references from the highest in the NL hierarchy (next to the "Great Leader" himself), almost in effect ambassadorial letters of credence, and *this* was the paradoxical response! He had been told – no, ordered – to remain in Washington and stay incommunicado for the last three days while "checks" were carried out. And now here he is being kept on ice while awaiting his interview with the deputy head of naval intelligence – and why *naval* intelligence, in the name of Billary? Was he suspected of trying to steal a frigate or corrupt the entire US Navy?

Harold stands, summons up all the dignity he can muster as an Englishman abroad, and follows the naval officer into the rear admiral's office. It is a spacious and elegant room and he is a little taken aback to see sitting at the desk a very handsome, rather craggy, auburn-bearded man not in naval or any other uniform but wearing an elegantly tailored black lounge suit and a bright silk tie. He has vivid blue eyes under thick eyebrows and is about fifty. He gives Harold the most charming of smiles as he stands and extends his hand. Harold finds him extremely attractive, but is determined not to allow that to distract him from his righteous anger at his treatment hitherto.

Randy is aware that Harold's case could be sensitive and is resolved to treat him with kid gloves. Mistakes have already been made and he doesn't wish to be the patsy who carries the can for them. But he hasn't got where he is without developing the most refined political sensibility. He has come a long way since those days seven or eight years ago when he had first befriended Francis in San Diego and had played a seminal role in the unfolding story of the Schlesinger family.

He had originally become involved in naval intelligence partly as self-protection against the prying eyes of other intelligence officers into his own sex life and partly because, with his particular mixture of diplomacy, ruthlessness and charm, he felt himself to be superbly well suited to an intelligence career. Once launched, he had climbed with ease the greasy pole of the intelligence "community". He had shrewdly decided that, in the battle of "don't ask, don't tell", it was safer to be not asking than not telling; not that he was directly involved in the prosecution of gay servicemen but had it arisen, his posting would have placed him nearer the prosecution than the defence. At the fund-raising dinner for a reactionary conservative association to which Francis had taken him as escort, he had started a brief liaison – Randy was nothing if not versatile – with the enthusiastic wife of the assistant Secretary of the Navy. And by some unaccountable coincidence he had, just a few months later, been appointed ADC – to use the European term – to that same public official. After nearly a year in that post – replete with the best ambassadorial hospitality – he decided that he didn't want to return to mundane service life; intrigue and the inner workings of diplomacy were clearly his forte, so which milieu would better suit him than naval intelligence? With excellent contacts – many of them ex-shags, of course – the posting was no problem to obtain, and along with it came his long-anticipated promotion to commodore.

And then – about two years prior to our meeting him again, at a time when Randy had been emotionally involved, though not in a profound way, of course, with a certain Irish lawyer with Washington contacts, and he and Tony had almost set up home together but Randy had naturally decided to put his career and his independence first – Randy had provided invaluable lubrication in easing the passage of Ben Schlesinger Senior from the GOP to their tribal rivals, much to the delight of the highest Washington circles, and in so doing had effortlessly eased his own passage to his present eminence as a rear admiral. He now had a magnificent Washington apartment near the vice-presidential residence, tied to his newly acquired post as assistant director of naval intelligence, and a charming country house of his own to which he retreated – not always alone – at weekends and vacations. And through it all he had retained that easy, apparently lazy, sensuously masculine manner that many men and quite a few women found got under their defences, into their bloodstream; he oozed a cool, comfortable sexuality – he couldn't help it. Which is why Harold, in spite of himself, feels attracted and disarmed by this warm, very manly naval officer who now sits smiling across his big, imposing desk at him.

"It's good to meet you at last, Mr Rosen. May I call you Harold?" Randy asks in his soft, almost conspiratorial way.

"Now look here, Admiral…"

"Randy, please call me Randy."

Harold laughs almost in spite of himself.

"You can be as charming as you like, Admiral – which is admittedly very charming – but it doesn't change the unpalatable fact that I, a citizen of an extremely friendly country to this one—"

"Your oldest ally…"

"No, that's Portugal—"

"Your closest ally then."

"Will you stop interrupting me, Admiral?"

A flicker of annoyance passes over Randy's face, and then is gone.

"Please continue, Mr Rosen."

"I have been held here against my will and I demand to see a representative of the British ambassador."

"You can see Her Excellency herself tomorrow evening as my guest at the vice-president's ball."

This stops Harold in his somewhat overheated tracks.

"That's bollocks."

"If that means what I believe it means, then, yes, balls certainly have their uses." Are his hands touching his own under the table or is that Harold's vividly aroused imagination? "But that's not what I'm talking about today, Harold. As a small apology for our unfortunate cock-up – would you Englishmen call it that? – I want you to be my guest at the veep's annual ball tomorrow evening. It would also give us a chance to talk in a more conducive ambience, don't you think?"

Harold decides to take a cooler line. Clearly the intelligence people want something from him, so he can name his price.

"Has there been some problem, Randy, about my security clearance? Relating to my new Third Way Consultancy?"

"There were some minor issues, Harold. Obviously, we're not too bothered about your sexual promiscuity—"

"Oh please…"

"Though very strictly speaking the entry into the States of promiscuous homosexuals and also those with drug convictions is—"

"*What?*" Harold feels he is about to explode. "Are you referring to the fact that twenty-odd years ago I was *cautioned* by Cambridgeshire police for smoking cannabis along with half of Cambridge University?"

"Well, it might be that," Randy smoothly replies, delighted to have struck a sore point by sheer serendipity, "But as I say it's of no consequence. No, what we *are* concerned about is your involvement with certain extreme right elements who are trying to infiltrate your consultancy."

"I'm hardly likely to get involved with the KKK with *my* name and provenance, am I?"

"There are certain far right royalist groups – not dangerous, a bit zany perhaps – the White House wouldn't want involved, of course."

Harold is vaguely aware that Zac and Armando have some royalist pretensions, but he really doesn't believe in this bluff.

"I have friends – who may or may not come in as partners – who have slightly wacky royalist connections. So fucking what?"

Randy pauses for effect.

"You do realise this interview is being taped, Mr Rosen? For your protection, of course. As indeed your detention – if one may even call it that – has been principally for your protection. We have reason to believe that you have been in considerable danger, Harold, so acting on a tip from British Intelligence we decided to hold you while we dealt with the problem."

Harold still doesn't believe, but he can't be sure.

He tries to sound as cool as possible. "And have you dealt with it?"

"I guess so. Broadly. Now we want you to do something for us."

"Answer a tricky question about opera perhaps? I'm very good on opera, you know."

"And sadomasochism and cocaine and a whole slew of things that could get you barred forever from these United States and fuck up your business plans completely, Mr Rosen."

Randy sounds a bit annoyed.

The two men glare at each other.

"Scotch or sherry?" Randy smiles. It is like sunshine after rain.

Harold feels uncomfortably drawn to him. Is it Stockholm syndrome?

"Scotch, if you insist."

"I do."

He pours it.

"I think you'll enjoy the vice-president's ball."

"Balls."

"You'd be lucky to see *them*. They say the second lady has a vice-like grip."

They both laugh.

II

The residence of the US vice-president is one of those fine old Washington mansions that everyone knows but no one admits to having visited. Like a grace and favour house in London, it has a surprising Old World charm, housing as it does, a gentleman who, like a Hanoverian Prince of Wales, is a breath away from great power but has none at all. Of course, there are always those who prefer to worship the rising sun, but this is a sun which, due to the vagaries of presidential politics, may (like that in Sondheim's Scandinavian operetta) stay suspended on the horizon apparently forever, and then sink.

Nonetheless, the vice-presidential residence is a mansion of some elegance and nobility. In fact, there are those who prefer it to the White House as more restrained, tasteful and "liveable". And it contains a ballroom – not huge, but handsome and finely proportioned – which bears a Victorian grandeur hardly matched anywhere in the United States. The second lady – to coin a rarely used and odd-sounding title – will generally hold a ball at least once a season (who being in possession of such a ballroom and for so short a time would not?) and the pre-Christmas season ball of December '97 was just such a special event, bringing together an alluring mix of writers, legislators, services' top brass, literati, glitterati – and major donors to the Democratic party, both rich and super rich; *everybody* in fact.

The butler, immaculate in white tie and tails – the only man who is – is announcing the guests as they enter to be received at the door by Mr and Mrs Veep.

"Senator Schlesinger and Mr Ben Schlesinger."

Ben comes in after his father who is sporting a black armband as if to trumpet his mourning. *Why have I come?* thinks Ben, who feels increasingly Hamlet-like, as he watches his father receive the warm hand clasps and too sincere condolences of the veeps. Then they turn to Ben.

"And you should have our condolences too, Benjamin, on the loss of your step-mother."

To see his father's fast-fading grief so pampered and his own so downgraded is more than Ben's ample flesh can bear.

"She was my mother actually, Mr Vice-President."

But the vice-regal couple – with that convenient political knack of ignoring reality – have already turned their attention to the next entrant whom Ben recognises at once.

What the hell is Harold Rosen doing here? he thinks. He also thinks he recognises the handsome daddy-admiral on whose coat tails Harold has evidently got his invitation, his eyelashes fluttering at the brilliance of his catch. His father nods to the admiral who moves over to exchange a few friendly words; at which point the penny drops. It is Randy Baker, the strangely omniscient naval officer who has played more than one significant role in the family revelations of the Schlesingers. Ben feels suspicious of him, as he now feels suspicious towards everyone connected with his labyrinthine family. He had agreed to come along partly to accompany his father – who was genuinely lonely as Annalise had to go back to San Diego for three weeks to tie up loose ends in her previous role – partly out of a snobbish inquisitiveness, but mostly because in his present morbid mood he considered that doing one thing was as good as doing another. He felt immobilised yet rootless. And despite several phone calls to Jonathan – who sounds increasingly concerned and pressing – he really can't decide if he wants to or should return to London. Drifting disconsolately here seems at least as attractive as doing the same over there. And his father's evident guilt has turned up the taps of paternal generosity to its highest yet with an offer of a new car and singing lessons with whomever, whenever. In these circumstances, why go back to a relationship grown distant in emotion as well as place? Why go back at all?

Harold, meanwhile, is beginning to enjoy the thrill of being at such an exclusive occasion and delighted that he had packed his dinner jacket. He can hardly wait to relay every detail to Celia; she will be *so* jealous. He has actually been introduced to the vice-president, who has the politician's knack of at least appearing to know who he is meeting; and when Harold had passed on greetings from some of the highest circles of the British government he had certainly betrayed no surprise. His message in return of "And give them my very best; I'm a great admirer of Prime Minister Blair" not only sounded impressively sincere but might contain a coded message. It would certainly be relayed word for word.

His escort is approaching with two glasses of Dom Perignon.

"Be my guest, Harold."

"Thanks, Admiral."

"Randy, remember?"

"Very well, Randy."

"You see, Harold, we want you to be our friend."

"I'm sure we're all friends here, Randy."

"I mean our *special* friend."

Harold hasn't yet drunk enough Dom Perignon not to realise that he is being in some sense importuned. He decides to get tough, catty even.

"What precisely do you want, Rear Admiral Baker?"

Randy gives him an intense, piercing look.

"We want *you*, Harold Rosen; just *you*. And in return you can name your price."

Randy turns and in a moment is dancing a waltz very expertly with his ex-fling, the wife of a former Secretary of the Navy, leaving Harold to ponder his precipitous offer of a starkly Faustian deal.

Ben, standing at the opposite side of the grand room, is also rapt in reverie, which is not pierced by the sounds of latecomers being announced – "Senator Nancy Idelbaum", "Professor Henry Lush-Evans, University of Artemisia" – *university of where?* muses Ben disinterestedly – until he hears the next name: "Mr Theodosius Rohan Van Duys the fourth". At this name, Ben looks to the door and sees the entrance of the darkly handsome man whom he has not ceased to fantasise about since meeting him as host of that gloriously outrageous wedding. He looks ravishing in a sharply cut black jacket with a gorgeously embroidered pale blue silk waistcoat over his sculptured chest. Ben thinks he looks more than ever like a young Greek archbishop, or more appropriately the priest of an earlier less censorious cult. How to approach him? But before he can make his move he sees Theo gravitate towards a big good-looking reddish-haired man whom he recognises as the arrogant bear from the wedding, and the club, and joining the group almost immediately is Ben's other nemesis, Harold. His plan to pay court to the lovely Theo will have to remain on hold.

His father appears beside him.

"Dorothea would want you to enjoy the evening, Ben. It's not often we hold balls like this anymore in Washington. Don't mope. It doesn't become you."

"And does it become *you* to enjoy your outward mourning so obviously?"

His father – deeply handsome as always – lowers his eyes a moment, then looks at him seriously.

"We've never understood each other, Ben, and I can't expect it to happen now. But believe me, I'm mourning in my own way. Dorothea – and I knew her better than you did – believed in *life*. Maybe it's time you got yourself one."

Ben feels as if his father has kicked him in the stomach.

He goes straight over to Theo where he is standing talking to Harold and Jon Starr.

"Can I speak with you please?"

"Sure," says Theo.

They moves a little apart from the others.

"I've been wanting to tell you ever since that wedding that you are one of the most beautiful men I have ever seen. I really want you. Can we sleep together?"

Theo smiles; his teeth are brilliant. Ben notices a mole on his left cheek, dark brown against his almost sallow skin.

"Of course, Ben. You only had to ask."

III

Daniel is walking briskly, as he always does, up the Golders Green Road. It is a chilly day, not long before Christmas and, more relevantly to him and so many of the residents here, Chanukah, the mid-winter feast of lights. He passes a group of Chassidim with *payos* – long curling locks drooped over their ears – elaborate coats and big, black hats. He passes an Israeli café and two strictly kosher restaurants – one meat and the other milk – without even noticing them. He does notice another young Chassid – a few years younger than himself – standing outside a *shtiebl* (a small local synagogue) a bit further along, in the direction he is taking towards the tube station. Although Daniel and his family are not Chassidim – in fact his grandparents actively disliked them – *he* finds them quite charming, richly redolent of his Ashkenazi ancestors' Mitteleuropean provenance and outwardly displaying what his own mainstream orthodox clan preferred to keep under a pinstriped suit and only slightly outré trilby. And this particular young Chassid – whom Daniel often sees in this area but has never spoken to – is quite beautiful, like a photograph in an album of pre-war Vilna or Lublin: sweet-faced, about seventeen, with light brown ringlets, a rounded furry *shtreyml* on his head, superbly silky black frock coat and spotless long white socks above his patent leather shoes. Seeing him always puts Daniel in mind of Tadzio in *Death in Venice*, the ultra-sensuous film which he guiltily adores, rather than the book which, despite his love of reading, he had found too prolix to complete. Not that Daniel thought of himself as "gay"; he fully intends to marry and has had the usual rather dirty thoughts about girls since puberty, which however he has tended to repress as he wishes to remain a virgin until his marriage. The desire to produce a family and reproduce the traditional family life of his parents and previous generations is greater and deeper than any sexual desire he has experienced, at least so far, but it combines at times with a more lofty platonic need to evoke the soaring romantic vertigo he always feels on seeing that beautiful young man.

He has in fact devoted so much of his time to Talmudic study – and day-dreaming – that his school education had rather gone by the board, which was why he had ended up at the local college of further education, somewhat to the disgust of his parents who expected him to more than emulate his older brother Sam who had graduated well in law from University College London and was now almost ready to take his bar exams.

He has always enjoyed reading – practically anything including his mother's women's magazines and the sides of cereal packets – but it was his classes with the odd, eccentric but essentially very human Mr Darkside at the college which had sparked his fascination with literature and especially with George Eliot's novel of his namesake, *Daniel Deronda*. Certainly he had also enjoyed *Hamlet* and the other set books – First World War poetry and contemporary short stories – but it was, not surprisingly, *Deronda* which had taken his imagination hostage. He had even read *Middlemarch* for background, and had been deeply impressed by its breadth and detail and had almost fallen in love with Dorothea – she seemed both more sensible and more altruistic than Gwendolen in *DD* and so more to his taste – yet the book had not moved or inspired him to the same extent as the latter. And then just as he was getting into these books and preparing for his exams which he had originally opted to take this December but had now postponed until the summer, George Darkside had disappeared, left the college without a word and without even returning his essay.

Mr Darkside is clearly a solitary, rather dreamy figure, quite like himself, and Daniel feels drawn to him and worries about his progress and whereabouts. And once Daniel gets his teeth into an idea, a project, he worries at it until he has sorted it out. Which is why, with his habitually rather distracted look, he is now walking up the Golders Green Road to the tube with the aim not of going into college as he is supposed to do but of going once more to pay an unannounced visit to George's West Hampstead address to discover exactly what has happened to him.

Getting on the tube he looks in his bag for something to read. The beautiful Chassid – and most of his co-students – would be studying a tractate of the Talmud when travelling so as not to waste precious spiritual time and to avoid the temptations for lewd or inappropriate thoughts that might arise from looking idly around the compartment. But Daniel's interest in English literature is now such that the religious text he always carries, almost like a talisman, remains in his bag, while he takes out not the *Study Notes to Daniel Deronda* that he ought academically to be reading but found so *reductive*, but instead his latest acquisition, *The Manor* by Isaac Bashevis Singer, which he only wishes his embryonic Yiddish was good enough to read in the original. It isn't a set book; he is just enjoying it. It is also nestled in his packed and rather musty bag next to a couple of gifts he is taking for Mr Darkside. Provided, of course, that he finds his old teacher in a fit state to receive them. For Daniel's intuition – which is very strong though not always equally accurate – is telling him that George is not in a very good state of mind or health or *something* and will be in need of his presence. Only the previous night he had woken shouting from a ghastly dream in which he had seen George lying on the floor of his home desperate for food and unable to move. At that moment he had decided it was his bounden duty, like a knight errant of old (Daniel had also enjoyed reading his Arthurian legends) to come to the aid of his old mentor, and, this time, *nothing* was going to stop him. He would break any number of windows and climb in if necessary. But the truth must be revealed, and the soul in danger saved.

Daniel is so engrossed in the pious and worldly doings of Singer's late nineteenth-century characters that he almost forgets his own place at the end of the twentieth and notices he has arrived at West Hampstead just in time to jump off in a rush before the train doors close. Daniel is always a little absent-minded, a little distrait. But he is also focused when his determination, and moral indignation, are aroused; now he is the good Talmudic scholar, the Arthurian hero and the Hebrew prophet rolled into one. And as he strides purposefully up West End Lane and takes a turning just before Quex Road, he knows the knightly quest is well on its way.

He finds the block – he had, of course, been here, if fruitlessly, before – walks up to the first floor and rings the bell. He fully expects the long wait that follows and is coolly considering whether consulting the neighbours, ringing the police or trying to batter down the door is his best option when it languidly opens and Mr Darkside stands facing him.

Daniel's first thought is that Mr Darkside looks terrible; not perhaps as terrible as he had imagined, but as Daniel had imagined him dead and on the cusp of decomposing that is hardly a compliment. To say he looks rough would be an understatement of monstrous proportions. His hair – previously relatively neat and short and grizzled at the temples – is now mainly grey, quite long and unpleasantly matted. His skin, always a little blotchy, is now a parchment-like yellow suggesting several days without daylight or exercise, and his eyes are bloodshot. In his favour is the fact that his features, always quite handsome and distinguished, are now, through the pallor and weight loss of weeks with little nutrition, almost ethereally beautiful. He is wearing a very tattered, dirty green old cardigan and baggy stained trousers. He stands at the door with a marked stoop, glaring, only half-aware of his surroundings, at Daniel. He has aged several years in the few months since Daniel has seen him. Though he thought himself prepared for the worst, he is humbled, embarrassed and moved. George's gaze twitches. Then he speaks in a scratchy, low, grumpy voice.

"What do you want?"

He appears not to have recognised Daniel, or to be determined not to.

"Erm… it's me, Mr Darkside, Daniel Cohen from you're A level group at college. You remember me?"

George screws up his eyes and says nothing.

"How are you, sir?"

"Perfectly all right. Do I have an essay of yours or something?"

Daniel is relieved; at least George seems to be coming back to life even if he has obviously become extremely misanthropic and is clearly resentful of Daniel's intrusion.

"Actually, you do have an essay of mine, sir, but that wasn't the real reason I've come. I just wanted to pay you a visit. See how you are. Have you retired from teaching, sir?"

To Daniel's surprise, George laughs, or rather snarls and grimaces at once.

"You could say that, young man. Remind me of your name?"

That was George's usual tack; some of the old tricks are seeping back.

"Daniel, Mr Darkside. We were studying *Daniel Deronda*?"

"Why do people *do* that?"

"Sorry, sir?"

"That rising intonation at the end of a statement. Are you Australian? It drives me bloody mad."

Daniel can't help smiling.

"You mean like *that?*" he says, intentionally rising irritatingly.

There is a pause; four, five, six beats.

"I suppose you'd better come in. Just for a moment."

George considers whether to state the obvious: that the place is a bloody mess, a bloody embarrassingly awful mess. But decides not to.

Daniel, coming in and following George through to the kitchen, thinks that, all things considered, the place could be a lot worse. Admittedly it smells as if the windows haven't been open in some years and clearly no dusting has been done for months but at least there isn't excrement on the walls or piles of dirty washing or decaying newspapers all over the kitchen floor.

With an evidently huge effort George says, "I suppose you'd like a cup of tea?"

For a moment Daniel hesitates. He shouldn't really take any food – even a cup of tea – in a non-kosher household, especially one as dirty as this, but the Talmud enjoins politeness and respect for people's feelings and enormous respect for teachers and the elderly.

"Thank you."

George grunts and begins shuffling around to find clean cups and cutlery. As even the ones on the draining board suddenly look distinctly grubby, he decides to take down from the cupboard his best china. Why not? It is a huge effort but he has to admit to himself that he is quite enjoying it. As he empties and then refills the kettle, very aware of Daniel's gentle but decidedly intense gaze, he wonders for a second if this young man might be some kind of stalker or worse. *Well, at least,* he thinks, *it's something* different.

"I could probably find your essay… somewhere."

"Oh, don't worry about it, sir. Another time maybe."

Pouring the water onto the tea bags in the elegant china cups, he looks over at Daniel who recognises a touch of the old irony in his eyes. That is a good sign.

George hands him his cup and saucer.

"It's beautiful china, sir."

"My late mother's best."

He suddenly feels emotionally vulnerable.

"I'll see if I can find your essay. Help yourself to a biscuit from that tin there."

He goes into his study and finds the pile of essays remarkably fast; he had always been a methodical lecturer. But he doesn't pick any up. Instead, he goes into the bathroom and combs his hair. Then he goes into his bedroom, takes off his cardigan and puts on one of the slightly battered but respectable jackets he used to wear for teaching. He feels a bit more like the lecturer he saw reflected in Daniel's eyes. He goes back in. Daniel, who has not touched the tea, raises it to his lips and takes a minute sip. He has taken out of his bag a packet and some kind of brochure which he is scrutinising.

"Actually, Mr Darkside, if you don't mind, sir, I brought some cake – we call it *kuchen* – homemade, sir, by my mother. I can leave it for you?"

George suddenly feels an itch around his eyes. He rubs one vigorously.

"If you like." His voice has a slight catch; he clears his throat. "Thank your mother."

"Well, actually, she doesn't know, sir. But she wouldn't mind. Not at all. Do you like opera, sir?"

George feels punch drunk with all these surprises.

He feigns nonchalance.

"I used to. Mozart's damn good."

"Well, sir, I just brought along this programme from the British National Opera. You know that company at the Western Hippodrome?"

"Of course."

"Shall I leave the programme for you? To be honest, I have no one to go with, so if you did want to... Well, maybe you'd think about it, sir."

George sits down and drinks some of his tea. It tastes a lot better from his mother's best.

"I couldn't find the essay. But I think I know where it is. If you come back in a few days…?"

"Oh yes, thank you, sir."

Pause. They both drink and George opens the *kuchen* and cuts two pieces.

"How are things at… at college?"

"Very dull, sir. You were the best teacher."

George harrumphs.

"Mr Shah's pretty good too. Mrs Green is an old… well, you know what I mean, sir."

"I certainly do."

They both giggle.

"Actually, Mr Darkside, I suppose I should be going. I've already missed one lecture, not that it mattered. Can I come back on Monday… if you might have the essay by then?"

"I suppose so."

Daniel puts his coat back on and his hat over his yarmulke.

"Maybe think about the opera, sir. They say the Janáček one should be interesting. It's just been discovered by the guy who's their musical director apparently. I'm interested in Eastern European culture; I don't know about you. Anyway… Thank you."

George gets up and almost smiles.

"Yes… erm… thank *you*… for the cake."

He leads Daniel to the door.

"You could call in on Monday then. I'll probably be in. Late morning say?"

"See you then, sir. Goodbye."

George shuts the door and goes into the study. He goes online and immediately begins an e-mail to his only correspondent.

Dear Professor,

An ex-student has brought me his mother's cake and wants me to go with him to the opera. Is this weird or laughable? Am I an old fool? He is an orthodox Jew which complicates things further. Shall I take up his offer? Give me some words of wisdom for, as you may know, life has lost so much of its savour that unless I take a new path, all taste, all colour will be drained.

He clicks on "Send now" quickly, so as not to change his mind.

Good heavens, he thinks, *I'm becoming as mad as the weirdo I'm e-mailing.*

<h1 style="text-align:center">IV</h1>

Ben wakes up with a start, unsure where he is or whose is the alien presence breathing – and gently purring – beside him. He had been dreaming of Dorothea – the mother he had always wanted to know, had started to know, would now never know. He begins to cry noiselessly. It is painful. And he weeps silently so as not to wake the darkly handsome but oddly cold man sleeping next to him. For one moment he wishes it is another small dark man, a little older than this one, a bit less glamorous but someone he can reach out to, share his sorrow with, expecting tenderness in return… But *he* is on another continent.

The sex had been good, and pretty exciting if a bit odd (though not as good or exciting as Ben had anticipated, but was it ever?). Theo had been very keen; too keen really for Ben's taste. He had given no time for a build-up of desire but as soon as they had got in here – his luxurious suite in another hotel in which his family had a controlling interest – he had stripped off, got on his knees, opened Ben's flies with his teeth and knuckled down to oral pleasure. Ben didn't even have time to adequately take in his cappuccino skin, dark chocolate nipples, generous curly black fur, long circumcised cock and rather pendulous balls. Not that he objected to having this handsome and very hairy (even hairier than he had anticipated) man paying homage before him. But it was not how he had imagined it; for it was *he* who had expected, even wanted, to pay homage to this gorgeous, remote icon. Whereas it was clear that to Theo this was just another welcome bout of hot sex. Theo was a letch, an addict. It spoilt the pleasure Ben had so sensuously anticipated.

And something else had spoilt it too. As Theo went down on him – or rather on his cock, which was often complimented on being as fat and juicy as its owner – images began to flash up in his mind, images which were totally inappropriate to what he was about to do – and which made what he was about to do totally inappropriate. First, there was a picture of Dorothea the last time he saw her: radiant, full-faced, hair like a dark brown halo round her laughing face. His erection went flaccid (Theo didn't even notice, he was chewing so hard) and a pang of guilt at indulging his carnal desires while he was still very much in mourning – or perhaps was still in shock preparatory to mourning. Then he looked down at Theo who withdrew a moment and actually smiled – as if he had realised for the first time that there was a person at the end of that dick. His teeth were brilliant, but the imperfection of that mole made him even more desirable, and Ben's erection hardened up at once.

After a while he decided to take the lead; maybe that was what Theo wanted or perhaps he just responded to anything (you could hardly be expected to know such things the first time, yet by the second time that unique thrill was gone). So, using his superior strength, he pulled the smaller man onto the bed and pushed his legs up so revealing his arse as perfectly placed for his own cock to enter. Ben didn't often fuck – hardly ever, mainly due to his fear of AIDS – but this suddenly seemed the ideal occasion. And Theo looked at him as if to say – as they still sometimes do in the porn films – "Oh yea, take me, baby." Ben was inebriated with a sense of power and felt a definite surge in his balls. The spermatozoa were preparing to make their hot, fast journey into colonic darkness. He looked vaguely around to the elaborate bedside table and Theo said, "They're in the drawer. Let me put it on your big, fuckin' cock."

Ben did not demur. But just as he was reaching over to pull the drawer out, he got a mental picture of his father passionately kissing Annalise Crump. That was momentary. He recovered his position; his cock stood to attention and he handed the condom to Theo who opened it with his teeth. But suddenly he saw Francis lying on that bed, instead of Theo, as he looked on the morning he died, smiling pleasantly and saying, "I don't advise fucking a stranger, dear, even with a condom; you never know where they've been."

At this Ben completely freaked out and turned his head away. Was he going crazy?

Theo asked, "Are you OK, Ben?" He actually sounded quite concerned. "Are you sure you want to fuck?" he added, rather gallantly. "I'm not sure I'm in the mood."

For his answer, Ben went down on his long, thin and very pleasant- tasting cock. Now *he* was paying homage; it felt less threatening. Eventually, Ben pulled Theo in front of him and, the rich smell of his body filling his nostrils, brought him off with vigorous strokes, Theo shooting great wads of cum all over the heavy bedclothes; clearly if he weren't so rich he could make a good living as a porn star. This Ben hugely enjoyed, but just as he was vigorously stroking his own cock, with Theo watching intently, he heard Dorothea's voice saying,

"Maybe it's time you went home now, my dear," and he shot but with the most minimal orgasm, followed nonetheless by total exhaustion.

Yes, he thinks, musing about it on waking, *it had been an odd session.*

He is doing too much of this; waking up in some stranger's bed, feeling emotionally dislocated. He will have to face up to the pain of loss, face up to his dependence on his father and decide where his future lies. It is time to grow up. What else can you do without a mother?

He turns over and sees Theo looking at him, quite sweetly. Maybe he is more than just handsome, more than just sex.

"I get the feeling you have issues to resolve, Ben. Not that I want to be an amateur shrink. But you know what I mean."

"I have issues to resolve," says Ben. "You know I just lost my mother."

"Sure. And remember fat is beautiful, Ben. Especially in *my* book."

Ben hadn't even realised that was still one of his issues.
He laughs.
"I know that, you sexy little cunt."

V

Christmas Day. The usual, almost traditional party at Jeremy Groves' elegant Knightsbridge flat (the one he inherited from Francis) which his friends go to not because they like him but simply because they have nowhere else to go. Even so, they like each other and somehow Jeremy collects around him a pretended family that feels, with all its niggles, envies and suspicions, remarkably like a real one. Jeremy never does anything; as he puts it, he "presides", so this year it is Adelina and Tallulah's turn to cook the turkey and they are in the kitchen from which a weird but enticing melange of sounds and smells is emerging. Celia and Jonathan are lounging in the sitting room chatting amiably while Jeremy and Pip are standing by the drinks cabinet, pretending to have a real conversation though both know that Pip's attention is entirely on his future ex-wife as she lounges on the sofa.

"And how are GLOW doing, darling? Have they survived my ever-so-polite refusal to appear in that camp musical?"

"Of course, my love. They'll survive anything. Hard as nails these amateurs. And *so* competitive. There's an unbelievable battle going on between my deputy, a feisty dyke called Flora, and Charles our pianist. He's extremely talented but utterly self-absorbed."

"Have you introduced him to mine host? Could be the perfect match."

"Could be. But could two such super egos co-exist?"

"Maybe not, but just imagine the collision."

"Boom! Have another beer, Celia; they obviously agree with you."

"Don't! I'm sitting here getting blotto with you," she sighs melodramatically, "My only true friend – while Pip uniquely for him stands there hardly sipping his Scotch. Do you think he's trying to impress me?"

"Maybe he's fallen in love with you all over again, lovey."

"Can you induce catatonia twice?"

"Not unless you're called Cerys."

She giggles. "She's good."

"And very attractive." Jonathan gives her an old-fashioned look.

"Oh dear, so *you* think I've gone queer as well."

"Well, bi, anyway, my dear. And why not?"

Celia lowers her voice. "OK, I fucked Addy – which was… *interesting* – and then the girlfriend very surprisingly made a pass at me – which was also quite fun – then told me in no uncertain terms to leave Addy alone. Which I totally understand and agree with. You see, it's not for me, dear. I'm not a dyke."

"But a taste of pussy's fun occasionally?"

"Sure, but you can't beat a mouthful of the dog."

They both fall about laughing.

"So, what's happening at GLOW this season?"

"We're doing *Little Night Music*, with Charlie directing and Flora's girlfriend playing Desiree. Far too young but what can you do?"

"And how's Ben? Coming back soon?"

Jonathan turns pensive. "I don't really know, Celia. I keep telling him to come back home but I don't think he knows where home is now. He's very cut up about his mother dying. And he'd thought she was his step-mother. It's really traumatic."

"Weird family. But rich families usually are. *All* families usually are." She takes a gulp of beer. "Do you want him back?"

Jon looks away. "I think so. I don't know."

"Have you seen that strange, attractive young man again?"

"What?" Jon's look of embarrassment confirms her suspicions.

"Young Jeb. Horny young devil. He had the chutzpah the other day to ask me if I knew what had happened to Harold. Who seems to have disappeared Stateside."

"What do you mean?"

"Gone to ground. Actually, I got a weird text message from him yesterday. Not that I'm really into this texting thing myself, but there it was. I've even got the phone in my bag with the thing saved." She leans behind the sofa and fishes in her handbag. "Here it is."

It read: *They want my soul, Celia. Can't leave with it. Can't leave without it. What should I do?*

"Did you reply?"

"Sure, here it is. 'Get what you can for it, dear, then come home. Love, Celia'."

"Do you think he's gone nuts?"

"No more than usual, dear. Look, there's something I need to do in the kitchen."

"Do you think they need a hand with the stuffing?"

Celia ignores Jonathan's jibe and goes for it. As she enters the kitchen the girls turn and go coldly silent. She marches straight up to them and says, "Ladies, you are both beautiful and you obviously belong together. Thank you for… what happened, but now I just want to be your friend. Can we do that? Please?"

There is a moment's pause, then Adelina says – sounding very Australian, "You never did really learn how to eat pussy, did you, Celia? But you sure can lick that Janáček!"

Tallulah smiles – Celia notices with a tinge of regret what a radiant smile it is – and says, "You must be getting hungry. How soon will this lot be ready, love?"

"Ten minutes max."

"In that case…" says Celia, heading back in, purposefully.

In the kitchen there is a slight pause, then Addy says, "I think we've survived that."

"Of course we have," Tallulah replies, taking the potatoes and parsnips out of the oven. "And by the way, I think we should buy a house *together*. Do you want to see a nice four-bedroom in Richmond?"

"You try to fucking stop me, bitch."

And they kiss over the sizzling parsnips.

Meanwhile in the living room, Celia goes up to Jeremy and says, "Butt out, Jeremy. I have to speak to my ex. Now."

"Fine, darling, fine. I'll go and help the ladies of Llangollen."

Pip and Celia glare at each other warily. Jonathan sits on the couch pretending to read a CD cover.

Pip is the first to speak. "I miss you, darling. I do love you, in my own odd way. Very much. Can we try again?"

"You sound like a tired pop song, Philip. We love each other as friends. Let's stay friends always – divorced friends. I'm sure it's best."

Pip looks as if he is going to cry.

Celia takes his hand. "We *will* be friends – promise. But not husband and wife."

Jeremy and the women process in from the kitchen singing the peers' chorus from *Iolanthe* and bearing the golden turkey and a huge tureen of vegetables.

There is a moment's silence as they survey the scene.

"Everything all right?" asks Jeremy.

Pip cracks a little smile and says, "Sorted."

VI

Christmas Day in Washington. The elegant home of Senator Schlesinger. The senator (though officially in mourning) is in high good humour. Not only has his lady friend, Annalise, returned to spend the holidays with him, but they were both feted at a White House reception the previous evening by a grateful president, as always in need of congressional support. Now he is preparing to receive just a few guests – about twenty – for a festive, if officially muted, dinner.

Ben is, of course, moping around the library wondering why he is still here, knowing it's time he went home – went anywhere – and got himself a job, made himself a life, independent of his father. Annalise enters. He prickles, but still has respect for her as his former teacher. Annalise is a tough old cookie; she knows Ben needs taking in hand and that his emotionally reticent father will never do it. She also knows it isn't really her business.

"How are you, Ben?"

"OK, Annalise."

"Are you still set on a singing career, Ben?"

"I was." He sighs. "But I'm still waiting to hear from the Met."

"They keep people waiting a long time, Ben. Look, I've heard that, back at San Diego U, there's a three-year fellowship available in Renaissance music studies – wasn't that precisely your field? Just between us, with my recommendation there wouldn't be any problem in your getting it. It could be the making of you. I always felt you were happy there."

"Yes, I was… Thank you, Annalise. I must think about it."

"Of course, but don't think for too long, Ben. I need to know by New Year's. And, by the way, happy Christmas."

She comes over and, very self-consciously, kisses him on the forehead. It may be worth returning to California just to get away from her, and everyone else.

As soon as she has left the room, the doorbell rings. Ben thinks it far too early for the dinner guests to arrive. The maid must have gone to the door. He hears her in the hall just outside saying, "If you'd wait in here please, Mr Rosen, I'll check if the senator can see you."

Before Ben can escape, Harold is in the library. He looks profoundly worried. Ben decides that, as this is his own home – or at least his father's – he can afford to be civilised.

"I didn't think I'd have the pleasure so soon, again. Can I get you a drink?"

"No thanks, Ben. I'm hoping to see your father."

"Why?"

"I want him to help me."

"To do what?"

Harold looks very frightened. "To escape."

Ben feels exasperated. "What are you talking about, Harold?"

"They're holding me here against my will. The intelligence people. They're trying to turn me. Your dad's got such a lot of influence…"

"Just go, Harold."

"But I haven't seen your—"

"I mean, just leave the country. They can't stop you."

Harold looks surprised. "But they won't let me back in."

"Of course they will. Just leave."

Harold looks hugely relieved; liberated.

"Thank you, Ben." He turns to go. "Do apologise to your dad."

"Bye."

Harold almost runs out.

Ben feels for once he has got the upper hand.

And "leave" suddenly seems the very best advice.

VII

Celia has worked very hard and has great fun learning her new role as a timeless Chinese dominatrix, but as always opening night is a terrifying experience. Everything is now amicable with Adelina, who has sent her an enormous box of chocolates and a huge bouquet with a card which reads, "Break a nail – from your most Sapphic admirers." Even so, Celia is glad it is Jeremy conducting. She has the greatest confidence in him; his acidity, his emotional intensity, always help to keep any performance together and bring out the finest in everyone. She is particularly nervous as this opening has been brought forward – due to the cancellation of a return visit by the famous Las Balletes de Horchata de Chufa who had made a huge success there back in the early nineties (their lead ballerina, a six-foot-six TV, had been crushed by the collapse of a huge phallic banana, but was now fortunately on the mend) – by three weeks to this ridiculous date in the dog-days between Christmas and New Year. But as this may be her last major role – and her first as a reconfigured singleton – she is determined to make it her best. The only trouble with the part – glorious in its range and power – is that it is so long and tiring. But it is also enormously dramatic and will give full rein to those acting talents which she may well be called upon to use in order to make her future living.

She hears the gorgeously haunting overture welling up from the pit. Fred, the ageless doorman, shouts for overture and beginners; she feels nauseous to the pit of her stomach – so *that* was in order – and she girds up the train of her magnificent costume, makes sure her whip is secreted as it should be beneath her skirt, says a silent, private prayer, and makes her way along the corridor to the wings in preparation for her first, magnificent entrance.

"Fantastic, darling; sublimely wonderful!"

"Harold, how lovely to see you. When did you get back, sweetie, and who is your handsome friend?"

"My love, I got back this morning, and rushed straight here to grab the last two decent tickets, and this is my Irish friend Jim. Isn't he a dish?"

"Absolutely. But what happened to you? We were terribly worried, you know. Someone told me you'd disappeared, and then you sent me that text…"

"Darling…" Harold theatrically lowers his voice. "I have been through such dramas, such traumas, they make your little opera here look like a nursery rhyme; *they* really put me through it."

"But who are *they*, darling?" asks Celia, fascinated.

"The powers of darkness, duckie – you really don't want to know more. But I've survived, stronger, and one day I'll tell you *all* about it. But now, here's that bottle of Veuve Clicquot I promised you."

"Sweetie, you shouldn't have, but I will drink it."

In the crush Celia spots a serious-looking Jewish young man with a yarmulke and a rather distinguished older man in tow; he reminds her a little of Francis. *Dear Francis, if only he were here.*

"Miss Greyfield?" It is the young Jew. "We just got in through the stage door – that gentleman brought us in." He is pointing at Pip who is present, re-united with the gangling, indeterminate Stefan.

"That's all right," says Celia. "He's my husband – was my husband. Whatever. You're welcome."

"Thank you. It was wonderful."

"More than wonderful," says George who is standing beside him in a best suit he hasn't worn for about five years. He feels – and somehow looks – completely re-born. He can't stop staring at Celia. Her scene as a dominatrix had walked straight out of one of his waking visions. Was this the woman he had searched for all his life?

"My name's Daniel and this is my teacher – well, ex-teacher – Mr Darkside. He's... an expert on George Eliot."

"How fascinating," says Celia. "You must tell me all about him... her."

"That would be marvellous, if I could pay you my respects some day."

"You must," says Celia. "Here's my card."

They disappear in the crush – it had been a hugely successful evening – as Celia turns to see Jeremy still resplendent in white tie.

"Giving your card out this early in the evening? And to very raddled old men?"

"I thought he looked quite sweet, actually. Not entirely unlike Francis."

"Celia, please. And look who's come to offer congratulations: our dear colleague, with a nice friend?"

Jonathan is standing there smiling. He embraces Celia. Jeb is beside him.

"We didn't come together," Jon says.

"How unfortunate," says Jeremy.

"Why did you bring *him*?" Celia whispers.

"I didn't," Jonathan replies, equally *sotto voce*. "He just turned up. But he's very sweet."

"Very strange, you mean." Then speaking louder and clearer adds, "When's Ben coming back?"

"Funny you should ask that. He rang this afternoon. I'm expecting him on New Year's Eve."

"Excellent. You must bring him over." She switches to *sotto voce*. "Ben, not your weirdo."

"Well…"

"No buts. I'm hosting a little party for Jeremy. We think he'll have something to celebrate."

"Oh?" says Jon.

But Celia has already turned to embrace Pip, and to look around for George.

VIII

Two days later Daniel is at home, frustrated and bored. His whole family have studiously ignored Christmas and are now determinedly blanking the forthcoming secular New Year. Daniel has decided that he finds this immature and anachronistic. He loves the Jewish festivals and greatly enjoys celebrating them, but why should that prevent him from enjoying the secular – or even non-secular – festivals of the rest of the world? When he put this view to his older brother Sammy the reply was, "Be careful, Danny. You can't keep a foot in both camps – it'll pull you apart. What's so attractive about Christian festivals? I've seen it all at uni and, believe me, you're better off with the beauty of Yiddishkeit. You don't need anything else."

But whereas a couple of years before Daniel would have been satisfied with that answer, now he no longer is. He wants to know what is happening beyond his parents' doors, beyond the bounds of his community; despite his admiration for the beauty of the young Chassid, he knows it is the beauty of a by-gone age. He wants to connect with the spirit of *now*. There is a character in the Isaac Bashevis Singer novel he is reading with whom he empathises, even, a bit ludicrously, identifies: a young woman who, being the daughter of a respectable Jewish tradesman in Poland, elopes with the handsome son of the local count. They marry, she has a son, and then he abandons her in Paris – such a romantic city to be abandoned in. And there she is, attending Mass with her baby, but also paying secret visits to the synagogue, consulting now the rabbi, now the priest, divided and confused between two cultures. He doesn't want to become as disorientated as she, but he can vicariously understand her predicament.

So, flushed by the fantastical experience of the opera – and especially the inspired performance of the diva, Celia Greyfield whom he had actually had the honour to meet – he decides to pay another visit to George who has clearly been deeply affected by the experience, so they can talk it over. And he has been delighted to see the big change which has taken place in George in such a short time since his first visit. For the opera he had dressed himself smartly, more elegantly than Daniel had ever seen him. After the show he had seemed rapt, entranced even more than Daniel, who wanted to check that he had not come down from the experience too suddenly – which to some extent he realised had actually happened to *him*.

He is glad, if a little surprised, to see that even Golders Green has Christmas lights up; all white and glittery but carefully non-religious in design. Well wrapped up against the bitterly cold wind, he is a bit disappointed not to see the sweet-faced Chassidic youth on the street but he does pass a group of older, bearded Chassidim one of whom is wearing the biggest, heaviest rounded fur hat he has ever seen; about a foot in height it seems to be shouting, "I am the biggest, most religious Chassid of you all."

Half dismissive, half amused, Daniel makes his way to the tube station for the now familiar journey to George's house, hoping he will not find his old mentor too depressed. As he sits down on the platform to wait for his train he decides to give Bashevis Singer a rest and instead takes out of his bag a volume of essays on George Eliot he has just bought; it was edited, he notices, by a Professor Robert Lush-Evans, whom he has never heard of before. The train snakes in almost at once. As Daniel steps onto it he suddenly thinks, *If I were Deronda, I would have married Gwendolen.* And a cultured faintly southern American voice says quietly in his head, "That's fine too. We all have our own paths to follow. And remember: that includes your former mentor. He will choose his own master – or mistress."

George feels like a new man, or rather, if the atrocious pun can be forgiven, he has realised that he feels like a new *woman*, and that woman, that diva, that Domina, was indubitably Miss Celia Greyfield. Or, as George loves to think of her, the Lady Cecilia, his mistress, his muse, his goddess of music. He had returned from the opera totally oblivious of his ex-student Daniel's presence kindly guiding him home. He had thoughts only for his heroine, the light of his life, the woman he had always dreamt of. For her, he would buy himself new clothes; for her he would start life over. And if she was interested in no closer contact, he would happily worship her from afar, his cynosure, his guiding star.

But dare he even think of approaching her? This is his dilemma, and how to solve it? Naturally – having hustled Daniel away and put on the kettle for his night cap – he at once switches on the computer and logs on to the internet, the world wide web of fellowship and hope as it seems to him now, the link to *his* mentor, that strange, southern, half-mythical being out there in the heartland of Georgia who appears to have a direct link to the soul (and brain) of his other and (apparently) long dead heroine, the mistress of English letters, Madame Eliot herself. Having tapped out the address – *Lush-Evans@ middlemarch.com* – he types:

My dear professor,

I have met a lady who, living, embodies the power and greatness of our literary heroine. I wish only to worship at her feet. She is, not surprisingly [the parallel has only just occurred to him], *like Daniel Deronda's mother, an opera singer, and a wonderful one. Would it be ludicrous to throw myself on her mercy? And what have I to offer? Your ever-wise advice will be my guide.*

Your friend and student,

GHD

George has made his tea and – as he has somehow grown to expect – by the time he has drunk it with the last piece of Daniel's mother's kuchen, an answer is ready to appear on his magic screen. He brings it up and it reads:

Time waits for none of us, friend; pluck the moment and pursue your goal. But two considerations I now warn you of. One: the lady may not be free or able to accept your service in the form in which you offer it; and two: there is work here *– a fellowship – that calls out for you to take it up. And by here, of course, I mean*

Georgia. Can you refuse to penetrate the land whose name you share with your heroine of first choice? Or will you abandon her whom you have always followed for your latest fancy? Answer me with care; and answer me within a week of the New Year.

George is a little taken aback by the tone – and rhyme – of this latest Delphic e-mail, and even more by its content; is he really being invited to take up a *fellowship* at an American university, and on what recommendations? *Curiouser and curiouser*, thinks George, suddenly perceiving that his until recently so-empty life has now acquired a surprising fullness, and that he now stands at an exciting crossroads; one which he will very soon be obliged to resolve.

So, as he sits now on Celia's extremely comfortable beige sofa, George feels even more astonished at the recent twists and turns of events. For here he is, facing the object of his utter devotion and speaking to her as one would – or almost as one would – to a mere human being.

"I'm so delighted to be sitting here with you, Miss Greyfield. No, delighted doesn't say it; honoured, enthralled."

"Thank you, Mr Darkside. I'm enjoying it too. But you must call me Celia."

"Oh... I think I'd rather continue to call you Miss Greyfield if I may. But I very much hope you will call me George."

"As you wish, George," Celia replies, rather titillated by the idea.

"I don't know how well you remember *Daniel Deronda* – I hope I won't bore you with it—"

"Not at all, George. Another gin and tonic?"

"Yes please, ma'am. It's just that I feel very much as the baronet does towards Daniel's mother who is, like yourself, a great operatic diva."

"How kind…"

"He practically worships her…"

"How *interesting*…"

"So much so that he adopts her son – without ever revealing his true provenance – in order to enable her to continue with her magnificent career…"

"Maybe that was going *too* far…"

A pause.

"I don't know how I could be of service to *you*, Miss Greyfield…"

"I'm sure we'll find a way, George. You also remind *me* of someone a little, an old friend of mine, no longer with us, very distinguished, and a man of letters like yourself."

"How flattering, ma'am. I hope it's not too late for me to become one."

Celia is suddenly deadly serious. "It's never too late to become what you could have been."

George looks at her in even greater admiration. "That's almost exactly what George Eliot said. I could almost think you were she."

Celia feels a little awkward for a moment. She wonders, subliminally, if George is a few notes short of a full scale.

"And where is that nice young man you had with you the other evening; he's not someone you adopted, is he?"

George laughs; he had practically forgotten about Daniel, which he realises was pretty selfish.

"No, rather the other way round, actually. He's been very kind to me. I suppose I've had a sort of breakdown since retirement – early retirement, of course – and he's been a great support."

Celia feels a great rush of almost maternal feeling for George; he *does* remind her of Francis, though – for once – an admirer is apparently not gay. However, he clearly has a particular proclivity of his own and she sees no reason not to fulfil it. *Bloody hell,* she thinks, *I've done practically everything else in the last six months.*

She kicks off her shoes; they were actually hand-crafted, silver open-toed sandals (Manolo Blahniks she had bought self-indulgently on her last trip to New York) and they have stiletto heels – she had not omitted to prepare for this encounter.

"Do you like shoes, George?"

George's throat begins to go dry. Could this be the great experience he has thirsted for and never dared try since an unsatisfactory fumble with a professional lady in Amsterdam in the early eighties?

"High-heeled shoes?"

"Yes, ma'am."

"Would you like to pick them up?"

Pause.

She re-thinks her role. "Pick them up, George. Place them under that chair in the corner. Then remove your jacket and tie and come and sit on the floor by my feet."

"Yes, ma'am."

George just about gets the words out. He follows her instructions to the letter. His dream is coming true.

About twenty minutes later, the door opens suddenly and a serious dark-haired young man comes in. He sees George, shirtless, kneeling on the carpet in front of Celia Greyfield who has one foot on his neck while he eagerly licks the inside of one of her high-heeled shoes. He is making passionate moaning sounds; she is lighting a cigarette in a long holder.

She sees him first, and seems almost unfazed.

George stops suddenly, with his surprisingly long tongue deep inside the shoe, and looks up at the newcomer sheepishly.

"You could have knocked," says Celia rather casually, realising that in her eagerness she had left the front door unlocked.

"I'm glad to see you're getting on so well," says Daniel, trying to keep shock and resentment out of his voice.

He turns and leaves.

Celia thinks better about going after him. It is too late for that.

Half an hour later, shoes cast aside, Celia has her stage whip securely round George's neck while, with deeply satisfying exactitude, he licks out something far more intimate.

IX

That same evening Jonathan is at the Squarehouse, taking a rehearsal which is not glowing but freezing due to the fact that nobody has bothered to inform the caretakers that this mad band of amateur musicians was intending to rehearse in the dead, cold days between Christmas and New Year. Even Peter, eternally resourceful, is unable to locate either the relevant switches or the resident caretaker, so shiver they must all evening except insofar as Jonathan could inspire them with passion and warmth for their coming production.

But as he enters the rehearsal room Jon can see at once that Peter is not shivering but full of enthusiasm and pride as he stands at the table with a large figure by his side, swathed in furs and wearing three inches of make-up. For a second, Jon thinks he recognises his old pal Miss Fleurice, the TV diva of the fat men's scene, but as he approaches them Peter calls out.

"Jonathan, you must come over and meet Mummy."

"Mrs Hore-Commodore…" says Jon but already she is addressing him with the eagerness of a pampered terrier.

"Mr Gordon, Jonathan if I may, I've heard so much about you. I'm *agog* to see your first production with us."

"I'm delighted to have met *you* at last, ma'am. I can certainly see the resemblance to Peter."

This has evidently hit a chord.

"Really? How splendid. You are just as charming as I had been told you were and…" She leans forward confidentially, "Actually better-looking."

While he is deciding how he should take this, she continues. "I hope you won't mind if I stay to watch the rehearsal. They're so much more interesting than performances, don't you think? You probably know that I'm sponsoring this production of what Petey and I like to call *Eine kleine Sondmusik.*"

"I don't think the word was *Sond* last time we mentioned it, Mummy dearest."

Jonathan is well aware he has no choice as to whether she stays. He decides she is a cross between Princess Margaret and Lee Bowery, with a dollop of Barbara Cartland thrown in; she is a tad frightening, but he rather likes her. And anyway, he is feeling distinctly nervous this evening, as he knows that Ben is returning to England just after New Year and he will soon have to make a significant choice. If Jeb turns up tonight – and it is never predictable if he would or not – would he, should he, try to arrange to meet again or even spend tonight with him? Jeb is still frequently in his thoughts as the sleek, sensuous, mysterious not-bear, the man whom he still guiltily wants. Yet at the same time he is looking forward to seeing his long-time partner, who needs him now more than ever, and isn't it good to be needed by someone of worth?

He looks up from his reverie to see Charles carrying his music over to the piano; his bulging left bicep sports a new tattoo: *Bach rocks.*

"Hi, Charles, OK?"

Charlie gives him the most cursory of nods as he arranges his scores.

"What's got *his* goat?" he asks Flora who has just arrived beside him drinking a cup of tea.

"Oh, I wouldn't worry about it. He's still pissed off 'cause you made me your deputy instead of him."

"Bloody hell, this group! I've asked him to direct *Night Music*, and promised to give his poxy Arthurian opera at least a workshop next year. And anyway, he couldn't be pianist and assistant MD at the same time. It wouldn't work."

"Charlie always wants to do everything, love. And everyone. Even me, I think. That's just Charlie. He'll get over it. Shall I take the warm-up?"

"Guys, can we just run through 'Twilight' again? Then we can call it an evening and get totally pissed."

"Unless you're giving me a lift," shouts Charlie from the piano.

"That could mean *anybody*," says Peter archly to Mummy, who giggles.

It is just after ten and Jon is exhausted and desperate to finish. As the ensemble start up – "You're still not quite on pitch, Bill," he shouts petulantly at the tenor, thinking he never had these problems working with pros – he feels a sudden arrhythmic heart beat as the handsome not-bear (his head completely shaven, making his appearance even more sharp and sexual) walks casually along the back of the group. Jeb looks over and flashes a quick enigmatic smile, which gives him a warm feeling.

"Lovely, guys, that was much better. Have a great New Year. Now, bar time!"

As he turns, he sees that Peter is standing immediately behind and Jeb is just approaching him. As usual, they share a conspiratorial grin; *perhaps*, he thinks, *the same one I had believed intended for me.* Flora comes up, breezy as ever.

"Don't look so worried, mate. He's not worth it – whoever he is. Let me get you a drink."

A couple of hours later, they are sitting in the bar, commiserating about Flora's ups and downs with Sophie ("She's a gem, Flor, stick at it" was Jon's sage advice), and his insecurity and uncertainty at Ben's imminent return.

"Maybe you should take your own advice on this one, mate."

"What?"

"Stick at it. Better the devil you know. That's not very positive though, is it? I mean, basically what it comes down to is: do you love him?"

"Yea, I do, but I also love my family and I love… you, but it doesn't mean we should live together."

"Not unless you want a great fat dildo up your arse twice a night, mate."

"Now you're talking, gorgeous. 'Nother round, love? You know you are the only friend I've got in this place. In fact, come to think of it, you're about the only friend I've got period."

"I fancy that pint before my next period, thanks, mate."

Thinking tipsily, *I really, really love that dyke,* Jon lurches towards the bar and practically falls into Mummy who is just being presented with her fourth Margarita by her adoring son.

"It was super tonight, Jonny," says Mummy. "You're so talented. What a pity you're not at the Whippo anymore."

"I still do some repetitit… coaching there, you know."

"Mummy means in a major capacity," Peter drops in acidly.

"How nice of you," says Jon, ambiguously.

"But with Jeremy going off for a year…"

"What?"

"It could be longer, of course. Cleveland's a lovely city and they pay a huge salary there."

"Oh, Cleveland, *that* job." He tries to pretend knowledge. Why does no one ever tell him anything?

"Of course," says Peter, "Adelina's already got both feet under the rostrum."

"Yes," replies Mummy, "But I'm sure a job share could be arranged. I shall speak to Lord Masters when he comes to lunch tomorrow."

Jonathan gulps. Lord Masters – "God" as he is known at the Whippo – is chairman of the board. The gorgon suddenly looks a lot less repulsive.

"Assuming you're interested in that arrangement, Jon?"

"Oh yes, absolutely. That would be very helpful of you, Mrs…"

"Just call me Mummy."

"Oh, how very… Do excuse me one moment."

Emboldened by that conversation and the alcohol, he grabs Jeb as he pushes past.

"Hi, Jonny boy. How's it hanging?"

"It's not hanging. It's standing up, 'cause you're here. Come back with me."

"Not tonight, sexy. I've got a very early start. Meet me on New Year's Eve at Traffic. About ten o'clock. I'll give you one to remember."

"Will you?" asks Jonathan, looking at him piercingly.

Jeb kisses him. His tongue, tasting like milk and honey, snakes into Jon's mouth and fills it with the sweetest of flavours. His balls feel warm and full. It is a second intoxication.

He realises he is still standing there with Jeb gone. He orders the drinks and goes back to Flora who now has her arm round Sophie's shoulders.

"Wow," she says observing his face, "That Jeb must know how to kiss."

X

New Year's Eve. At ten o'clock precisely Jeremy opens the door to his first guests.

"The Empress Domina herself; deliciously early for once."

"Darling."

He ushers her in and, while taking her coat, says through almost clenched teeth, "And who is this gentleman?"

"Don't you remember from our opening night, darling? It's my good friend, George. George Darkside."

"Hello, Mr Darkside."

Jeremy's smile is so evidently false it is honest.

"Why did you bring him? He's so… *plain*," he whispers.

"That's what *you* think, love. Actually, he reminds me of Francis."

He feels her forehead. "You haven't got meningitis, have you? Take your friend through and… well, do something."

A few minutes later, the bell rings again.

"Harold," says Jeremy. "Come *in*. I heard you were kidnapped by the CIA. Glad to see you escaped."

Harold wisely ignores this.

"Jeremy, love, *The Lady Domina* is fabulous. You are a huge, incandescent star – and so is our Celia, of course."

"She's already here, dear. And she's brought some dreary old bugger with her. Unlike your handsome companion."

334

"You must know Jeb. Isn't he gorgeous?"

"I can't help it," says Jeb.

"Though apparently," says Harold, "He has to leave us shortly to meet someone, though he won't say whom."

"I think I can guess," says Jeremy. "Do go through."

The bell rings. It is Adelina and Tallulah, Zac and Armando, all arriving at once.

"We have an announcement to make," says Addy. "The four of us are going to get married – to each other. It'll solve all our Home Office problems."

"Fabulous," says Harold. "May I kiss the brides?" he adds, going over to embrace the two men.

Jeremy is bringing drinks over to Celia and George.

"You're a very lucky man to be escorting this diva, Mr... what was it?"

"Just call him George," says Celia.

"I know," says George. "It's an enormous... fulfilment after years of futility."

"Really?" says Jeremy suddenly intrigued.

"It's a lovely friendship," says Celia. "But George has been called away."

"Must I answer the call, Lady Domina?"

"I think so, my dear."

"Are you two *on* something?"

"Life, dear, just life. He's going to pursue his other passion at the U of Artemisia, in Georgia."

"Isn't that where they live to be very, *very* old?"

George looks quite disconsolate.

"Why am I always making good men look unhappy?" says Celia.

"Because you're a bitch, dear," says Jeremy.

"If this weren't your house, Mr…" says George.

"I don't think it's Mr any longer is it, sweetie pie?"

"That's the bloody doorbell again."

"I'll go," says Celia.

A dark young man is standing outside looking sheepish.

"So, this *is* the right flat?"

"Absolutely. Daniel, I must apologise to you for taking your friend away. So, I invited you to introduce you to some new ones. Come in and meet Sir Jeremy Groves. Oh shit, I've given the game away before midnight."

Meanwhile, at Traffic, Jon is hanging around nervously, guiltily, unsure whether he should be here, but anxious to fulfil his tryst. It's busy and, though cold outside, it's hot in here. It feels an odd place to be on New Year's Eve, especially when he could, and probably should, be at Jeremy's in the bosom of his extended, chosen family (to quote Sir Elton). The jukebox is playing the Spice Girls' Christmas number one; it's tuneful and cosy and the video playing with it on about five screens shows the girls coming in from the cold to a luxurious warm interior. And Jonathan feels he shouldn't be here. But he is, awaiting his destiny.

Suddenly, he sees a familiar face; he's relieved, but anxious not to get too involved, as he keeps an eye out for the man he is meeting.

"Hi there, you old shit stirrer," says Grant, looking big and manly and smelling even manlier. He is wearing a white T-shirt with a hand-painted image of a bear on it, looking faintly ludicrous yet lovable. "So, what ya doin' here, me old luv? Thought you'd be at some posh party tonight with your opera crowd."

"I thought I'd just hang out for a while. New Year parties get me down anyway. What about you?"

"I'm meeting some mates here. Where's that gorgeous bear of yours? Not still in *America*?"

"Actually, he called today. He'll be arriving at Heathrow about 1 a.m. He said I shouldn't go to meet him there – not on New Year 's Eve. It'll be manic."

"And you took him at his word, you little cunt?"

Jonathan looks shifty.

"Are you meeting someone here?"

"I might be."

Suddenly his eyes are drawn to a shaven head just entering the bar. Jeb takes a look round, doesn't see him and goes downstairs.

"So, you've come 'ere to meet *her* when you should be meeting your husbear?"

"It was a prior arrangement." Jonathan feels his cheeks burning.

"She's a rightun is that. Called Justin, isn't she?"

"No, you've got the wrong guy. This one's called Jeb. And he's very… hot."

"A good shag, you mean. True."

"You've had him?"

"Who hasn't? You're not infatuated with *her,* are you? She's been around, mate. And I mean *around.* Works for the cops, you know. Kind of a nark."

"Absolute bollocks, Grant. She's… he's called Jeb, he's a decent bloke and he's some kind of musician."

"Could be, but she's also connected to Special Branch. I know whereof I speak, matey."

Grant's big pockmarked, masculine face comes very close to Jon's. And he isn't about to kiss him.

"If you drop Ben for *that*, you're a bigger loser than I took you for, me old luv. Like some bloody politician said, swapping real diamonds for paste."

Then he does kiss him; it is salty with a taste of beery tongue.

Grant is gone. Jeb is downstairs. Ben will soon be at the airport. Jon makes a dash for the door. If only for old time's sake, he shouldn't be here. With luck he can still make it to Heathrow in time. But before he can get out of the bar, his mobile rings. Switch it off and dash for the tube? Probably that gorgeous irritant Jeb calling; best to ignore it. But there's something very hard to ignore about an insistent mobile playing "Fur Elise". He answers it.

"Yes," he says irritably.

"Hi, babe." It is an American voice.

"Oh, hi. Where are you?"

"In a taxi almost in the West End. I got an earlier flight. I hope you're not on your way to Heathrow."

"Er… no. I'm at Traffic. Just had a drink with Grant, actually."

"Great. I'll be with ya in about twenty."

Jon goes to the bar. He isn't going to hide, but nor is he going to search for Jeb. Things will take their course.

When he's finally been served, he looks round and there is Jeb, suave and smiling as ever, standing at the top of the stairs from the basement bar. And then the door of the bar swings open, and a big ungainly guy with a pretty unkempt beard lumbers in carrying a suitcase. His walk is a cross between a swagger and a waddle and though his big, open face has sweetness and character, it isn't by a long way the handsomest in the bar. His jeans, which are much too new, just stretch over his large arse, and his thighs are clearly chafing within them. He spots Jonathan and ambles towards him. The jukebox starts to play Kylie singing, "I should be so lucky…"

In the forty-five seconds it takes Ben to walk over, Jonathan, like a drowning man, sees his whole life kaleidoscope before him. For some reason he remembers a metaphysical poem he had studied for A level: "Why should I ever sigh and pine?" where the poet absolutely determines to be free, then hears the quiet voice of the Almighty and replies, "My Lord." He thought of the local, inhibited, learned rabbi of his childhood saying, "True freedom means the liberty to choose your own master, your own discipline." (Mind you, this was the man who would ask for "the, excuse me, toilet.") He remembers waking up each morning with that broad back in front of him, and that early wrestle on the floor at Jeremy's party, and accompanying Ben's warm, not quite operatic baritone in some Mozart aria, and lying squashed against that big belly as they both fell asleep.

Then he thinks of Jeb, sees him in fact, sleek and sensuous and enticing, and imagines that fabulous sense of freedom to cruise, to love, to be lonely at times but also to be totally oneself that he has tantalisingly glimpsed once again in these past months.

He walks straight past Ben, grabs hold of Jeb, gives him a long, deep and passionate kiss and says, "Let's go to your place for some really hot sex."

But that is in a parallel universe called Perverse (they say it's fun there). In ours, Jon smiles at Ben who says in a cross between American and Noel Coward, "Strange how potent crap music can be."

"It's good to have you back, love. I'm really sorry about Dorothea. I wish I'd met her."

"Me too."

They embrace. And kiss with just a touch of tongue.

"Do you want to go to Jeremy's for midnight?"

"Do you? I'd rather go home."

"Me too."

Ben goes first with Jonathan following, his hand on Ben's arse. As they pass, he gives Jeb a non-committal smile.

"Who was that cute guy?" says Ben.

"Oh, just some loser," says Jon.

And they walk out, into their future, together.

1998

Following Jeremy's knighthood, he goes off for a year as guest MD at a major American opera house. Adelina and Jon are appointed – in his absence – as joint acting MDs at the Whippo. They work together remarkably well, despite or because of their rivalry. Jonathan also leads two productions for GLOW, both of which set the Squarehouse on fire; the first figuratively, the second literally, but the fire hydrants prove adequate.

Ben gets a proper job for the first time as GLOW's general manager, which he loves, and begins a successful career doing voiceovers for adverts.

Celia is invited to make a pop record with a huge (in all senses) rock star called Beef. It goes to number one in sixteen countries and they start a passionate relationship. She also keeps in touch with George, who takes up the fellowship at the beautiful University of Artemisia, and is now near completing the definitive life of George Eliot. The university has never heard of Professor Lush-Evans.

Daniel is accepted at Durham University to read English literature. His parents and older brother Sam are still working on him to read for the bar.

Harold gives up his plans for the USA and switches his business and travel plans to Australia and Japan (and Thailand). In 2000 he is appointed director of communications for the

Millennium Imaginear Consultancy, a global futures think-tank, on a six-figure salary.

Pip and Stephan settle down together, basically as friends. Pip channels his unhappiness into his second mould-breaking opera: *Carry On Carrying On,* a tragicomedy in three acts.

Tallulah is welcomed into the spanking new Mutatrix Chambers. She still aims to be Lord Chancellor, but her increasing interest in human rights law may bring her into conflict with the government.

Zac and Armando buy a large plot of land on Nob Hill, San Francisco, set up a centre for ecumenical peace and understanding and re-construct their wedding for US national TV.

Dorothea is contentedly embroidering a halo in petit point, while Francis lounges on a chaise-longue-shaped cloud.

"I do hope Ben and Jonathan will be happy," she says.

"We must make sure they are," says Francis with a characteristic twinkle, "While ensuring they don't become complacent. Do you think those seraphim are a touch out of tune?"

They both smile.

THE END

www.ingramcontent.com/pod-product-compliance
Lightning Source LLC
Chambersburg PA
CBHW051439190726
48289CB00001B/262